MISSING MOLLY

NATALIE BARELLI

The Last Word
NSW Australia

Print ISBN: 978-0-6482259-0-4
eBook ISBN: 978-0-6482259-1-1
v1.1b
Cover design by Coverquill.com

ALSO BY NATALIE BARELLI

Until I Met Her (*The Emma Fern Series Book 1*)
After He Killed Me (*The Emma Fern Series Book 2*)
Missing Molly
The Loyal Wife
The Accident
The Housekeeper

www.nataliebarelli.com

ONE

I was looking forward to coming back to work this morning after my break, but now that I'm here, something doesn't feel right. I think it's because everyone is hunched over their computer keyboard, deep in concentration. There's no banter, no atmosphere. It's just... wrong. Mike looks up and shoots me a small smile. "Hey Rachel," he says, then goes back to peering at his computer screen. I would have thought he'd be happier to see me. I've only been away for two weeks, but still, I was expecting a bit more of a welcome than that. For a moment I wonder if I've done something wrong.

I look around for Vivian but she's not here yet, so I walk over to Mike, undoing my coat at the same time.

"Hey yourself, good morning," I say as I perch myself on the corner of his desk. "You look busy, for a change," I add, with a wink.

"Welcome back!" he says, with a little forced bravado, I think. He swivels in his chair and leans back into it. "How was the holiday?"

"It was good, thanks. Cold, wet, you know..." I smile.

"Yeah, well, I could have told you that. As a holiday destination, Manchester is…"

"It's lovely." I interrupt, smacking his shoulder playfully. "It's where Matt's from. His younger sister still lives there."

"Right! Of course! It's great then!" He chuckles. Mike likes to tease me, but something's off.

I cock my head at him. "What's going on?"

He leans forward, moves his chair a little closer. I bend down a little, instinctively.

"The boss says the paper might have to close." Then he shrugs his shoulders in apology.

I smirk, anticipating the punch line. *Because without you, Rach, it's all gone to pieces.* Or something like that. But no, Mike doesn't say anything else. There's no grin on his ruddy face. He just sits there, looking at me with almost pleading eyes.

"You're serious?"

"Sorry to break it to you, but yes. We're not making enough money anymore. That's what the boss says. Not enough advertising sales. He could sell it to one of the publishing groups, but even if that happens, some jobs will have to go."

I feel my chest constrict a little. There's only a handful of us working here and if jobs are being lost, as the part-time bookkeeper slash admin person, mine will be the first to go. Our little paper, the South Hackney Herald, is a relic of a bygone era. When most other local papers around the country, and certainly in greater London, are managed by regional media groups, we're still independent. And media groups don't employ people like me at the local level. That work would be handled from Head Office. Even I know that.

I look towards Vivian's desk, willing her to materialise. Vivian is my best friend, and the person who got me the job here, so I'm surprised she didn't tell me, but then again, I've been away. No doubt she didn't want to ruin my holiday.

There's no way I can lose this job. I can't bear the thought of having to go through a whole other interview process somewhere else. I put on a brave face and pat Mike on the shoulder, then I walk over to my desk. I put my puffer jacket on the back of my chair and my handbag in the bottom drawer.

My desk looks nothing like the way I left it. I like it clean and tidy but now, it's covered with random pieces of paper and yellow Post-it notes. I begin to rearrange up all the bits into different piles. Things to be paid, things to file, things that don't belong on my desk to begin with.

I glance towards the door of Chris Masters' office, the boss, and watch him through the gaps in the vertical blinds. He's talking to someone just off to the side of the glass wall. I tilt my chair onto its back legs, crane my neck and see that it is Jacob. The new guy. He won't be happy. He only just started working here, barely a week before I went on leave. Abruptly, Jacob turns his head and looks right at me. I lower my eyes and fiddle with bits of paper, just as Chris's door opens and the two of them walk out into the main office area.

Chris claps his hands. "Okay everyone, into the conference room please."

Mike winks at me and I smile. The conference room—as Chris calls it—is basically a corner of the open plan office. There's a table no more than three feet square, covered with old copies of the Herald that always seem to end up there until I tidy up and find a spot for them.

"Grab the laptop please, Rachel. If you could take notes that'd be brilliant," Chris says.

"No problem," I reply. I spring out of my chair and quickly disconnect the laptop from the wide computer screen, and when I pull it away, the mouse and the keyboard fall to

the floor. I'm sure everyone is looking at me, and I feel myself
blush crimson.

"Where's Vivian?" Chris asks. He checks his watch with a
quick flick of the wrist. Then he looks right at me.

"Welcome back by the way, Rach."

"Thanks, Chris."

"You wouldn't know where Vivian is, would you?"

"Sorry, I don't." I wonder if she texted me. I wish I hadn't
left my mobile back at my desk.

Chris sighs. "I don't want to start without her."

Just as he says this the door opens and Vivian comes
flying in.

"I'm here!" she says, a little breathless, her black curls
bouncing around her face. I smile. If that was me, late like
this, I'd be quiet and apologetic. But Vivian just fills the room
with her energy.

She raises one arm in greeting. "You're all here! Sorry I'm
late. Are we having a meeting? Did I miss anything?"

I can't help but laugh. We all do.

She brings a chair over and positions it next to me. I'm
dying to talk to her about what's going on here, but I'll have to
wait. Vivian turns to me, puts a finger on my knee and
mouths, "How was the holiday?"

"Yeah, good, I'll tell you later," I whisper. She leans closer
and says, "You heard the news? About this place?"

"Yeah, I don't know what to say," I reply. She makes a
grimace. Vivian would be fine I suspect, if she lost her job,
because she inherited a lot of money. But that doesn't mean
she doesn't care. She works here because she likes what she
does and it's a step closer to her goal of becoming a journalist.
"A proper one," she likes to say, although never to Chris's face,
I noticed.

"Can we all concentrate, please?" Chris says. I look

around the room to see if anyone was expecting this meeting, but from the look on their faces, I'd say not. In fact, everyone looks terrified.

Chris clears his throat. "Now, you all know our situation has been dire, to say the least." He looks right at me and says, "Rachel, Vivian can fill you in later."

"Mike explained so I have an idea what's going on," I say.

"Okay, that's good. So, people, listen up. We have probably eight weeks to turn things around—"

"Eight weeks?!" That's Perry, almost shouting. He's the other senior writer. "What are we going to do in eight weeks we haven't done in the last eighteen years!" he bellows. There's a wave of murmur around the table.

I can feel the corners of my mouth drop. Eight weeks? I look at Vivian. She's biting her bottom lip.

Then Chris lifts his hands, palms out, and we're all quiet again. "Like I was saying, unless we can turn things around." He turns towards Jacob who is standing next to him, and says, "Jacob has an idea that just might get us out of this tight spot."

Jacob nods gravely to himself and clears his throat. "I don't know if it's the solution yet, but it is something I've seen other newspapers do successfully. If I can put it into context, there seems to be an upward trend in—"

"Just tell them," Chris interrupts. "No actually, I will. It's a podcast."

"A podcast?" Vivian asks, taking the question right out of my mouth.

"That's what I said."

"Am I writing this down?" I ask.

"And how's a podcast going to help?" Mike asks.

"Ever heard of *Serial*? The podcast phenomenon? Downloaded a billion times across the world? What about..." He turns to Jacob. "What is it again? The one about Daniel Morgan?"

"Untold."

"Right, *Untold*. Ever heard of that?"

Mike shrugs. "I might have."

"Well, so you know what I'm talking about then."

"But what does it have to do with us? We're still a local paper, last time I checked," Mike says.

"It's coming, hold your horses. Jacob here got the idea from—what was it, Jacob?"

"Well, as I was saying, there are a number of newspapers who are doing this successfully. By that I mean, introduce an investigative podcast as part of—"

"It will bring audiences," Chris interrupts again. "And what comes after audiences?" He asks this as if we're in a classroom and he's the headmaster.

"Jeez let me think, advertisers?" Mike replies.

"That's right! Sponsors! Advertisers!" Chris is now rocking on the balls of his feet. "Podcasts are all the rage these days and sponsors love them."

I can tell he's waiting for us to say something, but we're all confused, or in shock. A podcast?

"I can see how that would work," Vivian says.

"You do?" I ask.

"Sure! How good was *Serial*! We loved it, Rach, remember?"

I don't think I *loved it*. I know she did. I remember her waiting for the next episode every week. She'd download it as soon as it became available. Then she'd call me and dissect everything that had been said. Personally, I never really understood the attraction. These were real people. I thought it was awful. I don't know why I never told her that.

"Right now, it's the best we've got," Chris says. "Vivian,

I'd like you to work with Jacob who will be the producer and in charge. He'll need some research done and maybe some legwork. I expect everyone to chip in as needed. On top of your usual scribbles, mind you. We're trying to save the paper and our jobs here, got that?"

I turn to look at Vivian, I wonder what she thinks about Jacob being in charge, but she's just nodding along, unfazed.

"I'm expecting you all to pull up your socks and do your best. It's a good plan and we can make it work. We're putting out the first episode in two weeks."

"Two weeks?" we all say at the same time.

"No time like the present."

I put my hand up. "Can we propose ideas?"

"No need, Rach, we already know what we're going to do. It ticks all the boxes." Chris begins to count on his fingers. "It's a true crime story, it's not too far from here, because it's not like we have the budget to send you lot across the world, and it's unsolved. Sort of."

"Okay, I'll bite," Mike says. "What is it?"

Everyone is silent while we wait for Chris to tell us. He puts his hands behind his back, still like a schoolmaster at an assembly, and again rocking on his feet, he says,

"We're going to find little Molly Forster."

I can feel the colour drain from my face. My heart starts to thud in my chest so hard I can't breathe, and all I hear is the blood roaring in my ears.

Because I *am* Molly Forster.

TWO

"*NO!*" There's a noise behind me as my chair bounces back and suddenly I find myself standing.

They're all looking at me, but judging from their faces, I don't think that I screamed out-loud, only in my head. I open my mouth, but nothing comes out.

I scramble to pick up the chair. "Sorry, I didn't mean to… I'm so clumsy today." I'm stunned no one can hear the thudding of my heart.

"You have a question, Rachel?" Chris asks.

"No, thanks I'm good, sorry," I say, brightly I hope, and sit back down. If Chris thinks I'm behaving strangely, he's keeping it to himself.

"Okay, well I think most of us here are old enough to remember the Forster case, after all it was only twelve years ago, but Jacob, how about giving us a refresher?"

Jacob steps forward and nods to himself. He lifts the small notebook he's been holding. I hadn't noticed it before. He adjusts his glasses and begins to flick through pages. I manage to resist the impulse to bring my hands over my ears.

"Okay, so, Jack Forster was a small-town solicitor in Whit-brook, so not too far from here."

Chris nods approvingly at that. He is thinking about the costs, like he said. I'm thinking that I didn't move far enough. I should have gone to the other side of the country.

"Jack Forster ran his own practice, and by all accounts, he and his wife Mary and their two daughters, Grace and Molly, were well liked by everyone, and active members of the community."

Chris makes a gesture with his hand to hurry things up, and Jacob gets a little flustered.

"Right, okay. So, Grace had a sixteenth birthday party at home. A small party, just her family and half a dozen of her friends. Later that evening after the guests had left, a neighbour discovered the entire family murdered, except for twelve-year-old Molly, who was missing. Their gardener, Dennis Dawson, was arrested at the scene and later convicted of their murder. Molly is still missing. There have been reported sightings over the years, but nothing that led to her being found."

Everyone here knows the story, so when Jacob finishes, no one speaks or asks any questions. But my heart is beating so fast it hurts. My hands are shaking. I'm afraid to betray myself, that Vivian will notice. I rub them quickly against my thighs.

"I don't know, Boss, do we really want to revisit that tired old story again?" Perry says. I could kiss him. I raise my hand.

"Wouldn't it be better to do something more… positive?" I say, standing up. "A feel-good story, that's what people like, right? What about… a series of local histories! We could do a podcast about people who are *not* famous."

Chris is about to say something, so I quickly speak again before he does. I don't usually speak up like this in meetings, but today I can't shut up. "Something about parenting,

9

maybe? There's got to be an audience for that, surely." I'm aware how ridiculous I must sound.

"I don't think *Serial* would have been the same if it'd been about early childhood development, Rach, no offence," Chris says.

"But that case is closed!" I almost whine.

"What's wrong with you? Didn't you hear what I just said? We're not going to solve the Forster murders, we're going to find little Molly! And can you sit back down, please?"

I do as I'm told. I look at Jacob. He's looking at me too, of course. They all are. I try to read the expression in his eyes, but he just looks slightly puzzled.

I can feel a headache coming on. Chris makes a point that I can't argue, not without calling even more attention to myself, so I shrug as if defeated, and say nothing. He talks about the practicalities and logistics after that, deferring to Jacob now and then.

"We're calling it, *Finding Molly*," Chris says.

Oh God.

"Um," Jacob leans across to him. "I thought we agreed on *Missing Molly*?"

"Yes, that's right, sorry. *Missing Molly*."

"I do like a good alliteration," Perry mutters.

"There's going to be a website dedicated to the podcast where anyone can post tips, anonymously if they wish. Then we'll have a phone number so people can call and leave a message, also anonymously. Old school I know, but people think phone calls are harder to trace, and some people might be reluctant to send an email or a comment," Jacob says.

I bite the inside of my cheek, hard, while I take notes on everything that's being said.

"In terms of social media, there will be the usual. A Facebook page, a page on Reddit," Jacob continues.

"Which is what?" Perry asks, and everybody laughs, me included, because I need to join in with the banter, try to be normal again. Vivian keeps staring at me. She knows something is wrong so I make a joke about nothing and wink at her.

That's the thing, when you've gone through what I have. You learn to become someone else, and you learn to convince anyone and everyone of that lie. It's what you have to do when you're me.

If you want to stay alive.

THREE

Rachel Holloway is my third fake identity. I'm twenty-six years old. No I'm not, I'm twenty-four, but I tell people I'm twenty-six because that's how old Rachel Holloway is. Was.

Twelve years ago, I ran away from home and never went back because if I did, he would kill me. I know he would. So, I hide in plain sight. It's easier that way and safer too. If you try to be invisible, people will notice.

My birth certificate says that I was born on June 16, in Newcastle-upon-Tyne. In reality, I only visited twice, to get my bearings, should anyone ask.

I tell people my mother is dead, and that my father is in Australia, with his latest wife and brand-new kids. *They live in Avalon, by the beach. We don't get on. I don't have anything to do with them anymore,* I say.

I looked up Avalon on Wikipedia. *An idyllic beachside suburb of Sydney*, it said. I had to look up the word *idyllic*.

I keep glancing at Jacob who has returned to his own desk and is deep in conversation with Chris. I haven't really paid attention to him before, so I do now. He looks about thirty but

I think he's older. He seems harmless, a bit geeky with his large glasses and his thin moustache and trimmed, pointy beard, low on his chin. He reminds me of a painting I saw in a magazine recently. Edward the First, I think.

I've barely exchanged ten words with him, outside of 'hello how are you'. Chris was thrilled when Jacob joined us because he used to be a radio producer with the BBC, and Chris is impressed by that sort of thing. I didn't think anything of it at the time. Plenty of people move away from stressful jobs to simpler ones, even with the cut in pay it implies. But now, I wonder. It does seem like a strange career move, producer at the BBC to editor at a nondescript small local paper?

I squint at him. As if somehow that will help me see beneath the facade. *What are you really doing here, Jacob?*

Because the summary he just told about the Forsters' tragedy, as it's come to be known, is not the real story. There are only three people left in the world who know the real story. Two of whom were there that night, and I'm one of them. And I can't figure out whether Jacob knows something.

When Chris walks back to his office and past my desk, I'm on my feet. I have to stop myself from grabbing his arm. I'm about to follow right behind him but Vivian stops me.

"So? How was it?" she asks.

I stare at her blankly.

"Your holiday!"

"Oh yeah! Sorry, it was brilliant. We had a really great time."

"So why are you so jumpy this morning?"

"Jumpy? I'm not jumpy."

She narrows her eyes at me, then her face relaxes and she says, "I'm sorry about the job situation, here. But don't worry, okay? Maybe things will work out, with this new podcast. If not, something else will turn up. You'll see." She brings me into her arms and hugs me. For a crazy second, I consider whispering in her ear. *I need to tell you something.*

"Let's catch up at lunch, okay?" Vivian says, releasing me.

"Of course," I reply. "I better get back to it." I give her a quick smile and rush over to Chris's office. His door is open, so I step inside.

"Can I just ask…" I say, closing the door behind me, "was it Jacob's idea? The whole podcast thing?"

"To do a podcast? Yes. *Finding Molly*? I mean, *Missing Molly* —that was mine." He sits down and immediately starts to make corrections on the article that is laid out in front of him. "Why?"

"No reason. I mean I thought you would have talked to everyone, about the future of the paper. Jacob hasn't been around that long after all."

The words are coming out all wrong. He's going to think I'm put out that no one asked for my opinion, when I know they wouldn't have anyway, it's not my job around here.

"I just meant the others, Perry and Mike at least, they've been here a long time. They'd have ideas too, how to help the paper survive. Do well even."

He puts his pencil down and looks up at me.

"I didn't intentionally talk to Jacob. He just happened to be here when I got a call from the bank, okay? He took it upon himself to come up with a solution. And the podcast is a great idea—you have to admit that. We've only got eight weeks. I don't have the time to put it to a committee."

"Fair enough. I'm just saying that, given the opportunity, I would've liked to suggest topics, for podcasts. Good ones too, I think." I'm biting my bottom lip. I can't help it.

"I didn't realise you wanted to be involved on the editorial side of things, Rachel. That's good to know. And you can submit for an editorial role next year, if we're still around by then."

"Sorry, but I don't think it's the best we can do. *Missing Molly*. I think we should discuss it." Do I really expect Chris will listen to me? No. But I'm desperate. I'll try anything. He shakes his head, eyebrows raised, and I'm about to say something else when he dismisses me with a flick of the hand.

"Okay, go away, I'm busy. I've had enough of you." He picks up his pencil again and returns to making notes in the margins.

"I'm just saying."

"Go back to work, Rachel."

"Okay sure," I reply.

Back at my desk, I do my best to look busy, get some work done even. I can't get over the fact that the local paper I work for is going to do a podcast about finding me. But then I guess I'm still the most famous missing person case in the country. If you're going to do a true crime podcast, finding out what happened to *Little Molly* is always going to be up there as a top contender.

Still, I just don't trust Jacob.

I only work half a day on Monday, and then Vivian and I always have lunch together. I think it's best to keep up the routine but I didn't say much on the way here, I just listened to her talk about the podcast, about how exciting it all is.

"I'm starving," she says now, as we sit down at our usual table.

"Me too." I'm not. My stomach is tied up in knots and I can't wait to get out of here and go home.

"The usual, ladies?"

Carla has materialised next to us, pen poised above her

notepad. We do indeed order our usual, Caesar salads for both of us, and then Vivian starts chatting away. About the podcast again, the odds that the paper will close, my holiday. I do my very best to seem normal. I watch her pick up her napkin and wipe the rim of her glass. We're regulars here, and she's done this for so long that no one gets offended anymore. It's just one of her little quirks. Suddenly, I wonder if we'll have to move on, Matt, Gracie and me, and leave Vivian behind. It brings a prickle of tears to my eyes.

We were both working at Marks & Spencer when we met, Vivian and I. I was working in the bakery. My official job title was "customer assistant" but really, I served behind the counter. Vivian would come in to get her coffee every morning and eventually we got talking. She's three years older than me, but she seemed like a real grown-up to me. She worked in the marketing department. She explained to me what she did once, but it was over my head. All I know is that it had to do with branding and social media, and bringing customers into the store. Some days she had lunch there too, which used to surprise me. I spent enough time at work already, I didn't want to eat there too. I thought maybe she was saving her money, because we did give the staff a discount, but that wasn't it. Vivian doesn't need to save money. She's already got plenty.

One day, it was a Friday, I finished a bit later than usual and when I came out I almost bumped into her. She was standing alone, watching both sides of the street.

"I think I've been stood up," she said when she saw me. "I was supposed to go on a date, and he's not here."

"Maybe he's late?"

"Half an hour late. Do you think that's long enough to wait?"

"Oh yes. I don't think anyone should keep you waiting for that long. He hasn't called?"

"No." She waved her mobile in my direction. "And I tried to call him but there's no reply. Oh well." She sighed, then she turned to me, her face brightening. "Would you like to go for a drink?"

"Now?"

"Yes! We could go to the pub, or do you have other plans?"

I didn't have other plans. I didn't have a lot of friends either. I was pretty shy, back then, and I didn't—and still don't—make friends easily.

"Okay."

That's how our friendship started, and we've been friends ever since. It's funny really, because we're a bit like chalk and cheese. We're very different people, from very different backgrounds. I used to think it strange that we became close, but as I got to know her over the last few years, I realised we are much more alike than I'd thought. We're both lonely. We're both abandoned, really. Her parents don't seem to give a shit about her, which I just don't understand. She's a grown woman, but still. Sometimes I don't know which one of us has it worse.

Back then, I didn't really care what I did for a living. I just wanted to stay alive. Everything else was a bonus. But when I got pregnant with my daughter Gracie, I decided I didn't want to serve food behind a counter for the rest of my life after all, so I started doing night classes in bookkeeping.

"Why bookkeeping?" Vivian had asked.

"Because I figured I would always have stable and steady work."

"You're so practical, Rach, I love that about you. You know what I really want to do?"

"What?"

"Journalism. I always wanted to be a journalist."

"You never told me that. Like the *Daily Mail?*"

"Maybe, I was thinking politics, or investigative journalism. TV anchoring even, who knows?"

She was beside herself when she got a job at the *South Hackney Herald.*

"I'll be reviewing art and culture to start with," she'd said, proudly, "which sounds awfully grand but really, it's about flower shows and local music gigs. But I want to write a lifestyle column someday. Once I prove myself there, I'm sure, I hope, they'll let me have a go."

She was so excited, and I was pleased for her, but sorry for myself as well. I missed having her at work. But two months later, just when I got my diploma, Vivian said her newspaper was looking for someone to do the bookkeeping. She'd already told them she knew the perfect person.

"We'll be working together again!"

I hugged her when she told me. I was so happy, not just that she got me a job, but that she wanted us to work together.

Now I can't help but think it was a huge mistake, to work at a newspaper. Even a small local one. I go back over my conversation with Chris. He said *Missing Molly* was his idea, but the true crime podcast was Jacob's. But how hard would it be to nudge Chris in the direction of Molly Forster as a topic? And then make it seem like Chris thought of it himself?

I can't stop wondering if Jacob just happened to be here by accident.

18

FOUR

There are some things I never do on my home computer. Like look up anything remotely related to Molly Forster. Just a habit I picked up and have no reason to drop. So when I leave the cafe, I don't go straight back to our flat. Instead, I stop at a place around the corner that still rents out PCs to use the Internet.

This place is aimed at students and gamers. The front of the shop is a small convenience store that sells mostly junk food and soft drinks. The computers are at the back, behind tall black panels. It's dark in there but you can make out the users. They look like teenagers, hunched over, often they've got their hoodie up and some of them use some kind of console.

"Can I get thirty minutes, please?" That's the maximum time I can spend before I have to go and pick up Gracie from preschool.

The man behind the counter is always friendly. I get my ticket and find a spot out the back. I type in Jacob's name in the search bar. The first results that come up are all from the

19

BBC. What I want to see is a photo of him. There's a link to his LinkedIn profile, which I am pleased to see isn't set to private, since I never signed up.

A relaxed and younger Jacob smiles at me from his profile picture. I peer at it, but there's no need to study it. It's obviously him.

His summary is generic. *"I'm a dynamic, creative, talented and experienced audio content producer etc etc"* so I skip to his experience section. *Producer,* it reads, along with the relevant dates. He mentions a couple of programmes I've never heard of, a breakfast music show *Up Beat* and more recently a religious programme called *The Spirit.* He's listed skills like multi-platform and agile and some podcasting but even I know anyone could build a LinkedIn page and write whatever they like.

I check the BBC website next, and find the pages related to the radio programmes he worked on, but there's no mention of Jacob Whitelaw. There's no mention of any producer, so maybe it's no big deal, but it still makes me nervous and I write the phone number of the programme on my hand.

"Excuse me?"

I instinctively close the browser window, and then I turn around and look up at a young woman with heavy black eye makeup.

"Yes?"

She glances briefly at the screen and raises her eyebrows. She must be wondering what I'm so keen to hide. I mentally chide myself for being so obvious.

"Yeah, sorry," she says. "I was sitting here before and I lost a glove." She lifts her hand to show me. "Would you mind?" she points to the floor.

"Oh sure." I push against the desk to roll my chair back, then stand as she bends down.

"Got it!" she says, brandishing the other glove. I hadn't seen it there. I'm not even sure it was there to begin with, but maybe I'm just being paranoid. Nothing new here.

"Thanks," she says. "See ya."

I nod briefly. I don't know what else I can find out here anyway, so I grab my bag and go to pick up Gracie.

My daughter is almost three years old. Sometimes when I'm at work, I catch myself picturing what she might be doing in that instant. I imagine the feel of her little feet in my hand, the sweet plumpness of her legs.

I see traces of my sister in Gracie's face, but she has hair like mine. Fair and fuzzy, like pale yellow fairy floss that frizzles in the rain. Mine is more the colour of light copper, somewhere between blonde and red, and I suspect Gracie's will be the same in a few years.

I used to colour my hair. All part of my disguise. Clairol Chestnut. I styled it straight too. I even darkened my eyebrows. But when Gracie was little, the sight of her angelic pale curls gave me a pang of nostalgia for my own early childhood. Or that's what I told myself because deep down I suspect it's just that I've relaxed a little too much. First, I forgot to be scared and then I forgot to be careful. So a couple of years ago I got it cut really short and let the colour grow out. Now it's down to the base of my neck, thick and wavy.

"I love you like this," Matt said once, caressing my newly styled blonde hair. "It's like you're a different person, Rach."

"Not that different, I hope."

"You look beautiful. Why would you colour it?"

"Oh you know me, slave to fashion," I said. Which was funny because I'm not that at all. I'm more the jeans and sneakers variety unless I have to go to work, in which case I'll wear a pencil skirt and a white shirt, the office uniform for women all over the world.

I touch Gracie's soft curls and pull myself out of my memories. As we walk home, she chatters about her day, her friends, her little life, already so full. I stop myself from thinking about what's going to happen to us if this podcast goes ahead. I just want to be in the moment with her.

In the kitchen I peel an orange and set its quarters on a small plastic plate shaped like a flower. Gracie is standing next to me on her toes, holding onto the worktop with the tips of her fingers, her arms stretched up and her face upturned. I smile on one side of my mouth.

"I love you," I say, handing her the plate.

"I love you more," she replies, in a sing song voice.

That's not possible, I whisper to myself.

I clean up and make myself a cup of tea, turning over the Jacob situation in my mind. He started at the paper a month ago. Chris had advertised the position on a couple of jobs websites. I'd posted the ad for him. Then Chris interviewed four people and picked Jacob. "Heads above the rest," he'd said to Vivian and me.

I take my tea into the living room and settle down on the sofa. Gracie is sitting on cushions and glued to the TV screen. She's watching some kids' programme and eating in slow motion. I pick up my mobile and dial the number I wrote on my hand earlier. I spin a story about checking the spelling for the producer of *The Spirit* programme for a local credit, and I find out her name is Alice McGrath. I hang up, then I wait for twenty minutes or so, listening to the sounds of Gracie singing along with the TV.

When I call again, I ask for Alice McGrath.

"One moment, please," I am put on hold briefly and then a different voice comes on the line and announces herself,

"Alice McGrath" in the clipped, professional tone of someone who doesn't normally answer their own phone.

I try to match it. "Hello, it's Catherine Morgan, I'm calling about a work reference for one of your ex-employees. Jacob Whitelaw."

She doesn't say anything. For a second, I think I've lost her, but then she blurts, "Where are you calling from?"

"*The Acton Express*," I reply, which is a lie. "I have an application from Mr Whitelaw. Just checking up on past employment. How long—"

"And he put my name as a reference?"

I don't know how to answer that question. Something in her tone makes me think maybe I contacted the wrong person. So, I ask a different question instead. "Mr Whitelaw was the producer of your programme, is that right?"

"One producer on this programme, yes."

I don't know why I am disappointed.

"Ms…"

"Catherine Morgan."

"Ms Morgan, I'll be honest with you. If Jacob put my name down as a reference he must have thought you wouldn't check. That's his bad luck. I fired Jacob Whitelaw. He was with us for less than a year and when he was sober he wasn't so bad, but since that was a rare occurrence, I never got to find out how good he was. I gave him three warnings as I am required to do by our internal code of conduct, and the fourth time he screwed up I let him go. I don't recommend him to any future employer. Was there anything else?"

I am speechless. "No, thank you," I finally stammer.

"You're welcome. Goodbye," she says, and hangs up.

When Chris introduced Jacob, he made it sound like Superman had flown down from the heavens to work at the paper, and we were incredibly lucky to have him. What story did Jacob spin? I wish I'd looked up who he put down as a reference before making the call. Did Chris even check?

"Hello!"

"Daddy!"

Gracie runs down the corridor, pounding the floor with her little feet and throws herself against Matt, wrapping her little arms around his legs. He picks her up and bounces her in the air to the sound of her happy giggles.

"Hey, you're home early," I say.

"Yeah, we had a cancellation," he puts Gracie down on the floor and kisses me softly on the lips. "I figured I may as well come home."

I met Matt at the pub, four years ago now. Not long after I met Vivian in fact. I'm always careful when I meet new people, but I don't avoid them either. That night, there were four of us from work. It was Vivian's idea that we go out, as usual. She was always trying to meet a guy. Her dream is to settle down and have babies.

Matt was there with a couple of his own friends, and we all ended up at the same table. There was a band and the others got up to dance, leaving Matt and me behind. We started talking. Hours later, we were still talking. He's only my second serious relationship and everything I ever wanted in a guy: he's very honest. He always wants to do the right and the fair thing. I think it's because he grew up without a dad. His father left when Matt was ten, and his mother raised him and his two sisters. But even back then, he took it upon himself to be the man of the house and do all he could to help his family. That's the kind of person Matt is. As soon as he could, he jumped into an apprenticeship, and now he's an electrician. He's always looked after the people he loves, and now he looks after me too.

Meeting Matt changed everything for me. Not for the first

time, I could see a glimpse of what my life could be like. Normal. Happy. Then I fell pregnant really early on into our relationship, and we were both ecstatic. That's when I made a decision, that enough time had gone past, and I could stop cowering and hiding and begin to live a little. So I let Rachel Holloway come out a little more into the light.

"Daddydaddydaddy!"

Matt laughs and picks her up again, wedges her on his hip and takes her into the kitchen. I follow them. He grabs a beer from the fridge, offers it to me but I don't want it.

"How was work?" he asks. Gracie has wriggled her way out of his grasp and she slides down his side to the floor. I want to tell him about the paper possibly closing, but that would mean telling him about the podcast and I'm not ready yet. I'm scared that I will betray myself.

"I wish we were still on holiday," I say.

FIVE

Back at work, I do my best to keep things normal all day. I actually have a lot to catch up on after my holiday, so I have a good excuse to keep my head down. It doesn't stop Vivian from asking me if I'm okay. She thinks I'm worried about my job, and that's fine with me. I would be worried, normally, so it's a good cover in that way. But then I hear Jacob's voice behind me, calling my name. He wants to talk about the podcast. He needs to tally up the costs, he says, and could I help him with that? Would I have the time today? All I can hear is *Missing Molly, Missing Molly* and I can't bear it anymore. I tell him I have a headache and I leave work early.

I need to plan. I can't decide whether Jacob knows who I am and is connected to *him* somehow. I'm scared Jacob is trying to flush me out, and that's what this fucking podcast is really about. Once upon a time I might have discounted my fears. I might have put it down to paranoia, but not anymore. I've been there. I know *he's* looking for me. I don't think he's given up.

All I can think of is protecting Gracie. On impulse, I get

on the bus and I end up near London bridge. I've tried to walk across this bridge before, but not lately, because why would I bother? But suddenly, it feels important. I think of my child. I need to break through this fear that paralyses me, otherwise how can I protect her?

I picked London bridge because at first it doesn't feel like a bridge. It's more like a continuation of King William street. But now I can't breathe. I should have known what would happen. I started to feel light-headed when I reached the part that hangs over water, but I kept going anyway. *You can do this. Come on Rachel, be brave, try harder. Push yourself.* The only other time I tried, I remember the same feeling of vertigo, the wobble in my legs, my heart pulsing in my ears, and I turned around and almost ran back. But this time, I was determined. I shut my eyes, felt the cold railing under my hands and inched forward, step by step.

Now I'm stuck.

I give myself pep talks that I already know will do nothing to help. Come on, Rachel, put your skates on and stop whining. Keep going, just walk faster. It's not that hard. But the cold sensation running through my arms, like ice in my veins, tells me it's too late. I can't go back, and I can't go forward. I have nowhere to go.

My eyes dart from side to side, looking for a way out, fear pounding in my chest, but all I can see is a blur of people moving past me against the grey sky. I'm losing all sense of direction and I have to grip the railing, on the river side, and I hold on as hard as I can, taking big gulps of air that won't go down my throat.

I'm going to die.

No, you're not. You're not going to die.

I'm going to die.

I drop to the ground, huddling into a ball with one arm

pulling my knees up against my chest, my other hand searching for something to hold on to. I can't breathe. I can't get the air in.

Run! Molly, run!

There are dark spots dancing in front of my eyes now, the edges of my vision melting into a dark, ragged shadow like a burning old photograph.

Call Vivian.

My arms and hands are tingling as I pull my bag closer to me and feel my way around the leather folds until I find my phone.

Call Vivian.

I press the button and lift the phone close to my mouth and say, somewhere between a whisper and a plea, "Hey Siri, call Vivian."

The sound of ringing at the other end comes through dim and distant and her voice, like a miracle, says, "Rachel, wow that's amazing I was just about to—"

"Help me."

In the silence that follows, I can't tell if I have spoken the words out loud or merely imagined them, until she asks, "Where are you?"

I'm gasping for air. I won't be able to tell her because I can't speak, and I'm propelled into an even deeper state of panic. But then her voice comes through again, dim and distant.

"Listen to me, Rachel. You're okay. You're all right. Listen to my voice, honey. I want you to slow down your breathing now. We're going to count together. Concentrate on counting, Rachel. One, two, three, that's it. Slow down, you got it. Four, five, six. Okay, you're doing great Rachel. Now tell me where you are."

"I'm on … the bridge."

"Okay just breathe and count. Everything's all right. Breathe and count with me."

So I do, and the pressure on my chest begins to loosen ever so slightly. I am still crouched on the ground. I feel someone put a hand on my back, hear the distant sound of a voice, asking if I need help. I shake my head and rest my forehead on my knees.

Twenty-seven, twenty-eight—

Without looking, I lift one arm to the railing on top of the concrete barrier and pull myself up. Vivian's voice is soothing, soft and distracting at the same time. She breaks up her counting with anecdotes about our past. *Do you remember the time we laughed so hard you peed your pants?*

I release a shaky breath. "I'm walking now," I whisper.

"You're doing great, Rach, just look at the ground and take your time."

In what feels like an eternity, but was probably only a couple of minutes, I'm off the bridge and the relief floods my entire body. I close my eyes and tilt my face to the sky. Vivian's voice is stronger, clearer now. I just relish the feel of the ground under my feet, the sense of peace and safety that has returned to me. I pull a crumpled tissue from the pocket of my coat and wipe my tears, blow my nose.

"I'm sorry, it was going to pass. I should have just waited it out," I say into the phone.

"I'm glad you called me, honey." Vivian's seen me like this before. She's helped me out of a panic attack more than once. I don't know what I'd do without her.

"Thank you," I say softly.

"You're welcome. Go and sit down on a bench somewhere, you want me to call you an Uber?"

"I'm okay now Viv, I can do it. I'm sitting down."

"Okay. Whose bright idea was this by the way? Your shrink?"

"No. Mine."

"I see. Did you tell her? What you were going to do?"

I start crying, more out of sheer exhaustion and disappointment than anything else.

"Oh, honey," she says into my ear.

"I'm okay, Viv, really. Let me take a moment, I'll get home and call you back."

I say goodbye, drop my head between my knees and wait for the crushing disappointment to abate.

SIX

I've spent the past two days driving myself crazy, looking into Jacob's background, the little of it I can access online. I can't find anything that ties him to me. We haven't crossed paths before, in any capacity, and I can't quite picture him as the hired assassin trying to flush out his target. But that doesn't necessarily mean anything. What's the expression? Just because you're paranoid doesn't mean they're not out to get you.

But I have come up with a plan which is breathtaking in its simplicity. The only person who has the required expertise to produce this podcast is Jacob. Therefore, get rid of Jacob, and no podcast. Magic. We'll think of something else to save the paper. There's another way. There always is.

I'm back at work now, and it's Friday. Normally, I like Fridays, because what's not to like about Fridays? But also because Vivian and I, and Jenny from work, often go for a beer at the Cat & Mutton, the pub around the corner, and Matt will pick up Gracie from preschool so I can have a break with my friends.

But that's hours away. I've only been at the office for five minutes, and Vivian is telling me something about a TV show as I turn on my computer and catch sight of Jacob in peripheral vision, walking right up to my desk.

"Hi, Rachel."

"Hi, Jacob. How are you?" I barely look at him. He smiles a little awkwardly. "Yeah, good, thanks. Can I have a few minutes of your time?"

"Of course. Did you want to work on budget?"

"Yes, Chris said I should check with you on some costs, for the podcast."

"All right." I hesitate for a second, then I add, "Do you want to pull up a chair?"

I indicate the space next to me. He looks around, spots an empty chair at one of the other desks and wheels it over. I catch a faint whiff of aftershave. I look down at my hands on the keyboard. They're trembling. I rub them together as if to warm them up.

"Okay, so breaking down what we need..." He's flipping through pages of his notebook as he speaks. "Can you tell me any costs I haven't thought of? The first thing is the website. I think a blog, so we can post some updates and also let people post any tips, anonymously."

"Right." I scribble a note that makes no sense. It reads 'blog tips ££.'

"Okay. There shouldn't be any expense for the website. I thought *missingmolly* as a domain name had a nice ring to it—"

I close my eyes and will myself to breathe.

"—but Chris doesn't want a dedicated website, he wants it on the paper's site, so we're good there."

Jacob tells me about contact forms, and the message bank with a unique phone number, and the various social media channels he wants to set up for this podcast. If anyone has anything to say about me, they'll have plenty of opportunities to do so.

"Money's tight, as you know. So anything that costs extra, it's probably out," he says. Maybe I could make the whole thing sound unaffordable.

"And if we're over budget, let me know, and I'll make it work. I'm willing to cut any costs down to make sure this happens."

I nod. There goes the unaffordable idea.

"Can I ask you something?" I say.

"Of course."

"Is there any way I can work on the podcast too? I was thinking it could be a great experience for me. Maybe I could monitor the social media, or the phone messages, or the email account. I could make sure nothing gets missed."

"That would be great, Rachel, thanks. I'll mention it to Chris if you like." He even writes it down in his notebook.

Vivian lays a hand on the back of Jacob's chair. "We're still going to the pub later?" she asks me. Jacob keeps scribbling, aware the question is not directed at him.

"I sure hope so," I say.

Jacob and I wrap up the rest of our work and by the time he returns to his desk, I have a list of things to do that will take me a good part of the day. I make myself a cup of tea first, after all, it's not every day you're asked to set up a website to search for yourself.

Have you seen Molly Forster?

Yes! I have! She's right here! In the office!

I work through my list all day, waiting for the right moment, which never comes. I'm massaging my temples when I hear Vivian behind me.

"You ready?"

I turn around. She has that long taupe coat on, over her

shoulders. She's wearing her floppy hat, the one that makes her look like she's on her way to the French Riviera. I check my watch, shocked that the day has gone by so fast and I glance at Chris's door. It's closed, but I can see through the vertical blinds behind the glass wall that he's still there. I only have a small window of opportunity to do what I have to.

I turn back to Vivian, who by now has her hands on her hips. I'm scrambling for an excuse to catch up with them later so I can get a moment alone with Chris.

"Why are you looking at me like that?" she asks.

"No reason," I stutter. "You look great, Viv."

Jenny comes and stands next to her, looking at her up and down. "Yeah, you do, Vivian," she says. "It's a great look on you."

Vivian flicks her hair back. "Good. Because I'm going out, and later I'm catching up with Tommy. He says he wants to talk, and I reckon there's big news coming." She wriggles her fingers in the air.

"Really?" Jenny asks. "He's going to ask you to marry him?"

Vivian bursts out laughing.

"No! Of course not! But I think he wants to move in with me. He's over at my place all the time anyway." She's beaming with pleasure.

I look over at Jacob, hunched over his notebook, scribbling furiously.

"You want to come too, Jacob?" I ask.

He looks surprised by the question.

"To the Cat and Mutton, for a beer," I continue. Of course he's surprised. I've barely said boo to this man and now I'm asking him out for happy hour. But I'm desperate.

Jacob's smile says everything about how rarely he gets included in something like this. "Okay, yeah, thanks," he says, and returns to his notebook, the smile not quite vanishing yet from his lips.

"Great!" Vivian says brightly, as if it was settled, as if it had been her idea to ask Jacob. But the look she gives me is more puzzled than put out.

"I don't know about you all, but I'm ready to go," Jenny says.

Jacob stands at that, grabs his jacket from the back of his chair and bends over his computer, shutting everything down.

"Ready, Rach?" Vivian says.

"Okay yes. Let's go." I turn back to my screen and shut everything down too. I stand up, fish my mobile out of my bag, and pretend to read a text. I make a frustrated noise.

"I just need to make a call, I'll join you all there."

"We can wait," Jenny says, dropping her bag from her shoulder to the floor. Jacob is standing behind them, his hands deep in his pockets, a large brown leather satchel hoisted on his shoulder.

"No, no you go. I won't be long. Get me a pint of the Truman, will you?"

Vivian does a mock salute. "At your service," she says, and turns on her heels. I make a show of tapping on the screen while they leave the office and bring the phone to my ear. I have a pretend conversation, in case one of them comes back, feeling like a complete idiot for another few minutes, then I head to Chris's office.

"Give me a sec, will you, Rach? I just need to finish submitting this form," he says when I walk in.

"Sure." I pull out the one and only spare chair and sit down, drumming my fingers together. It's a really small office. There's a cork board that takes up half of the wall behind him, and I gasp as my hand flies to my mouth as I stare at the flyer that bears a photo of my twelve-year-old self.

Missing. Have you seen Molly?

I begin to cough to cover my shock.

"Do you need some water?" Chris asks.

"No, thank you, I'm okay."

He gives me a moment to recover. I can't stop staring at the flyer. I've never seen it before.

"Where did you get that?" I ask.

He turns to look at it. "I don't know. Jacob got it from somewhere. It's an original too. Anyway," he turns back to face me, leaning back in his chair. "What can I do for you, Rach?"

I make myself look at him and clear my throat. "I don't know how to say this…"

He cocks his head. "Give it a try."

I lean forward and cross my arms on the desk. "I have a friend," I begin, "who has a friend, who works at the BBC."

"Okay."

"I'm going to cut a long story short here."

"I would appreciate that."

"I mentioned that Jacob was working with us now."

"Okay,"

"And my friend mentioned it to her friend—"

"This is the short version?"

"I'll get to it, sorry. But actually, before I do, I'd rather you didn't say the story came from me. I would prefer if you left me out of it."

"Okay, out of what?"

I pause. "It gives me no pleasure to tell you this, okay?" That part is actually true.

"Just tell me, Rachel."

"You told us that Jacob was a real hot radio producer, right? That he did all kinds of really interesting things at the BBC, correct?"

"That's right."

"Well, my friend told me…"

I can tell from his face he doesn't like where this is going. Chris is a good guy at heart. "Rachel, gossip—"

"Did you know he got fired?" I blurt out. "From his previous job? From the BBC?"

The way he jerks his head tells me that he did not.

"They gave him three warnings. Apparently, he was really unreliable. And not just because of his drinking problem. Did you know about the drinking problem? Maybe he got help for that, I don't know. All I know is that he really messed up a lot, and they tried to help him, gave him three warnings, but he screwed-up one too many times, and they fired him. And maybe you already know all this and you're giving him a fresh start. But I wanted to make sure because we have a lot to do over the next couple of months. If we want to survive, and keep our jobs…"

I breathe out.

"You're sure about this?" he asks.

"Positive. I'm sorry."

He shakes his head, eyebrows raised. "I'm stunned. Is your information verifiable?"

"Call his boss. His ex-boss. My friend said her name is Alice McGrath. She will be happy to confirm."

He sighs, picks up a pen and makes a note. "I don't suppose you have a number?"

I stand, push the chair back against the desk. "No, sorry. Just call the main switchboard. I'm sure they'll put you through."

When I close the door behind me, I manage to do so without looking back at the flyer that bears my name.

SEVEN

Now I just need to get through the weekend which shouldn't be too hard. Today is Gracie's birthday party. She's turning three. I'm frantic. I want everything to be perfect. I want her to have the best time.

"We can just do it at the preschool you know, parents do that all the time," Matt said a month ago, but I wanted her to have a proper party. So he has spent the entire morning blowing up balloons. They're bouncing off the furniture everywhere I look. I baked a cake. The living room has been transformed into a playroom with all kinds of activities for the kids. But I'm nervous. Anxiety is stalking me. It makes me worry about everything. I'm worried no one will turn up and she will be scarred for life and it will be all my fault. I'm worried that one of the children will fall over on the stairs. Or the kids will get food poisoning. Or—

"My God! Did I just walk into the wrong birthday party? It's very quiet!" Vivian erupts into our narrow hallway, too many shopping bags for me to count dangling from her arms.

"You came early! Thank you!" I kiss her cold cheek. "Here, let me take some of these. What's all this?"

"Oh, you know, trinkets."

"It doesn't look like trinkets," I say, peering inside the bags.

She shrugs. "I couldn't decide between the Karaoke set and the princess outfit, so I bought everything."

I laugh. "She's three years old! You're outrageous. You shouldn't have!"

"It's not for you, Rach, it's for my goddaughter. And anyway, you're calling *me* outrageous?" Her eyes are fixed on the colourful balloons that cover the ceiling.

"Where's Matt?"

"Out for a run. He'll be back in a minute."

"Auntie Vivian!"

"Happy birthday, my little princess," Vivian's arms are high and open wide and Grace bounces into them, giving her a tight hug. She's wearing a pink tutu and yellow tights, and some kind of tiara on her head that falls off as she nestles her face into Vivian's neck. I pick it up and watch Vivian hug her tight.

The presents are given and opened, to Gracie's squeals of delight. I propose that we take them to the living room and all the kids can play with them later, and I'm relieved that Gracie agrees. I caress the soft spray of freckles on her cheeks with the back of my hand. I had those too, once. But I always wear enough makeup to make them disappear.

"Let's go and finish up in the kitchen, your friends will be here soon." Gracie hops on one foot in front of us. Vivian picks up a square pack from her handbag and slips her arms into the crook of mine.

"I brought some cupcake mix. Have you ever made cupcakes?" she asks.

"Never." I let out a chuckle, forcing myself to relax.

"Me neither. But it's a packet mix, so we should be safe," she says, and I laugh.

The kitchen table is covered with slices of buttered white bread. I'm making fairy bread. When I put the butter away, I knock over the jar of multi-coloured sugar beads and it spills everywhere.

"Fuck!" I snap, not catching myself in time. Vivian gives me a shocked look, even though she swears like a sailor. Gracie tries to pick up the sugar beads from the floor.

"Sorry," I say quickly, belatedly. Vivian picks up Gracie and I sweep the floor clean.

"Is Tommy coming?" I ask.

She makes a face, purses her lips. "Tom has gone back to his ex, would you believe?"

I've never heard Vivian refer to him as *Tom* before.

"What? What happened?"

"The bastard decided to go back home after all, his tail between his legs. Told me last night that they were going to give it another shot. Normally one decides this *before* getting divorced—as I pointed out to him."

"I thought he couldn't stand her? His ex?"

"Exactly. As it turned out, the moment she beckoned him to come home, he went running."

"Oh, Viv. I'm sorry, that's terrible."

"That's okay. Good riddance. I'll think of something to make it up to him. I know all his passwords, believe it or not, because he wrote them down carefully in a little notebook which he forgot to take with him when he went back to his—" she pauses, covering Gracie's ears, "fucking ex. Or should that be to fucking his ex?" Gracie squirms, pulls at Vivian's hands and manages to escape. She hops out of the room on one leg.

Vivian sighs. "Anyway, she's his current now I guess. Maybe I'll hack into his Twitter account and post photos of his dick for all to see. He sent them to me often enough. Why should I be the only one to suffer?"

I laugh, but I check her face to see if she's really okay, and not just putting on a brave face.

"So, it's back to Tinder for me! Cheers!"

I want to ask her if she's heard anything, about work, about Jacob. But she wouldn't have. It was only yesterday. I just wish I knew.

"Hello, ladies, I hear there's a party going on here." Matt appears in the doorway, smiling. He comes over to us in two long strides. He kisses Vivian on the cheek. "Hi, Vivian, how are you?"

"Hello, handsome, I'm very well, ready to party. You smell nice."

Matt chuckles. He stretches his tee shirt to dab at the sweat that is dripping down his face.

"You should have a shower, your mum will be here soon," I say.

"I'm about to." He leans towards me and pushes a strand of hair behind my ear.

"Did you invite any good-looking blokes for me?" Vivian asks.

"What about Tommy?"

"Who?" she says, eyes wide in mock innocence.

"Oh, it's like that, is it? Well you're in luck, Gracie is very popular with the boys at preschool, I'm told. There should be at least four of them arriving any minute now."

I check my watch, surprised to see the time. "It's almost twelve already." I grab the packet of cake mix, put it down again and open cupboards at random, looking for a mixing bowl.

"I'll do that," Vivian says behind me. "You finish whatever you were doing."

"I'll leave you ladies to it then, I'll go take a shower," Matt says.

"Typical. Runs off as soon as there's work to be done," Vivian mutters.

We make cupcakes while Matt gets himself presentable, and suddenly our small flat is buzzing with people. His mum is here, and she has baked a cake too. Hers is much better than mine, and it's shaped like a castle. "I know you said you had one, Rachel, but I couldn't help it. Maybe they can have both?" She smothers her granddaughter with kisses, and Gracie loves every minute of it. One of Matt's sisters is applying glitter on Gracie's eyelids. We play songs the kids like to dance to.

Vivian turns to me.

"Don't you ever want to call your dad?" she asks softly. She means Mr Holloway who lives in Australia and hasn't seen his daughter in nine years.

"No, why?"

She points at the children. "You don't get tempted? It might be different now, with Gracie, surely."

"I'm pretty sure he wouldn't be interested."

"Yeah, I understand." She puts her arm around my shoulder and squeezes. "I bet you miss your mum at times like this."

I told Vivian about my mother once, because she had asked. She thinks my mother's name was Jane, and that she died when I was young. At least that last part is true. I simply nod. I do miss them. I miss them all.

Vivian isn't exactly estranged from her parents, but as far as I can tell, they're completely uninterested in their daughter. They live abroad mostly and only spend a couple of months a year in London. Vivian has mainly been raised in boarding schools by the sounds of it. My idea of boarding schools comes from books at the library, and they're all pretty scary. Vivian's an only child, 'like you' she said once, and I wondered if my dead sister could see me then, and if she hated me for denying her even a correction of her existence.

Matt's mum asks when we're getting married. I change the topic, like I always do. It's not that I don't want to marry Matt, but I can never be sure that my ID is completely safe. Marriage certificates live closely with birth certificates and death certificates. My birth certificate might not withstand the scrutiny. It's also why I never applied for a passport and never travelled far, and probably never will.

Matt puts an arm around my waist and we chant happy birthday. I help Gracie blow the candles on the cake.

I would never have dared to hope I'd have a life like this, and I am desperate to hang onto it. I don't care what it takes. Vivian is saying something that I can't quite hear and she laughs, so I laugh with her, and I look at Matt and Gracie and can't help but wonder if life will ever be this happy again. I want to bottle a little bit of the afternoon in a corner of my mind, for the future.

EIGHT

When I get to work on Monday, the first thing I do is look across to Jacob's desk. He isn't here, and his desk looks normal, tidy, the way he left it. Maybe he's just late, so I try to be natural. Mike and I have a usual moment of banter. I notice Vivian is already in Chris's office. I make myself a cup of tea and suddenly she's by my side.

"Jacob's gone!" she whispers.

"What?"

"He's quit. Chris just told me this morning."

"What happened?"

"No idea."

"He didn't say why?" I am fairly sure Chris wouldn't have mentioned my name, but my heart gives a small flutter of anxiety anyway.

"No, that's all I know. I asked if he had another job, I thought maybe he got a better offer, but Chris didn't say. Something happened, I think, I don't know what."

"Vivian! Come back in here, please," Chris says loudly.

Mike lifts his head to look at us. I move towards my desk, just as Chris adds, "You too please, Rachel".

Of course, me too. I am so relieved I could sing. Chris is going to tell me not to worry about the budget, or anything else. I am grinning, I can't help it. I have to pinch myself till it hurts to make it stop. I dodged a bullet, and I can't tell anyone about it, but I'm still happy.

Chris closes the door behind us and Vivian perches herself on the corner of the desk, so I sit in the chair.

"How can I help?" I ask. "Vivian just told me. Do you want me to take down the Facebook page?"

"Why would you do that?"

"I thought…"

"You thought what?"

"It's my fault," Vivian says. "I just now told Rachel that Jacob had left. I didn't get the chance to explain."

"Explain what?" My chest has started to constrict a little. It's what happens when I get tense. It stops me from taking a proper breath.

Vivian hops off the desk and raises her fists in the air in a gesture of triumph. "I'm doing the podcast!" she yells.

"Not quite," Chris says.

My jaw drops. It's such a shock, it takes me longer than it should to react. Finally, I find my voice. "What are you talking about? Jacob's gone, isn't he? you just said—"

Chris clears his throat, but Vivian beats him to it.

"That's right," she says, "he's gone, and we're sorry about that, aren't we Chris? But here we are, so Chris asked me!" she pumps a fist in the air with a whispered "yes!"

Chris shoots her a stern look. "Vivian, do you mind?"

"Sorry, boss." She brings her arms back down and looks at him, with an expression somewhere halfway between wide-eyed innocence and chastised sheepishness. "You were saying?"

Chris turns to me. "Jacob left us, but there's no reason for us not to go ahead with *Missing Molly*. Vivian's going to do it."

The words tumble out before I can stop myself. "But we don't know how! We've never done anything like this before. We'd have to hire someone with experience!" I am working hard to keep the panic out of my voice.

"How hard can it be, Rach? It's not that different from what we do here, we're all about content."

"Good content. Content that grabs you by the throat and won't let go," Vivian adds in a funny voice, her arm swinging. Normally I'd laugh at her antics but right now, she's annoying the crap out of me.

"What about recording the podcast? How would you put it out there?" I ask. "We have no idea how to do that, do we?"

"That's where you come in."

My mouth opens but no sound emerges. Vivian grins at me. "It's going to be a hoot, Rach! It's going to be our project. You can do all the tech stuff, with me of course. We'll have to learn together but once we know what we're doing, it can be your department!"

"My department?"

"Yes! I heard you say to Jacob the other day that you'd love to work on the project. And now that he's gone we need all the help we can get. Isn't that right, Chris?" Chris nods. "See? Chris agrees with me. You're great with numbers, Rach, you've got a great brain. You could do this with your eyes closed. You just need to learn how."

I don't answer, so she leans forward, gets closer to me. "You *are* pleased, aren't you?"

"I'm—I'm shocked to be honest. Shouldn't we put it off for now?"

"In an ideal world, yes," Chris says. "But we can't. The press release went out last Thursday afternoon."

"Thursday afternoon?" I can feel the corners of my mouth pulling down. I am crushed with disappointment. So much for my breathtakingly simple plan.

"Yes. Thursday. That's all right with you?" he asks.

I blink a few times. "Yeah, of course, I'm surprised, that's all. Has it been picked up? The press release?"

"You bet." He shuffles papers around the desk. "Ah there it is, the *Metro* ran it. Not prominently mind you, but that's okay, early days yet. We put it on the front page of the *Herald*, obviously." He points at the floor next to where I'm sitting. I haven't seen this week's *Herald*, but there's a small box of them beside me. I reach down and pull one out.

Missing Molly, a true crime podcast delivered to you by the South Hackney Herald.

"Catchy," Vivian says.

"Yeah well, Mike wrote it."

"Figures."

The words are dancing in front of my eyes. All I can think is that he's going to find me now. This podcast is going to lead him straight to me.

I'm going to die.

Twelve years ago, Molly Forster disappeared from Whitbrook—

I point to the text. "Technically, it's eleven. You've got twelve here."

They look at each other before Vivian slaps me on the shoulder. "Well done! So you *have* been paying attention. I told you it was a good idea to get Rach involved," she says to Chris.

Vivian looks like a kid who's been told she was getting a big red bicycle for Christmas. She puts her arm around my shoulders and squeezes. "We'll be a team, like Thelma and Louise!"

"God help us all," Chris mutters.

That's Chris's nickname for us. Thelma and Louise. He says it's because we're as thick as thieves. I didn't know the reference so I had to look it up. It's an old movie about two friends who go away on a trip together and end up dead.

"Anyway, back to the article," Vivian says, lifting her arm. "It doesn't matter. It'll be twelve years in November. Close enough."

There's a small sound that comes out of me then. It's because I'm in pain, real pain, but Chris interprets as lack of confidence in the project.

"Come on, Rachel, it can't be that hard. Everyone's doing a podcast these days. You'll figure it out."

I've lost, again. I know that, so I begin to rearrange my face from crushed to excited and say, "Well, that's amazing! I can't wait! When are we putting out the first episode again?"

"Friday," Vivian says.

"This week? Surely not!" I quickly scan the article, looking for the confirmation.

"With Jacob leaving we're a bit behind, I won't lie to you," Chris says. "He was going to line up some interviews with the locals and that hasn't happened because frankly, no one's had the time."

I nod gravely. "So we're already behind schedule?"

"You might need to put in some extra time, is that okay with you?" Chris asks.

"Of course. Happy to. When do we start?"

"We already have." They both stand. "Come and see the recording studio."

NINE

We have a storage room in the office. It's next to the kitchen area, where the electric meter is. It doesn't have any windows. Anything that is no longer of any use gets dumped in here, along with the vacuum cleaner. Once in a while we'll do a big cleanup. Last time I checked, the room contained boxes of old newspapers, a printer that no longer printed anything, and a couple of desk lamps.

Vivian opens the door with a flourish. I gasp. It's unrecognisable. There's a small desk, with a microphone on a stand and a pair of headphones next to it. There's a computer screen too, but the most bizarre sight is the padded material on the walls.

"So, what do you think?" Vivian asks. She leans into my ear and whispers. "I couldn't wait to tell you. We finished it yesterday." She looks at Chris.

"You did this? Over the weekend?" My voice sounds softer in here, too quiet almost.

"Jacob did most of it," Chris says behind me. "He started it anyway. Vivian and I put the finishing touches."

49

How come I didn't know? But why should I have known? I was on holiday. And anyway, I am a part-time bookkeeper slash admin person. Until today, apparently.

"Can we afford it? I only finished the budget on Friday."

"It was donated," Vivian says.

"By who?"

"Jacob. It's his old equipment."

"Won't he want it back now?"

"Don't worry about that, Rachel," Chris says.

Vivian sits down and swivels in the chair. She's like a child, grinning. She lifts the bulky headphones and puts them on her head. She pulls the desk mic closer to her, puts on her radio voice, and says, "Good evening, everyone, my name is Vivian Brown, and you're listening to *Missing Molly*."

"You can't say *evening*, you don't know when they'll be listening to it." I hadn't meant to sound so curt, it just came out that way. She makes a face. "Thanks, Sherlock. I was just pretending."

"So, you see here, the mic is being fed into that rack over there," Chris says, oblivious as always to what is going on around him. An odd quality for someone who runs a newspaper. "It's connected somehow to this computer here, or so I was told. You can take a look later, Rach. But it should be good quality, good enough for our purposes."

Maybe I could sabotage something here. Pretend Jacob didn't really know what he was doing with all those cables, and this setup was never going to work. But what would be the point? That would simply delay the inevitable.

"Anyway, Rach, we just wanted to bring you up to speed," Chris says, moving back out of the room. Vivian is put out, I can tell from the way she's avoiding my gaze. I've seen her face light up with excitement. It might not be the job she's dreamed about, but it's the closest she's ever come to it so far, and yet I'm being a complete buzzkill. She thought I would be thrilled, but instead I have found fault with everything.

I wish I could tell her. *This podcast is going to get me killed, let's not do it please?*

"Okay," I say, "it's great. Great news. I'll get right on it." Chris is standing against the open door, I assume he means to be polite, ladies first, that sort of thing. But as I walk past him and into the corridor, Chris goes back inside. He has one hand on the door handle, and says, "Vivian and I are having a production meeting, so feel free to get on with the rest. Maybe do some research on the technical side of things. Thanks, Rach."

I put my palm against the door. "A production meeting?"

"Yeah, we don't have much time, so we need to finalise the script asap." Vivian claps her hands. "I love saying that!"

Chris nods in my direction. "So, if you don't mind, I've got truckloads of work to do, so let's get this done, Vivian. Rachel?"

Finalise the script?

"Can I stay? Maybe I can help?" I say.

There's a beat where Chris looks to Vivian, and she shrugs. "Sure! Why not? Let's just get to it."

I walk back inside the small, stifling room.

TEN

I watch them, sitting at the desk. Vivian is doing something on the computer. I am standing behind them, leaning against the door, grateful for the dim light in here. They can't see me grinding my jaw.

Do they really think they're going to find me? How? I've never setup any social media accounts, not even in my new name. There are no websites out there that are looking for me, no banners screaming '*Have you seen Molly Forster?*' partly because my entire family was wiped out that night, so there's no one left to care. Also, Edward Hennessy, Chief Constable in Whitbrook, has always maintained the investigation into my disappearance is ongoing, and best handled by the police. He is on record as saying that websites and amateur sleuths will do more damage than good, and they should leave it to the professionals.

I wonder how he'll feel about the podcast. Does he know? Has he picked up on the small item in the Metro? Probably not. But he'll hear about it, and he won't be pleased. Well, that makes two of us.

"We're fine for the first episode," Chris is saying. "Even the first two episodes, because they're going to be recap, mostly. The family murders, what happened to Molly, background on the killer, etc. etc."

Vivian is making noises of assent. She's typing something on the computer, then she says, "I know Jacob hasn't had any luck lining up some good interviews, because the town has closed ranks on us. I made some calls, but I haven't been able to access anything either. Nothing from the school, for example. No one wants to talk to us. I think they're worried we'll make them look bad and they need the tourists. But we have this."

Vivian is fiddling around with the mouse and I am unprepared for what happens next. I am staring at an old clip of Channel Four news. Chief Constable Hennessy's voice fills the room.

"We are pleased to report the arrest of a Mr Dennis Dawson in conjunction with the Forster family murders. Mr Dawson was known to the family, he was employed by Mr Forster as their regular gardener, he had access, and a motive. Without going into too much detail, we want to reassure our community that this attack was not a random occurrence, the reasons for which I'm not at liberty to discuss at this time."

This scene, almost twelve years later, has as much power upon me as it did when I first saw it. I can taste the bile rising up, I don't know if it's for the tragedy of the situation, or because back then, my reaction to it almost cost me my life.

Vivian pauses the video and turns to Chris. "Generally speaking, all we have right now is footage of old news items, like that one."

The room feels way too small. I feel for the door handle behind me and open it a crack, hoping for some air.

"Can I see the rest?" Chris asks.

Vivian resumes the video.

"We are appealing to the public to help us find young Molly Forster, who escaped from the residence while this individual was committing this atrocity upon the family. Our priority is to find young Molly and keep her safe. If you see her, or if you have any information as to her whereabouts, please contact the police immediately."

A wave of nausea engulfs me. Then it happens.

I am back there, in the old abandoned train station. It's cold. I'm in shock, and I'm terrified.

I don't know how long I'd been crouched there when I heard footsteps outside, on the gravel. I squeezed my eyes shut and leaned into my knees to muffle the scream. Then I heard him, whispering. "Molly, are you there?"

I bolted outside and saw his silhouette near the door. His hand reached out to me, and I felt the tip of his fingers brush my shoulder just as I turned around and ran. I should have gone to the police station then, but all I could think of was to get away from him as I heard his ragged breath behind me.

I ran towards the river, to get away from the lights. Then I ran along the bank, ignoring the ferns and branches that cut and grazed my shins, until I reached the old bridge.

They called it the upside-down bridge, because the steel truss was built under the timber deck and railings. It was dark, a moonless night, I ran across and I almost smashed myself against the heavy barrier near the other end. My stomach lurched, and I lost my breath. I had forgotten that the bridge was closed. The abutment at that end had been damaged in the storm and part of the timber deck had collapsed.

"Molly…" he sang out, behind me, his voice hoarse as he took in raspy breaths. I turned, my legs wobbling under me. He was halfway down the deck, leaning forward, his hands above his knees to support himself. I could hear him catching his breath. Then he stood tall again and I turned to climb over the metal structure that had been erected there, but I couldn't. It was too high and I didn't have the strength. I screamed and screamed and in a flash he was almost level with me, his arm outstretched to grab me and I jumped in the river, praying that I wouldn't hit the rocks I knew were protruding below.

I must have fainted in the freezing water and I didn't know how much time had passed when I came to, wedged against tree roots a few hundred feet from the bridge. There was silence all around me, not even his footsteps, nothing. I managed to pull myself up the river bank, my clothes heavy with water and mud. I could see the outline of the bridge in the distance but I couldn't see him. I made my way back, shaking with terror and cold and when I finally ran inside the police station, pushing hard against the door, almost falling on the tile floor, there was only Chief Constable Edward Hennessy.

"Oh my God, Molly? We've been looking all over for you! Molly, sweetheart, are you all right?"

"Help me!" I said, sobbing. "He's coming for me!"

"Rachel?" Vivian's voice brings me back to the present. I blink a few times, aware they're waiting for me to say something.

"Sorry, what did you say?" I ask, shaking the vision out of my mind's eye.

"Do you need any help to get started? With your research?" Vivian says.

"No, I'll be fine." I open the door to the studio. I need some air.

ELEVEN

"What prompted you to do that, Rachel?" Barbara asks.

I give Barbara my most incredulous stare. She's my psychiatrist—or my shrink as Vivian likes to call her— and the NHS pays Barbara lots of money so that she can tell me things I already know. *You suffer from agoraphobia, an anxiety disorder. It's triggered by environments where you feel unsafe, or situations where you feel you can't get away easily.*

It's bridges actually, although I'm not crazy about tunnels either.

I had a breakdown after Gracie was born. It was pretty bad so Matt was adamant. Get help, he said. It doesn't matter if it's expensive, we can afford it. I can always work more shifts, he said. We can never go through this again, Rach, he said.

Poor Matt. It wasn't just him that had insisted. Social Services made it a condition for the first twelve months. Now I keep coming anyway.

"I want to get better. I thought that was self-evident," I tell Barbara.

She nods. "But that's what we're doing here, every week. And you're making progress, Rachel."

I make a sarcastic noise. "It doesn't feel like it. And I figured that if I just practised doing it, I could teach myself to do it." Which is a lie. I haven't practised attempting to cross a bridge exactly, not like *every day*. Just once or twice and then I sort of forgot to. It didn't bother me that much anymore, that I can't cross a bridge on foot. I can cross a bridge if I'm on a bus. I can drive across a bridge. I don't like it much, but I can do it.

"Why didn't you tell me?"

"I wanted it to be a surprise."

She raises her eyebrows. "We could have discussed it, I could have helped you."

"Then it wouldn't have been a surprise, would it." I say this a little petulantly. I don't feel like being scolded for attempting to heal myself.

"Why now?" she asks, after a moment.

"What do you mean?"

"You've been coming here for over two years for treatment, and I never heard you say you wanted to overcome this particular aspect of your phobia."

I nod.

"So why now?"

I look outside the window. The sky is pale grey, almost white. Small diagonal drops of rain land on the window.

"I need to get better. That's all."

I need to protect my daughter.

"Okay." She makes a note. "What happened after the panic attack? How did you get out of it?"

"I called a friend."

I can't help it, the tears well up and I can't speak for a while. She hands me a box of tissues. I've been crying ever since I went home last night. Matt couldn't get me to tell him what was wrong.

I blow my nose.

"Why are you upset, Rachel?"

"I'm frightened," I whisper.

"Why?"

"I don't think I'll ever be free."

TWELVE

Missing Molly - Episode 1 - Transcript

[Music]

Vivian: Every year, thousands of tourists descend upon the charming town of Whitbrook, on the edge of the Cotswolds. It's an ideal getaway location for families or couples alike. The medieval town is best known for its lime-stone architecture and its typical English village feel. The locals are friendly too, and a visit to the traditional stone-built pub will see you well fed and kept warm.

But Whitbrook is not just known for its hospitality. It's also the scene of one of England's most enduring murder mysteries.

[Voice over: Radio 1 evening news report of the killings]

Vivian: What you just heard is the news report broadcast on BBC Radio 1, the day after three members of the Forster family were brutally killed. The tragic event dominated the news in this country for months, and for those of us who are old enough to remember, one of the most disturbing aspects of this tragedy is that the youngest daughter of the family, Molly, disappeared that night without a trace.

Molly was twelve years old.

I'm Vivian Brown and you're listening to *Missing Molly*. If you have any information about the disappearance of Molly Forster, please contact your local police station, or you can leave me a message here on (020) 7946-0318. You can also go to our website and follow the prompts to leave a comment. You can choose to remain anonymous if you wish.

[Music]

Vivian: Jack and Mary Forster, and their two children, Grace and Molly, were a well-liked family in the town. Jack Forster, a solicitor, ran his own practice while Mary raised the children and volunteered for numerous local charities. Then, the unthinkable happened. Almost twelve years ago, on the fourth of November, Grace Forster was celebrating her sixteenth birthday with her family and six of Grace's school friends. The Forsters lived in a large comfortable house in Whitbrook that sits on two acres of what one would describe as a classic English garden. Jack and Mary Forster hosted the small party at their home that afternoon from about four p.m. The children enjoyed a birthday cake followed by a game of cricket in the garden. Grace's friends stayed until approximately six p.m., by which time the guests left and went back to their respective homes, all within walking distance of the Forster residence.

At seven twenty-two p.m., a neighbour walking past the house heard repeated screams coming from inside. He ran down the driveway and around the back of the house. The back door leading into the kitchen was wide open, and inside twenty-year-old Dennis Dawson was found scream-ing, cradling Grace Forster's broken and bloodied body in the hallway. Mary Forster was lying face down at the entrance of the kitchen near her husband's body. All three had been killed with a cricket bat, their skulls broken.

Molly Forster, the youngest daughter, was missing.

It's just Vivian and me, in the studio. She's sitting at the recording desk, the lamp illuminating the script laid out in front her. She suggested I sit next to her while she records the episode, but I said I'd make less noise if stood behind her, near the door.

It hits me with a cold sweat. The thing I dread. It was stupid of me to think I could control it. It begins as it always does, as a memory, fleeting, the sound of people singing *Happy Birthday*, and then it becomes a full-blown movie, one that I can neither stop watching, or stop playing.

Grace brought me here and told me to be quiet, and that she would come and get me. "Whatever you hear, whatever happens, don't move. Promise me." She was scared, I could tell. I promised, and she closed the door. I put my hands over my ears but I still heard the screams. I heard him run up the stairs and yell and shout and I heard Grace cry.

It's so quiet now, everywhere. Quieter than it's ever been. It's as if the air has been sucked out of the house itself.

I pull my knees up and wrap my arms around them. He must be gone but I don't understand why no one has come for me. I push apart the coats and squint at the thin sliver of light that is visible through the gap in the door. I tilt myself forward onto my knees and put a palm against the edge of the sliding white door. I move it slowly, and still crouching, crab like, I leave the wardrobe and I'm inside the bedroom.

I tiptoe softly on the thick carpet until I stand in front of Grace's bedroom door, I put the palm of my hand against the white timber and whisper her name. There's no one there.

Softly, as quietly as I can, I walk down the stairs, my hand brushing the wall, and even before I turn the corner I know that something monstrous has happened down there. At first, I don't understand why Grace is on the floor but then I see the blood. It's coming from her head. The wound is gaping.

I make a sound and Grace's eyes open. She looks right at me.

"Run, Molly, run," she whispers.

I scream for my mother but she does not come. I can't stop screaming. I run to the kitchen and there is blood everywhere, and I see my mother, her head, it's not right, her neck, there's blood. There's my dad, by the door. His eyes are open and staring at nothing.

I run down the hallway to the front door, and he's there, standing in front of it, with the bloody cricket bat by his side.

"Ah, Molly, there you are." He smiles and for one crazy moment I think maybe he just walked into our house and he's going to help us. I want to tell him that Grace is hurt, that she needs a doctor, but there's only a sob rising up in my throat. Then he lifts one arm high above his head, ready to strike me. I run back inside the house.

I must have cried out because Vivian's face hovers over mine.

"Rachel? What's wrong?" I recognise the studio. Then I remember. We're recording the first episode of *Missing Molly*.

My face hurts. I think I hit something. "I can't do it. I'm sorry."

"Can't do what?"

I sit up. I'm shaking. How long have I been like this? I can feel the edge of the nightmare trying to push its way back in. The door of the studio opens behind me.

"You're all right, Rachel? What on earth's happened? What are you doing on the floor?" Chris asks.

"She's not feeling well," Vivian says. She pushes him gently back out. "Give us a minute. We'll come and see you in a bit. Everything is fine."

She crouches next to me and helps me sit up. "It's this room. It's too claustrophobic. We have to keep the door open from now on. You okay, hon? Yeah? Good. Just take a breath. You'll be okay, just relax."

I get up from the floor and sit down on the chair. I put my head in my hands.

"You're feeling better, Rach?"

"I'm sorry. I really am. I'm a complete fuck-up."

"No, you're not. It's just that thing you get sometimes."

"Oh, Vivian, what am I going to do?"

"Don't be so dramatic, Rachel. You just fainted, that's all."

I've dried my eyes and we go to see Chris, who asks me if I'm pregnant. I blush and Vivian stares at me, her lips forming a perfect O.

"No! Not at all! Nothing like that!"

"Well, in future, don't skip breakfast. Get back to work. Get out of here. Both of you. And get me the first take, pronto."

THIRTEEN

"There! See? What did I tell you!" Chris stands in the centre of the room, a copy of the Daily Telegraph in his hand. He brandishes it like it's some kind of trophy.

"What's that?" Perry asks.

"This, people, is what happens when you put your mind to it and come up with a good idea. This," he slaps the paper with the back of his hand, "is a review of the first episode of *Missing Molly.*"

Vivian and I spring out of our chairs at the same time. She almost knocks me out of the way, her arm outstretched. Her face is already glowing with pride. I suspect mine is reflecting the fear I feel, but no one is looking at me.

We only put out the first episode on Friday. I did my very best to make it unremarkable. I tried to persuade Vivian to stay away from making it too dramatic. "I know it's not really any of my business," I said, "but I think it would be good if we didn't sensationalise things. Just keep to the facts." She just laughed at me. And now, a few days later, we have our first review of the podcast. Chris still has the paper in his grip, his arm up high, out of Vivian's reach. She's literally jumping up and down for it and we all crack-up laughing—or they do and I pretend to. But it must be good because Chris wouldn't be teasing her like this if it wasn't. Finally, he relents and hands it to her.

I lean to read over her shoulder, but it doesn't matter. She reads it out loud.

"Missing Molly *podcast review.* Missing Molly *has everything. A missing child, a family massacred for no apparent reason, a murderer so racked with guilt he took his own life.*"

"Jeez," Jenny mutters. "Won't someone please think of the sponsors?"

Mike laughs out loud. Vivian resumes.

"Missing Molly *is not for the faint of heart, but it's as gripping as any murder mystery you might pick up at the airport bookshop. An investigative podcast that assigned itself the task of retracing the steps of twelve-year-old Molly, the first episode is off to a rocking start. It's too soon to tell whether* Missing Molly *will emerge victorious from its challenge, but it's well worth a listen.*"

I don't need to hear anymore. I wear an expression that I hope approximates delight and sit back down. I have to. My legs have turned to jelly. The people looking for me may not have picked up on the small item in the Metro, but I bet they'll read about the podcast now.

"*To this day, there has never been a confirmed sighting of Molly Forster. If you have any information regarding the disappearance of Molly Forster, please contact your local authorities, or alternatively, you can leave a message for the podcast producers on...*" blah blah blah.

I close my eyes. I argued against the phone line, but Vivian insisted. Our dedicated phone number and message bank are ready to take your call. Anyone can leave a message if they have anything to pass on to us. And they can do it anonymously. It's to be the last sentence at the end of each episode, and now, the *Daily Telegraph*, circulation one squillion, has published it.

When I open my eyes, the entire office is looking at me.

"What?" I ask.

"I said, have you listened yet? This morning?" Chris asks.

"To what?"

"The hotline! You goose!" Vivian says.

To me, the word 'hotline' conjures up images of a dozen or more volunteers sitting by the phones, fielding the onslaught of calls from genuinely concerned individuals. The volunteers filter out the real ones in an ocean of possible sightings, 'I saw a little girl that looked just like little Molly. She was wearing pink pyjamas, like on the telly'.

Hennessy did set up the Molly Hotline back then. So that I would be 'returned to safety' as soon as possible. Almost twelve years later, I am given another hotline. But no matter how good this podcast might be, it's not going to generate a national emergency. There are plenty of other missing kids. What about them? There are children on the streets right now that no one is looking for. They're just adrift. Forgotten. I should know. I've met a few of those myself.

I've checked the messages. Of course I've checked. Every day. Every two hours pretty much, sometimes more. I have the number stored in my 'favourites' and I check obsessively.

Grace Forster was a fucking slag, she was a fucking whore, and she deserved everything she got. They all did. Put that on your fucking podcast, you slag.

That was only hours after we released the first episode into the world. I was at home when I heard it and it made me ill. I had to run to the bathroom so Matt wouldn't see me retch. It didn't help that whoever left that message spoke in a low voice, as if they didn't want to be heard.

We thought it might happen, trolls coming out of the

woodworks. You invite people with information about a missing twelve-year-old to contact you, you're going to get a bunch of crazies calling.

After I heard that I just hit delete, right away. Delete delete delete. I had to wash my hands afterwards, cleanse them from handling the phone that had delivered those disgusting words.

"No, yes—still nothing. I'll keep checking," I finally say.

It's funny that they keep asking the same questions. Has anyone left a message about Molly? Anyone know anything? Somebody must know what happened to her! But there's one thing they never ask.

Has Molly called?

They don't even realise it, but they all think she's dead.

FOURTEEN

"You're ready for this meeting, Rach?" Chris asks. Vivian is already at the door of this office, ready for this production meeting. She's beaming. I smile at her.

"Yes, give me one minute," I say brightly. He and Vivian disappear into his office as I retrieve my mobile from my pocket and quickly hit the buttons.

You have no new messages.

I feel the tension in my chest release a little as I stand up and follow them. The time has come to shut this down.

Reddit.com is another one of those endless social media sites. Like all social media sites, it can descend into chaos at times, but it's popular with podcast listeners and producers. Anyone can create a page—or a subreddit as they call it— about any topic, within reason, and anyone can join the conversation. If we hadn't created a page for the podcast, and it had become popular, then someone else would have done it, and that person would be controlling everything. Who can post, what gets deleted, who gets banned.

So I did it. I created a subreddit called *missing_molly*. So that I could control the conversation.

Vivian and I sit across from Chris, each with our notepads at the ready. Chris swivels his computer screen towards us. "You've seen this?"

I squint, lean forward. We're staring at the page. Chris taps the screen with an index finger, right on the latest post.

The one I put up last night.

Really sad news to share about Molly Forster!
Submitted 11 hours ago by friendofmolly
7 comments.

I hear Vivian gasp behind me and turn to look at her. She's thrilled, I can tell. We were only on episode 1 and already people had stories to share about Molly. From a *friend- ofmolly* no less.

Chris clicks on the post heading. Vivian and I both stand and lean closer, our hands on the desk. Her eyes are wide, and I pretend to read the post for the first time.

I never used reddit before so be nice to me if I'm not doing it right. But I knew her, and she was my friend. I live in Canada, I don't want to say where. Molly was in Canada but she called herself Melanie. We worked together at one of the Walmart supercenters there. I think it was 2011. We were both single then and we'd go to the pub after work and sometimes we'd stay there for hours, drinking gin and tonic. She started telling me stories, but I didn't believe her. Stories like that her parents were dead, they died when she was really young, and her sister too. Her whole family had died. I thought it had been a car accident, you know? but I didn't think she was telling the truth anyway because we all say things like that when we're really pissed and we're young. But one night she called me crying and slurring in the middle of the night and said that they all had been murdered, the whole family, and that her name was Molly Forster and her sister was called Grace and her dad was Jack and her mom was Mary and they'd all been murdered by some psycho, and she'd got away. I calmed her down and told her she just needed to get some sleep. That we could talk tomorrow after she'd slept it off. I went to her house the next morning and I thought she was asleep but she was dead. It was so horrible. She had taken pills, I don't know what, and she killed herself. I didn't know if her story was true until I heard about the podcast Missing Molly. So I'm really sorry for everybody, but Molly killed herself in 2011.

I've never set foot in Canada, but I figured that the further away from here the better. I could have gone further. I could have gone to Australia, but I'm already using that one for my neglectful father and evil stepmother. Anyway, surely Canada is far enough.

Vivian stares at the screen, her hand over her mouth.

I shake my head. "I don't know what to say."

"This is amazing," Vivian says.

"It is, I agree. I guess."

"How do you want to tackle this?" Chris asks, looking from Vivian to me, and back again.

I can already feel the relief washing over me as the words pour out. There's a little voice in my head that whispers, *it's okay. It's over.*

"I guess we record a short episode, and we say that we found her and explain what happened to her, the poor girl," I say, shaking my head again. "Maybe we can do a different podcast? It's still a great idea, and people like it, it's working, I mean we got a lot of attention for this one already. I found this website called sleuths or something," I'm aware I'm rambling but I can't help it. "Have you heard of it? People post about cold cases—"

"Will you stop talking for a second?" Vivian snaps. "You're not making any sense. Why would we want to do a different podcast?"

"What do you mean, why? She's dead!" I poke at the screen. "It says so, right there!"

"Actually, I'm more interested in the comments," Chris says.

"The comments?" My chest contracts again, making it difficult to take a breath. I stare at the section below the post. I saw that first response last night, but it was on its own. I didn't check for any comments after that. I didn't think there would be any more, and that if there were, I assumed they'd be irrelevant.

That's really sad, friendofmolly! Thank you for posting!
Submitted 7 hours ago by iamdore.

I'm a private detective and I was hired back in 2012 to look for Molly Forster. I didn't find her exactly, but I got close to tracking her down and I know for a fact that she was in Spain in 2012 so she couldn't have been committing suicide in 2011 in Canada.
Submitted 5 hours ago by anonymousfornow

OMG! That's amazing! But if you knew where she was, why do you say you didn't find her?
Submitted 5 hours ago by iamdore

You worked on finding her? That's awesome!
Submitted 5 hours ago by crymeariver

*The client decided to cancel the assignment at that point. I don't
want to say anything else.*
Submitted 5 hours ago by anonymousfornow

*Did you tell the podcast people? You should talk to them! There's
a number you can call, it's on the website.*
Submitted 4 hours ago by iamdore

I left a message already. Haven't talked to anyone yet.
Submitted 4 hours ago by anonymousfornow

I ball my hands into fists and put them on my lap to stop
them from shaking. There's a trick that Barbara, my shrink,
taught me, and it works most times. Breathe through your
nose and concentrate on the feeling on your upper lip. Shut
out all other sensations and concentrate on the air brushing
the skin below your nostrils.

"Rachel?"

"Yes, Vivian?"

"I said, did you talk to that guy? He said he left a
message."

She looks confused. I just told everyone moments ago that
there were no messages.

"I don't know what he's talking about. I just checked, like I
told you, ten minutes ago, and there were no new messages. I
think it's a prank. Why would he post on Reddit anyway? If
he's a private detective, wouldn't he—"

But then it comes to me, tickling the back of my brain. I
remember now, the disembodied voice.

You have two new messages.

It was horrible, hearing that bit of filth about Grace. It
was so unexpected, so shocking, that I just pressed delete

delete delete delete. I wanted it out of my head. I just forgot about the other one. I wonder if it's gone too. Did I delete it at the same time?

"Do you think it's a tech issue with the hotline?" Chris asks.

"I don't know, but I can reach him through Reddit," I say. "If he's real, that is."

Chris nods. "Good. Get on it."

I'm about to leave the room when Chris says, "How did you get on with Hennessy, Vivian?"

I sit back down. "Hennessy?"

"Yeah, I spoke to him," Vivian says.

"Edward Hennessy?" My heart is pounding so hard I'm surprised they can't hear it.

"What did he say?" Chris asks.

"He was really helpful, actually. He explained how hard they tried to find her back then. Put their whole police force onto it. For months. But they never got an inkling of where she disappeared to. He thinks Dennis Dawson probably killed her but of course the body was never found. She was just a child. He blames himself."

I wince.

"You didn't tell me you spoke to Hennessy," I say, trying not to spit on his name.

"I am now," she replies, her head cocked at me. "Why?"

"I just thought that we were working on this together. Thelma and Louise, remember?"

They both shoot me a funny look.

"It just so happened that you weren't here when he called me, what do you want me to say?"

"What else did he say?" Chris asks.

"He couldn't shed much light on where she might be or

what might have happened to her. He doesn't think we'll ever find her. His money is on Dennis Dawson having killed her and buried her somewhere."

Yeah, I bet.

"But, we talked about the older sister, Grace, quite a bit. It's funny," she turns to me, "I hadn't made the connection before, that Molly's sister is called Grace, just like Gracie."

"Why is that funny?" I ask. It was an innocuous thing to say, a matter-of-fact remark. She didn't mean anything by it, I know that, but I can't look at her.

She shrugs. "It's not. Just a figure of speech."

"So? What did he say? About Grace?" I ask through gritted teeth.

"It was a bit sad, actually. We were talking about motive. He said a bunch of stuff that never made it into the papers at the time, but apparently Grace was—how did he put it? Secretly promiscuous. Easy with the boys I think he said."

I flinch. "Seriously? He said that?"

"He's very old school, I gather. He said there were vague whispers back then, that she'd been caught behaving inappropriately, but he hadn't been paying attention to gossip. I said to him, it was twelve years ago, maybe more a sign of the times, you know? The way she dressed or whatever, maybe people jumped to conclusions, it's a small town, but he said no, it was nothing like that. As it turned out, there were pictures. Of her. He almost made it sound like she brought it on herself through her actions, you know the type of talk?"

"No!" It just comes out of me, but Vivian misunderstands my burst of anger for shock.

"Yeah, I know, I was surprised too! He said they kept it out of the papers for obvious reasons."

"What kind of pictures?"

"The kind that you don't want your mum and dad to see.

She posed. For blokes. For money, apparently. 'Playboy would have hesitated to publish them' he said. I thought he meant because she was so young, but he said, no, because they were that pornographic."

"Bullshit."

"That's what he said."

Chris lets out a whistle. "Did you record the conversation?"

"Of course."

"We can't use that!" I almost shout. "We don't even know if it's true!"

"Of course we do."

"How? Have you seen the photos?"

"I don't need to see them, Rach. He was the Chief Constable at the CID. He's the Mayor now. I think we can take his word for it, don't you?"

Chris laughs at something Vivian says, and Vivian laughs with him.

"Is something wrong, Rach?" Vivian asks. I'd been looking at my hands in my lap. I look up at her.

"Don't you find it strange," I begin, "that Grace and Hennessy's son were dating when she died?"

Vivian winks at me. "That's right. They were. Glad to see you're on the ball." She flicks through pages of her notebook. "Hugo Hennessy."

I feel myself grow pale at the sound of his name. "So Edward Hennessy just told you Grace Forster was a—" I almost say *slag* "—easy with the boys. And yet he let his son date her?"

She thinks about it but only for a second.

"He said there were only whispers, gossip he called it. He said he hadn't paid attention to it at the time."

"But you bring up a good point, Rachel," Chris says.

"Have you tried to talk to the son, Vivian?"

"I did ask Hennessy senior about it, but he said don't even try. It wasn't easy on him, losing his girlfriend in such tragic circumstances, and—"

"His secretly promiscuous girlfriend you mean," I blurt before I have time to stop myself.

"What's the matter with you?" Vivian snaps.

I raise one hand up. "Sorry."

"Anyway," she resumes, "I'll keep trying. It would be a scoop, right? He's never spoken publicly about it."

Over my dead body.

"Does Edward Hennessy have any other suggestions? Of who we could talk to?" Chris asks.

"Not really, as I said before, he thinks we're wasting our time. Molly's dead and Dawson killed her." She sighs. "I'm not having much luck lining up some good interviews, but I'll keep trying. I'll keep you posted."

Chris claps once. "Okay! Fantastic work. We might not have anything new on Molly herself yet—"

"But we do," I interrupt. "We have the post from that girl who knew her, the one in Canada."

"I don't think it's real, Rachel. Given the chap that's a private detective disproved it. It's probably a prank, kids or something. But we need to track down that bloke."

I nod. So much for controlling the conversation.

"We've got some good audio anyway, with the Hennessy interview. If we don't get anything on Molly for episode 2, we'll have plenty to talk about with Grace."

"You're going to play that?" I ask, incredulous.

"You're kidding? Of course we are! It's new material! It's great!" Vivian says.

We are done here, it's over. My attempt at shutting this down failed royally. No one believes my online post, supposedly from *a friend of Molly in Canada*. It's turned out to be a complete waste of time. I wish I could crumple the post, like a piece of paper. I picture myself reaching into the screen and doing it.

FIFTEEN

Had Hugo Hennessy not murdered my sister Grace, she would have turned twenty-eight next month. I was the baby of the family. I don't think I was planned, but if I was an accident, I'm sure I was a happy one.

Grace was beautiful. She had blond wavy hair and blue eyes, and dimples when she smiled.

Hugo was two years older than her. The first time I saw them together was at a local soccer game. We'd all gone as a family. Dad liked to support local sport activities. I think he even gave money to the club. I can still picture Hugo standing on the sidelines in his soccer outfit, watching players practice a few moves, his hands on his waist. He exuded so much confidence he might as well have been the coach. He was very handsome, like, look twice handsome, with blond hair that he was always pushing off his forehead and a square jaw that reminded me of a character in a comic book.

We were all seated and he waved to Grace, who waved back. When I turned to look at her, she was blushing. After the game we got up to leave, my dad talked to someone he knew, and suddenly Hugo was there. He was very polite, and after he said hello to my parents he started to chat to Grace. They looked like the perfect couple. I don't know how they met, at school I suppose, and not long after that soccer game, they started dating.

I think the whole concept of dating has changed a lot in the last twelve years. I'd be surprised if he and Grace were having sex, but then again, she wouldn't have told me. For them, dating would have meant a trip to movies, or a walk somewhere, maybe a bike ride, but all I know is that he started to spend more and more time at our house. He was always nice to me. Always nice to everyone actually. Mum loved him. Dad thought he had excellent manners.

It was a few weeks after they first met that I happened to be in Grace's room one night when she came out of the shower with only a towel wrapped around her. There were marks on her upper arm, like dark bruises.

"What's that?" I asked, reaching to touch it. She flicked my hand away.

"Nothing!"

It wasn't very long after that that he killed her.

That evening at dinner, I barely say a word. The third time Matt asks if I'm okay, I almost snap.

"I'm fine! Really!" I say too quickly, then I see the hurt on his face. "Sorry, love. Just a lot going on at work, you know."

I could tell he's put out, by the way he plays with his food for a bit. I want to reach out, lean into him, but I just can't.

"Why don't you just tell me what's really going on, Rach. Ever since we've been back from our holiday, you've been acting weird." He pushes the plate away and crosses his arms.

"No I haven't."

"When's the last time you've been to see Barbara?"

"Really? What's that supposed to mean?"

"You're not yourself. Just tell me."

"Last Tuesday, Matt, same as always, same as every other fucking week, okay?"

I get up from the table and almost throw my plate into the sink. We barely speak the rest of the evening and now, in bed, he won't even look at me. He has his back to me, and when I lay a hand on his shoulder, he shrugs it off.

I keep thinking about the private detective that was looking for me. I knew I couldn't convince Vivian and Chris that he wasn't real. The problem is, he was telling the truth, he must have been, because I *was* in Spain in 2012.

Terrible things happened there and at the time, I didn't think they were related to Hugo or Molly. But now I don't know anymore. And if there is a connection, then I'm really worried about what's going to happen to Vivian.

The thing about Vivian is that she's very good at every-thing she does. She's taking everything at face value right now, everything that Hennessy says. But at some point, she's going to look for Molly. Really look. And she's going to ask ques-tions, and she's going to want answers, and Edward Hennessy is not going to like it.

And if she gets too close to the truth, they'll kill her.

SIXTEEN

I watch Chris type, one index finger at a time, looking from the keyboard to the screen, and back again. That's how he types, and he's never made an effort to learn, or even to speed things up.

"Can I talk to you for a minute?"

"Jesus, Rachel! You scared me. How long have you been standing there?"

I ignore the question and close the door behind me.

"Sorry. Do you have a second?"

"Not a lot more, what is it?"

I pick up a rubber band from a small receptacle on the desk and start playing with it, looking for the right words. Chris leans backwards in his chair. I have his full attention.

"It's about the podcast. I…"

He lets out a puff of frustration. I steamroll over it.

"I did some digging. Over the last few days." I pull out a piece of paper from my pocket. I unfold it slowly and I lay it flat on the desk, smoothing out its creases.

"There," I say, pushing it towards him. "It's the phone number of Molly's schoolteacher."

"What are you talking about?"

"Mrs Callaghan, that's her name. She's retired, but she still lives there. Molly was in her class." I tap the piece of paper with my finger. "The number's current. I checked."

I don't remember what Mrs Callaghan looks like exactly, but I remember I liked her. We all did, in my class. I figured it wouldn't do any harm if she got on the podcast. What could she possibly say? That she knew me, and I was an average student?

I called Directory Enquiries and found two Mrs Callaghans in the town. I rang them both. I pretended I was doing a survey on behalf of the local council to do with public transport. I knew the second I heard her voice that she was the right one. It's funny, the things you remember. For me, it's the sound of voices. Anyway, it didn't take much for her to tell me she was a retired schoolteacher, and that more public transport would be a brilliant idea.

Chris is holding the piece of paper as if there's more to read than a bunch of numbers.

"That's good stuff, Rach. How did you get that? Vivian called the school, but they wouldn't give out any information."

"I have a source. And this, it's just the beginning."

He smiles. "A source? Really?"

I nod.

"That's great. Well done. Vivian must be thrilled." He looks through the glass pane towards Vivian's desk. I turn around and do the same. She's on the phone, making notes, oblivious to our stares.

"She doesn't know yet," I say. "There's a problem."

"Do they want money?"

"No, no, nothing like that."

"What then?"

"Well, it's like this. This source only wants to speak to me. They said they'll get me interviews and all they know, but only if it was me so… I want to be a producer on this podcast."

He thinks about it for a moment, then he says, "Do you know what a producer does?"

I feel myself blushing. "No, but we all have to start somewhere."

"Can you even handle the workload? It's not like you don't have a lot on your plate already."

"Yes, I can. I know I can," I reply.

He looks at me, silently, and shakes his head. "I don't get it. Why won't you tell me how you got that info?"

"You wouldn't believe me if I did. Trust me."

"Well, if you bring in this kind of material, I don't see why not."

I let out a breath of relief.

"Thanks, Chris. Also, I want to be part of all the decisions, like who we interview, what direction we take with the podcast, all of that." I bite the inside of my lip.

Chris leans back in his chair. "Vivian's in charge."

"I know, and I want us to work together, and make decisions together."

"She's got a lot more experience than you, Rach. What's the problem?"

"There is no problem."

"We can make you a producer and still have Vivian be the lead. I don't mind giving you the opportunity, but you'll learn a lot more that way."

I'm doing this all wrong but I'm in too deep now.

"And if I say no?" he says.

"Then you say no, but why would you? I have a lot to

contribute to this project." I point at the number with my chin.

Chris narrows his eyes at me. "You surprise me. I didn't pick you for being so ambitious. Not like this."

I feel my tears well up, and I will them away. "Call the number," I say.

He dials the number and puts it on speakerphone.

"Hello?"

My heart skips a beat.

"Is this Mrs Callaghan?"

"Yes, it is."

"Mrs Callaghan, were you Molly Forster's primary school teacher?"

"Yes, why?"

"We're producing a podcast about the disappearance of Molly Forster. We'd like to interview you. Is that possible?"

"How did you get this number?"

"Can I get someone to call you and make a time?"

"Yes, I—I don't know. I have to go."

"Thank you, Mrs Callaghan, we'll be in touch soon."

He hangs up, then without looking at me, he says, "You drive a hard bargain there, Rachel. What about hosting, is Vivian still doing that? Or do you want to be the voice of the podcast too?"

If I could leave Vivian out altogether, I would. She'd hate me for life, and I'd have to live with that. But there's no way Chris will let me host it. He's only asking because if I say yes, he'll tell me to go back to my bookkeeping and never to mention this again. Or he'll fire me.

"Vivian is still doing that. She's the best person for that job."

"It's big of you to say, Rachel."

He taps the end of his pen on the desk. *Tap tap tap tap.* I want to lean over and snatch it away.

"I tell you what," he says, "I'll talk to Vivian, and see what she says. If she's okay with it, we'll give it a go. For one episode, to begin with. Either way, it's just a trial, you understand? And I'm not paying you any more, you got that?"

"Yes."

He gives a small nod and goes back to his computer screen. I watch the slow one-finger typing. I figure we're done here.

"It was her idea, you know."

My hand is already on the door handle.

"The podcast?"

"No, of course not. I told you already. I meant for you to be involved. That was her idea."

He doesn't lift his eyes from his task, one finger painstakingly searching for the right key, then the other. I thank him and walk out.

I go right over to Vivian. I have to tell her, and I want to find a way to soften the blow, but just as I reach her I hear Chris behind me call out to her.

She looks up, walks over to him, raises a questioning eyebrow at me on the way. I want to find a way to explain but instead I shrug a timid smile. I find that I am relieved after all, that Chris will tell her instead of me.

I watch them through the glass pane of Chris's office, while pretending not to. I'm scribbling randomly on a notepad.

At first, she stands quietly, listening to Chris, then she starts gesticulating. I can hear her voice become louder but I can't make out what she's saying. Later when she walks past me she doesn't look at me. I extend a hand.

"Vivian," I say softly. She hears me, I know, but it's as if I hadn't spoken.

I stand quietly and walk over to her. I rest my fingertips on the edge of her desk.

"Can we talk?"

"It's a bit late now, don't you think?" she says without looking up. "Why didn't you tell me?"

"It's just that... it's complicated."

She shrugs. "You know what, Rachel? I don't feel like talking. Let me get back to work."

Not long after that she shuts down her computer, noisily, banging her mouse. She puts her coat on, the lovely black suede one she picked up at the vintage store on the way to my place, then without a glance my way, and without her usual "Bye, everyone! See you tomorrow, everyone!" she's gone.

I finish my own work quickly, and then I leave too.

SEVENTEEN

Vivian lives in a lovely flat in Kensington. She told me once she has some kind of trust fund set up. Not by her parents mind you, but by her grandmother. They were really close. I figured her grandmother must have wanted to protect Vivian from her own parents' neglect.

It's raining when I get there, and I don't have an umbrella. My hair is wet, rain dripping down my neck and down my back.

I ring the flat, and she asks who it is.

"It's me."

Nothing happens. I can picture her upstairs, finger on the button. I hold my breath but then the door opens.

When I get upstairs, she's standing in the doorway.

"Don't be angry with me, Viv."

"I'm not angry, Rachel, but I'm pretty fucking disappointed."

I wince. "Listen to me please, I'll try and explain."

She opens the door wider and lets me in. I follow her into the kitchen. There's a steaming cup of tea on the worktop.

She doesn't offer me one. She stands there, sipping her tea, waits for me to say something.

"The thing is—" I begin, without any clue of what I'm going to say, but she interrupts me immediately.

"How long have we known each other?"

"Vivian, listen—"

"How do you think it feels, to hear that you've gone behind my back, and essentially wiggled your way into my job."

"That's not true."

"You have never said that you wanted to do anything other than what you were doing, i.e. the accounts. But now I find out that you're going to be a co-producer of the podcast, that I have to run any editorial decision past you." She shakes her head in disbelief. "It would have been nice if you'd told me."

"I wanted to."

"I feel pretty betrayed here, you know? And I've been wracking my brain to figure out what I've done to deserve this, and you know what? I've been nothing but a friend to you. A true friend."

"It's not like that."

"Do you agree?"

"Yes, of course I do."

"So why would you fuck me over like this? You didn't even want this podcast to happen for fuck's sake. So what is it?"

"I didn't fuck you over—"

"You know I want to be a reporter. It's my dream job. An *investigative* reporter, Rachel. Then this opportunity comes up and it's fucking perfect! I love podcasts! It's the future of investigative reporting! And by some stroke of luck, it's been given to me!" Her arms are open wide, in wonder at the incredible fortune that came her way. Part of it had been luck, the part I played, in exposing Jacob and having him gone, sure, but the rest was all her. Vivian is great at what she does. This lead producer's job was a promotion, and she'd earned it.

"You wouldn't even have this job if it wasn't for me," she says now.

"Cut it out. You know that's not true. You told me the position was available, but I got the job, not you. I'm branching out. You told me I should be more ambitious often enough, well here I am."

"You should have told me," she says. "If you'd told me, we could have gone to Chris together, and—" then she cocks her head at me, the way she does, and says, "Chris says you have access to info, somehow. You have an in, a source, I think he said. Is that true?"

I flick my head in a 'maybe' kind of way.

"And you're not going to share that with me? You're keeping it to yourself?"

I blink. "For now."

She shakes her head in disgust, and I see the tears well up in her eyes. I'm betraying our friendship and she doesn't understand why. Her face collapses in misery. Suddenly I want to stop. I want to take her in my arms and tell her I didn't mean a word of it. I'm just trying to protect her.

"You know, I'd never say this normally, Rachel, never. But I feel I have to." She takes a deep breath and I know exactly what's coming.

"I was there for you."

And now it's too late. I cross my arms over my chest, holding back my own tears.

"Don't you dare," I say.

"When you went crazy," she continues, "I was there for you. Your postnatal depression episode, you have no idea what it did to us. Me. Matt. Gracie. What it took out of us. And I. Was. There."

I turn around for the door.

"I stood up for you," she says louder, "When they could have taken your daughter away from you, because of what you did? I vouched for you."

I'm crying now, I can't help it. Even if I wanted to speak, I couldn't get it out through the tears.

"I told the cops you were going to be okay. That your daughter was safe with you. I told the doctors the same thing. I told social services the same thing. I was there for you, Rachel. I was your friend! And now you're doing this?"

"I'm not listening to this anymore," I say, opening the door. I close it just as she says,

"I'm worried about you. I think you might be going crazy again."

EIGHTEEN

Matt is working late today and won't be back for at least an hour. I give Gracie some hot chocolate and she settles in with her pencils and paper. That's one thing she gets from Matt, she can draw remarkably well for her age.

Like most people our age, we rent our flat. It's an older flat. When the central heating comes on in winter, the pipes make a hell of a racket. But it's home for us. It's the only place Matt and I have lived in together. As far as I'm concerned, it's the most wonderful home in the world.

In the kitchen, under the sink, there's a cupboard where we keep cleaning products. Behind the down pipe, on the wall, there's a small panel made of old tin that's been painted over with the same colour as the wall. It looks like something that was put there to fix a big hole. It's affixed by four screws except they're not screws exactly. I don't know what they're called, and I didn't want to ask Matt, because he would wonder why I was interested. I described them to the man at the hardware store, and he sold me a tool that was shaped like a Tee.

Behind the panel there's a wall cavity and an old rusted pipe. The whole thing must have been sealed years ago. Whatever use it once had, it was no longer required.

That hole has become my hiding spot. It's the perfect size for my memory book. My sister Grace came up with the name, a memory book. It's a scrapbook, essentially. We both had one, Grace and I. Mine is filled with a bunch of clippings I collected over the years for one reason or another, along with a few meagre souvenirs that I feel should be kept hidden. Things that are important to me, to have and to keep.

Grace and I used to play in the old disused train station not far from our house. The doors and windows were boarded up, except for that one small window at the back. It was hard to get to it because of all the ivy that had grown over it, and the tall nettles against it. But Grace had found a path, and that window had never closed properly. It was just big enough for her to pass through. Then she would put her hands out and help me up.

I would line up my dolls against the wall, where the paint had cracked and peeled almost completely, and the wall had a soft, pale surface that left a chalky powder on my hands. They would become my pupils and while I taught them maths, my sister would write in her memory book, glue a picture of a famous pop star that she'd cut out of some magazine, or make a drawing. I'd stick stars in the margins for her, where she'd put something really special, or where she mentioned something about me.

I tell Gracie that I'm doing some cleaning. She doesn't pay attention. She's sitting in her chair, engrossed in her drawings, humming to herself.

I remove the bit of tin and pull the memory book out of its hiding spot. Back at the kitchen table, I unwrap it from the plastic bag I store it in and a few pieces of paper fall out.

Among them is a snapshot, the only photo I have of the man who helped me survive, and who was killed in a car accident.

When I turned fifteen I decided I had to get out of living on the streets. I was seeing too many kids like me ending up with lethal drug addictions, or dead. I fantasised about being a maths teacher, but I found out it wasn't going to work. I had missed too much school.

I had a job then, I washed dishes in a Chinese restaurant. The people who ran it were always nice to me, but I wasn't earning much. Not enough to put myself through school. A counsellor at the Youth Centre said I might look into an apprenticeship, that there was loads of options for someone like me. I started looking into it, and one thing became clear: I needed some kind of verifiable identification. I figured there had to be a way to get a fake ID, people did it all the time. There are various underground networks that help you do that, none of them that advertise on Facebook, but when you live on the streets for long enough, you become very good at finding out information, especially of the illegal kind.

That's how I met Gabriel. I suspect that wasn't his birth name, and he never told me one way or the other. And anyway, I wasn't going to give him mine.

He was considerably older than me, mid-twenties at least. Maybe because I was so young, and so vulnerable, but Gabriel helped me. I wanted a completely fake ID, but he explained to me why I'd get caught and told me to find a name of someone around my age, someone who had died, and he'd do the rest.

There was a girl, back in Whitbrook, called Susan Bishop. We weren't friends exactly, but we knew each other from the neighbourhood. She died when she was about seven years old. Meningitis. It was a tragedy in our town. I didn't go to the funeral, but I went to her grave a few times. She'd been the first person I'd known who had died.

I told Gabriel about her, and he got hold of her birth certificate, then he explained how to get an ID in her name. "You have the birth certificate, now you get the next thing. You might get yourself a library card. You build up slowly, bit by bit, a collection of identifying things. You start small, but the more evidence you have with your new name on it, the easier it becomes. You'll have a full ID in no time." He also told me never to get arrested, probably not to get married and always to pay my taxes on time. Other than that, it would do for most things, he said. He also taught me how to hide in plain sight and he taught me how to disappear.

I became Susan Bishop and I went back to school. Then when I was seventeen, I ran into Gabriel again and we started dating.

Most people who became adept at creating false identities started out running away from their own, and Gabriel was no different. I never knew what had happened in his life that made him hide, and he never asked about my past.

We went to Spain together because he had a job there, in Barcelona. You didn't need a passport to go to Spain, not then anyway.

We settled there, we were happy, but around a year later he became concerned about some activity he was picking up on his networks. He got scared that his past was catching up with him. I thought he was being paranoid.

We had plans to visit some friends in Sitges for the weekend, about 25 miles down the coast. At the last minute I fell ill, and I couldn't go, so Gabriel went on his own, just for the day.

He must have been halfway there when he called me. I couldn't hear him properly, but it sounded urgent. He sounded scared. I could only catch a few words, but it sounded like "They found me." He was shouting. Repeating the same words over and over again. There was too much noise, too much wind, and I couldn't make out the words.

Then he came through, *Go!*

I thought he wanted me to meet him somewhere. I thought we had to run away.

Go! Now!

Where?

It was a miracle they were able to retrieve the car from the bottom of the cliff. I thought he'd been murdered by whatever had caught up with him. It was our nightmare come true. The police said he didn't have his phone with him. That phone had been thrown out of the car a few miles back.

I returned to England, and I ditched Susan Bishop and became Rachel Holloway. I always assumed it was him they were after because he was always looking over his shoulder. But after reading the comment from that detective I think that it was never the case. I think what Gabriel had been trying to say was, "They found you."

He was warning me.

Go!

Run, Molly, run.

I hear the key in the door and I shove all my memories back into the book. Gracie is already chanting *daddydaddydaddy* and by the time Matt appears in the kitchen I've only had time to pull a bit of newspaper over the book. It's a copy of the local paper.

Missing Molly, a new podcast delivered to you by the South Hackney Herald.

"You're home early?" I don't know why I make it sound like a question.

Without answering, he goes to the fridge and pulls out a beer. He offers me one, but I decline. I notice he's wearing his tracksuit bottoms and an old hooded sweatshirt. When he removes it, his T-shirt is damp with sweat.

"Daddy!!!"

He picks up Gracie with one arm and she hugs him tightly, her face flush with happiness. Matt finally smiles.

"You went running?"

He nuzzles Grace, blows raspberries into her neck while she giggles and wriggles with joy.

"Yeah, we had a cancellation at work, so I got out early," he says at last. He sits down at the kitchen table with Gracie on his lap as she toys with the cord dangling from his hood. I turn a page of the paper, pretending to read. My heart is beating so fast it's making my mouth dry.

Please go away, just for a minute. I look at my watch and take a gamble.

"Do you want to give Gracie her bath? Or do you want me to?"

"I'll do it," he says.

He stands, throws her in the air a couple of times and she screams and squeals. They coo at each other and he takes her to the bathroom to run the bath. I let out a long breath of relief, quickly fold the paper and turn on the kitchen tap. Should he return too quickly, I am ready to make a show of cleaning. But there's no need, I can hear them chatting and laughing and pretty soon I can hear Gracie splash into the water too.

I secure the tin sheeting back in place.

NINETEEN

When I walk in the following morning, she's already here, sitting at her desk, typing at a million miles an hour. *Tip dancing*, she called typing sometimes. It made me laugh. We'd start speaking with a New Zealand accent, sending each other into hoots of laughter.

But not today. You can tell the atmosphere in the room has shifted. It's like we don't know what to say to each other.

At first, she pretends not to notice me. Which is silly. She knows I've arrived, I am standing a few feet away from her. Then she raises her head and says hi with a pretend cheerfulness. I reply with the same awkwardness. Mike looks up and though normally he would have said something, now he's mute.

I hook my bag on the back of my chair and take my jacket to the coatrack in the corner of the room, with its curly tentacles pointing up and a space at the bottom for umbrellas.

"Rachel, in here please." Chris is standing at the entrance of his office only a few feet away, but by the time I reach the door he's already gone back in. I don't sit down. Somehow, I don't feel invited to do so.

"It's not bad." He hands me the script of the new episode that I emailed him last night. He has printed it and made some corrections. "Give it to Vivian and see what she thinks."

I take the sheets of paper and notice the paragraph that he has crossed out. It's the part about Dennis Dawson's arrest. I point out that the only reason he got arrested was because he happened to go to the house. But the cricket bat was wiped clean, so it didn't have his fingerprints, or anyone else's for that matter. I explained that, in the script. It was the cricket bat used in the killing because it still had traces of blood, especially on the handle, where some of it had seeped under the leather. But why would he wipe the cricket bat clean and then stick around screaming for the neighbours to find him?

"What's wrong with any of it?" I ask.

"It's irrelevant. I appreciate that you've looked into it, and it's interesting, but it's not what we're trying to do. We're looking for Molly, not challenging the facts of the case. Okay?"

"Even if I'm the producer?"

"Even if you're one of the producers."

I take the script to Vivian and put it on her desk. She doesn't look at me, but she just picks it up and reads it.

"What do you think?" I ask.

"It reads like shit. It's like a twelve-year-old wrote it."

"So rewrite it then. Here." I hand her a red pen. "Rewrite it so it doesn't read like *I* wrote it."

"Call for you, Rach," Jenny yells out, holding out the phone.

"I'll take it over at my desk," I tell her.

There's one call I've been waiting for and I've been dreading at the same time. I did leave a private message on

Reddit for the user who calls himself *anonymousfornow*, asking him to call Rachel Holloway, producer, at *The South Hackney Herald*.

And now, Tom Sneddon, private detective, and I are having a short phone conversation. I'm desperate to ask him: *who was it? Who hired you back then?* But I know better than to do that over the phone. Instead, we agree on a time and a place to meet up.

TWENTY

I'm sitting on a wooden bench in the park near our place, watching Gracie play in the sandpit. She loves coming here and it's one of those warm autumn days where we still can. Sometimes we feed the ducks and geese and she squeals with delight at the sight of those big birds, her small hand reaching out to pat them, her little fingers opening and closing in the air. I find geese kind of scary, up-close like that, but not Gracie. She's pint-sized and already braver than I am.

We're not feeding birds today. We're just spending half an hour before I drop her off at preschool. I've arranged her hair into plaits that go all the way around her head, just the way she likes them. She's got her little pink basket with her. She's playing with a small dark-haired boy about the same height as her. He has a yellow rake and they seem very happy moving sand from one side of the pit to another, he with the rake, she with the pink plastic basket.

"How old is she?"

I turn to look at the dark-haired woman who has come to sit next to me.

"She just turned three," I reply. "And yours? How old?" I point my chin towards the dark-haired boy.

She smiles. "No, he's not mine."

"Oh."

I say nothing further, I just watch my daughter. I don't feel like making conversation with strangers. I've barely slept the last two nights. We finished the second episode and it's out there now. I can't get Hennessy out of my mind. The things that he said about my sister. That he would use this opportunity to sully her name like this. I tried to keep the recording of their conversation out, and managed to get some of it edited out, but Chris overruled me on the substance of it. I had to sit there and listen to Hennessy say the most awful things about Grace.

"She was disturbed you see, as we now know, although we certainly didn't then," Hennessy had said, his voice dripping with fake pity for her. "She even got Dennis Dawson to pay for these photos, although I don't know why, after all her father was rather well off I thought. The family didn't skimp on anything as far as I knew. Grace had all the things a girl her age might desire."

I pressed my fingernails deep into the palms of my hand, but I had to listen, it was important.

"Dennis was a simple boy, poor chap, I wouldn't say it wasn't his fault but—"

"You're not suggesting it's Grace's fault that he took a cricket bat to the whole family, surely." Vivian's voice had asked.

"Lord no, of course not. I just meant to say that Dennis was not the brightest spark in the firmament, if you get my meaning. He was a simple boy, simple of mind. He was twenty at the time, but his mental age would have been more of a boy of twelve or so. Which is not to excuse anything of course," he rushed to clarify. "But Dennis was in love with her, you know. To her, it was all a game," Hennessy went on, "but Dennis kept all the photos. In some ways, it was fortunate he killed himself before it went to trial. We were able to spare the memory of that poor family."

Listening to that garbage, I made myself a promise. I would go after that man, and somehow, I would punish him. Not just for what he's done, but for what he's said.

"Jacob is a good man."

I am so deep in my thoughts I forgot about the woman next to me. I turn to her, she's still sitting there, still staring straight ahead.

"I'm sorry, what did you say?"

"Jacob Whitelaw, he's my husband."

She's strikingly beautiful. She speaks with a slight accent, suggesting she comes from somewhere exotic, somewhere I've never been. Somewhere that smells of aromatic spices, and that brings up images of golden embroidery and colourful scarves.

"Jacob Whitelaw?"

"My name is Zoya Whitelaw."

"How did you find me?"

"I followed you, from your house."

"How did you know where I lived?"

"I followed you from your work once."

I stand up fast, furious and in a panic at the same time. "You followed me home, and you've followed me here? And my daughter?"

I turn frantically to find Gracie. She was right there, sitting with her dark-haired little friend, working on some kind of sand structure.

"Gracie! Honey!"

I stare at the spot where she'd been a second ago, my heart

thumping. I can see the pink plastic basket, it's fallen over on its side, and Gracie isn't there. The panic makes my chest hurt.

"Gracie? Gracie!!"

Gracie's blond head pops up from behind one of the large rocks in the corner of the sandpit. She's stood up quickly, her beautiful blue eyes searching mine, confusion clouding her face. Something in my tone.

"Sit down. Please. You'll frighten her. I just wanted to talk to you in a quiet place, that's all," Zoya says.

"You're pretty frightening, lady," I reply, but I sit down anyway, my legs like jelly.

"It's okay, honey! Just stay on this side, please." Grace's frown dissipates, and she nods. She says something and the little boy stands up as well, then they obediently move around the rock to this side of the pit.

"I simply wanted to tell you something, there's no need to be afraid of me."

"I'm not afraid of you."

Her eyes flicker towards Gracie who has resumed her games.

"Grace is a beautiful name," she says. "I was pregnant once. With a little girl. We were going to name her Laeticia. Jacob was driving, we were returning from a visit to his brother and his family for Sunday lunch. It happened at a crossroads, two streets from their house. The other driver went through a red light. Jacob didn't see him coming, and even if he had, there was nothing he could have done. I was eight months pregnant. We lost Laeticia in the accident."

I swallow. I see that she isn't crying, but I figure it's because she's all out of tears.

"Then we found out I could no longer bear children, also because of the accident. Jacob blamed himself. There was nothing anyone could say or do that would change his mind. You see, he'd had a couple of drinks, and he was just over the legal limit. But the accident was the other driver's fault. It had nothing to do with Jacob's reflexes. But he wouldn't listen to me. As far as he was concerned, he should have protected me and our child and he had failed. He was shattered. Immediately after the accident he started to drink—a lot. Anything to numb the pain, you see. He did a fine job at the BBC. You might think I'd say that anyway because I am his wife, but the truth is that the woman you spoke to—"

I close my eyes and let my head loll back in exasperation. Bloody Chris.

"Look, I—"

She puts her hand up again. "Really, it's all right. I just wanted you to understand. The woman you spoke to, she wasn't his boss then, she was his colleague and they were both up for the same promotion. She kept a close eye on Jacob, looking for anything that would make him unsuitable."

I shudder. I've essentially done the same thing.

"She found the bottles of vodka, in a drawer of his desk. She had her suspicions—they all did. He wasn't hiding it very well. There was a scene, a terrible scene. I think the organisation would have helped him find a way to deal with it, but he didn't want to. He walked out, went to the nearest bar and drank himself a little further into his grave. He stayed out all night. When he came home, he could barely walk. He was sobbing, like a child. I gave him an ultimatum that night: he would find a way back to being the man I loved, or I would leave him. I couldn't watch him kill himself anymore. I'd already lost a child. There were many more tears, and it's a testimony of how much we love each other that he came back to me, and he hasn't touched a drop of alcohol since. He found a new position, as you know, at your paper. He loved it,

I think. He thought he had something to contribute. He was finding his feet again, being appreciated. He liked working with all of you."

She stands, pulls the strap of her handbag a little higher on her shoulder. "He is not the man you made him out to be. And that's all I wanted you to know."

My cheeks are wet from tears. I quickly run a hand over them. "I'm really sorry, Zoya. I truly am." I sigh, thinking of all the mistakes I've been making lately. "I am not that person either."

She nods. "You're hurting, aren't you?"

I look up at her. "Why would you say that?"

"Women like us, who have known pain, pain that sliced something inside that can never be closed again, we can smell it on each other. Don't you agree? No. Maybe you're too young. You'll see."

TWENTY-ONE

The mood is up in the office. It's only the second episode and listening to them you'd think we'd solved the crime. I put a brave face on, and I am cheering with the best of them, because Chris tells us the number of downloads is huge. Tens of thousands at least.

We have a brief production meeting for the third episode this morning. Chris reminds me that I said I would come up with some good material. He wants to know what I've got lined up. I make up vague names.

"Friends of Grace would be good," Vivian suggests. "Friends of Molly would be even better," she adds.

What about Molly herself, would that work? I imagine myself saying.

That's the state of our friendship these days. She pretends to work with me, but really, she's giving me orders. She's punishing me. I know her.

Back at my desk, I try to keep myself busy, but I can't concentrate. I give up and make the call that needs to be made.

"Jacob Whitelaw," his voice says at the end of the line.

"It's Rachel Holloway." I squeeze my eyes shut as I say it, as if to prepare for the blow. But there's a silence that goes on for too long.

"You still there?" I ask.

"What do you want?"

"To apologise."

"Really?"

"Yes. I'm very sorry, Jacob. I behaved very badly. I know that."

"What brought that on?"

"Your wife told me, and—"

I hear his intake of breath. "Excuse me?"

"I mean it, Jacob. I apologise. I screwed up, royally and I'm sorry."

"What did you say? About my wife?"

Oh God. He didn't know. I can't believe it. It looks like I screwed-up, again.

"Your wife—Zoya, isn't it? She came to see me. She told me about... your history."

There's another intake of breath. "Zoya came to see you?"

"Yes. She wanted me to understand, that I was wrong about you. And I'm sorry, for what I did." There's more silence, but I figured I've said my piece.

"That's all I wanted to say, I wish you the best, Jacob."

"Wait."

"What?"

"I heard the second episode," he says, quickly.

I'm not sure why he's telling me. I'm about to ask, but he blurts out, "You're credited as a producer."

Ah. I get it. He thinks I went through all this so I could have his job. "So?" I ask, my tone defiant, but his response surprises me.

"It's about the photos—of Grace," he says, his voice low.

I lean forward, hold the phone tighter. "What about them?"

"Something's not right, Rachel. There are no photos. There can't be."

"How do you know?"

"Maybe we should have a chat."

My heart is racing. I don't want to have a chat over the phone. I tell him to meet me in the park around the corner, in half an hour. I won't have much time, I tell him. I'll have to pick up my daughter after that. Then for the next fifteen minutes I try to do some work, but I can't concentrate. Time doesn't move fast enough.

When I get there, he's already waiting for me. I think he's thinner than he was, if that's even possible. It's awkward at first, as we sit on the bench near the entrance of the park, then I wonder if he really has something so important to say. I look into his eyes and find that they are swimming behind curtains of sadness. I can't believe I have never noticed this before, but then again, I didn't know to look. I was too busy suspecting him of trying to have me killed.

"Tell me again," I ask. "What did you say before? About the photos?"

"I'm trying to explain to you that there couldn't have been any photos. I researched this case, when I was, before I—"

"Before I got you fired."

"I didn't get fired, Rachel. I left."

"Why *did* you leave? Since we're on the subject. Chris said the same thing, that he didn't fire you. So why didn't you stay?"

He pauses as if searching for words, and sighs. "I don't know how much Zoya told you." He turns to me, and his eyes search mine.

"You should ask her that, not me," I say.

He nods.

"They caught me out drinking on the job, last time. I didn't want to go through it all again. All the disappointment, and the distrust."

"You were a radio producer, Jacob. Not a brain surgeon."

That makes him smile. Just.

"That didn't stop people from looking over my shoulder all the time. The glances, the whispers. The knowing looks if I happened to stutter over a word. I just wanted to do my job, and a good one. But if my co-workers were going to be suspicious of my motives, well, screw them. It wasn't worth it."

I feel myself going crimson. "Did you get another job?" I ask. Please God. Let him have another job. A fantastically well-paid, fun, radio producing job.

"Not yet."

I don't have any appropriate response to that, and I don't think one was expected, so I move on.

"You said that before you left, you did some research on the podcast. Where is that research by the way?"

It's his turn to blush.

"It was at my place. I didn't see the point of coming back to return it."

"You took it, didn't you? Out of spite."

"Maybe."

I wonder what he had, but I can't think any of it relates to me. Still, it would be good to get my hands on it.

"Tell me what you know about the photos," I say.

"Dawson was arrested for multiple murders. He was taken into custody and he pleaded not guilty in the Magistrate's court."

"Okay, this is before the trial even started, correct?"

"That's right."

I glance at my watch, and he catches me. "Sorry, it's just that like I said, I have to pick up Gracie soon."

He nods. "I'll cut to the chase. The point is that the evidence was recorded right down to the minutiae. This was a big criminal case, one of the most violent criminal cases in the country for a long time. They had their guy, and he pleaded not guilty. They were not going to let him get off on a technicality. They threw everything they had at it, they crossed the Ts and dotted the Is. I have a copy of the pre-trial submissions and it includes an exhaustive list of the evidence that was gathered. Both at the scene, and his house. There's no mention of photographs of Grace Forster. Naked or otherwise. There are no references to any photographs of any kind."

"Is it possible they were found after the pre-trial submission was completed?"

I am playing devil's advocate here. I know there are no photographs. My sister has never been promiscuous. She was not *easy with the boys*. But I need to think like someone who didn't know her.

"I thought of that too. I made some calls this morning after I heard the episode, because frankly it made no sense. I'm still waiting to hear about what the local police might have on file, but whatever they have, I can guarantee you it doesn't include photographs of the victim."

I have nothing to say to that. It's nothing new to me. But it's so wonderful to hear it from someone else that it brings tears to my eyes.

"You know what I'd do, if I were you?" he says.

"What?"

"I'd go there and ask the people who were around then. I would try to find one person who could corroborate that claim. But I'll put my money on not finding anyone."

"Then what?"

"Then I'd look into why Hennessy would make such a blatant, easily exposed lie."

I sigh. "You must be joking. It's not just that he was the Chief Constable back then, he's the Mayor now. It's not that easy."

"Something worthwhile never is. There's something there, Rachel. I can smell it. I have a nose for this stuff. Something isn't right."

His words sink in and for the first time in my life, I hear someone inching close to the truth. I hear someone doubting Edward Hennessy. Someone who dug deep enough to see more than the story that's already been told.

He stands up. "You should go to your daughter. I don't want to make you late."

We walk out of the park together. Before Jacob goes off to the station, he says,

"There's another thing."

"Yeah?"

"You never changed the podcast website. My mobile number is still there, listed as the producer."

"Okay, so? I'll take it down today if it bothers you so much."

"Mrs Dawson called me."

"Mrs Dawson?"

"She's the mother of Dennis Dawson."

"Right."

"The man who was arrested for the murders."

"I know that. Why would she call you? Why wouldn't she call the hotline?"

He shrugs. "I'd say she wanted to speak to someone real, and she found my number, does it matter?"

"No, of course, you're right." My mouth is dry. "What did she say?" I ask.

"She said she has proof, that Dennis couldn't have done it."

TWENTY-TWO

It's the first time in my life that someone has suggested things may not have been as they seemed. It's not just making me dizzy with excitement, it's like there's a sliver of light at the end of the tunnel. The ghost of a possibility.

Which is why I'm back in Chris's office, begging, and praying.

"You cannot be serious, Rachel! Please!" Chris bellows. He's thrown his pen across the desk and it's bounced off to the floor by my feet. I bend down to pick it up.

"I've never been so serious in my life," I say, depositing the pen back on the desk.

"Don't be so dramatic. I've already got a headache." Chris drops an Alka Seltzer in the tall glass of water. It bubbles and fizzes. I point a finger at the glass.

"That's not going to help you. Those are for heartburn."

"I've got that too. Close the door."

He sits down with a sigh. I do as he says and as I turn I catch Vivian's eye. I give her a quick smile.

"Tell me again, Rachel, I just want to make sure I heard you correctly."

"You heard me correctly. Get Jacob back in, Chris, please. We can't do it without him. It's not working. He's the one with the experience. With the ideas, if you don't mind me saying."

"You asked me to fire him, remember?"

"That's not true, and you know it. I just related something I heard that seemed important to relay. That's all."

"I don't understand you. One minute you tell me not to trust him, the next you can't live without him. Which is it today?"

"It's about priorities. The podcast is good, really good. It's getting the downloads and the sponsors, which is fantastic. But now what? We have to do more than just recap what happened twelve years ago. I can get some interviews—"

"So you keep saying."

"—but so what? It's not called, *What Happened to the Forsters*, is it? None of this is helping us to find Mm—Molly." I can't say my own name. It doesn't matter how many times everyone around me says it. "We need more. We need dirt. Jacob has the experience we need for that. He worked as an investigative radio journalist. It says so on his LinkedIn page and—"

"You checked out his LinkedIn page?"

"I did, I'm not afraid to admit it. It's a public page anyway, it's not like I broke into the Internet."

Chris shakes his head quickly in confusion. "Okay. Stop. Let's backtrack here. What do you want, Rachel? Wait, I just got a weird sense of déjà vu when I said that."

"I want—I would like you to please call Jacob and offer him his job back."

"Three weeks ago he was a liar and a cheat. That's the Jacob we're talking about, is that right?"

"I never said he was a liar and a cheat."

"You implied it."

"No, I didn't. He was a liar, true, if omitting something is a lie, but I never said he was a cheat. But anyway that entire thing was a mistake. I have it on good authority that he's sober now. I also have it on good authority that he's as good as you thought he was. We never had anything to worry about. That ex-boss just had an axe to grind."

"Rachel—"

"I made a mistake. I'm admitting that. And I've already apologised to him personally." That raises Chris's eyebrows.

"Now, I'm apologising to you," I continue. "I'm sorry I made a mess of things, Chris. But I'm trying to fix them and we need him. We need him to get this podcast to the next level."

"I swear if you hadn't just been on a holiday, I'd tell you to take one."

He eyes the ceiling. "What does Vivian say?"

"I haven't told her yet, I wanted to talk to you first."

"Can you get her in here, please?"

This is good. If Chris wants to run it past Vivian, then at least he's considering it.

I lean back and look through the glass. I am sure she'd be looking this way, and I'm right. I make hand gestures to beckon her in. She raises her eyebrows as if she hasn't been looking at me, as if this is all a surprise.

"Come in here!" I mouth. She raises her eyebrows higher, if that was even possible. Oh I get it. *If you want me, you can come and get me.*

I stand up and pop my head out the door. "Vivian, would you please come in here? If you're not too busy?"

"Certainly," she replies breezily.

She's inside with a couple of long strides. I close the door after her.

"Sit down, Vivian. Rachel, the fickle one over here, now wants Jacob to come back and work with us."

She shoots me a confused and more than mildly suspicious look.

"Just listen, okay?" I plead.

"Personally," Chris continues, "I'm in favour. We haven't replaced him yet—frankly I haven't had the time. He's bright, he has good ideas, he's an excellent editor, and these days I find myself doing his job as well as my own."

Vivian bristles. "Excuse me? And what have I been doing? Chopping liver?"

"You're right. My apologies. You've been a great help with the editing side of things. Thank you. Anyway." He sighs. "If, and that's a big if, Jacob hasn't taken up another position somewhere, how would you feel about that, Vivian?"

I hold my breath. If things between us had been the way they used to be, then I would know exactly how Vivian feels about that, and anything else she happens to have feelings about.

"Who will be hosting the podcast?" she asks.

"You will," I reply quickly, before Chris has a chance to say anything.

He gives me a stern look, but doesn't contradict me, which is the main thing.

"You're doing a great job, Vivian," he says. "If you want to keep hosting, and I hope you do, then it's yours."

"You've got the better voice," I add.

She nods. "What would Jacob be doing?"

I jump in again. "I suspect Jacob would have some strong ideas about the direction. He's got the experience. He knows where to dig."

She scoffs. "I think I've done just fine on my own." I note that she's excluded me, but I don't bite.

"Yes, but things are really heating up now. I think between the three of us we can get this podcast to move in the perfect direction. We can bring the focus back to Mm—Molly."

"What about as news editor? Is he going to take over from me? I've been doing the bulk of it," she says.

I make a face. "Maybe you could share the load?" I suggest, just as Chris says, "Yes, he would take over from you," just as Vivian says, "Because I can't do everything around here!"

I laugh with relief. "I thought you wanted to do it! Keep doing it I mean."

"No way! The podcast? Yes! My own column? Absolutely. Editing the freaking paper? 'Scuse my French, Chris," he blinks his forgiveness, "but that's hard work and, no offence, but it's boring."

"Okay, then," he says.

I clap my hands.

"Let me think about it," he adds.

"Okay. Thanks, Chris."

When I get back to my desk I see through the blinds that Chris is already on the phone.

"What was that all about?" Vivian whispers beside me. I'm so surprised that she's talking to me the way she used to, I don't know what to say for a second.

"I kinda made a mistake," I reply softly. "I'm trying to fix it."

"What did you do?"

"I misjudged him."

She shrugs. "Sounds like you're making a lot of mistakes, Rach."

TWENTY-THREE

I've never met someone who works out of a coffee shop before. But that's what Tom Sneddon does. He didn't want to meet in our office and frankly I couldn't care less.

But I don't feel very confident handling this interview by myself, for the obvious reasons. I'm worried I would give myself away. He is a private detective after all. Since Jacob is working with us again I got him to meet us too.

It's a pretty ordinary coffee shop, which is fine, but it's not particularly inviting. There's no background music, no pretty flowers on the Formica tables. I don't have to ask for help in order to pick Sneddon out. He's the one sitting at a corner table that is covered with files dripping with papers. The only other people are a young couple at a table by the window, and an attractive woman in her sixties reading a newspaper.

"Are you Tom Sneddon?"

He stands and offers his hand for me to shake. "You must be Rachel. Please." He indicates a chair for me to sit.

I tell him that Jacob will be here shortly and order an espresso, then immediately regret it. I'm jittery enough as it is.

I hear Jacob's voice next to me. "Sorry I'm late."

"No problem," I reply. I'm so relieved to see him, I could kiss him.

I turn to Tom. "So, you still work as a private detective?" I ask, unsure how to begin.

"Not really, not anymore. I'm retired now, but I still get the odd job here and there. This place is handy for meetings, they don't mind me."

Jacob has introduced himself, and now pulls out what looks like a heavy-duty audio recorder. "It's a Zoom," he explains, watching me studying it up close. "Broadcast quality."

I nod.

He puts on a pair of heavy-duty headphones while Tom shuffles through the papers on the table until he finds what he's looking for.

"It's all a bit bulky, isn't it? Not exactly spy material," I say to Jacob, pointing my chin at the equipment.

"We're not spying on anyone, Rachel."

I wonder what Sneddon thinks of our mindless chatter. Then Jacob winks at me. "But I do have a wireless mic too."

He pulls out what looks to me like a small black box. He explains to me how it works, that it has a receiver which looks to me like the exact same box, and you plug that one into the zoom, and the other is wireless with a fifty-metre range, but it's not quite as good quality as the mic on the Zoom, and pretty soon I wish I'd never mentioned it.

"It was an odd case, that one," Sneddon says, flicking through a notebook. "Six years ago, I received a call to track a missing person. That's not an unusual task for me—it's the bulk of my work. I don't do divorces. Anyway, I remembered the case, of course, the Forster murders."

"Sorry, wait, who hired you?" Jacob asks.

"I don't know."

"What do you mean?"

He shrugs. "It's not that unusual. People want to stay anonymous for reasons that they're not prepared to share with me. But as long as they don't ask for anything illegal, and I still get paid, I don't care. My clients expect confidentiality. It comes with the territory."

"Okay. Could you start from the beginning?"

"Sure." He takes a sip of his coffee, licks his lips. "I got a call from a man—let's call him John Smith. I'd been recommended to him, he didn't say by who. Again, this happens. I don't need to know. He wanted to find Molly Forster. He said he was writing a book about the case."

"Was he?" I ask.

He shrugs. "Who knows? There hasn't been a book, but what does that mean? Maybe he gave up the project. But he wanted to find Molly, even though the Chief Constable at the time, Edward Hennessy, was certain that Dawson, the bloke who killed the Forsters, must have killed Molly outside the house and buried her somewhere."

"But Dawson had already left three bodies behind *in* the house, why would he go to the trouble of hiding Molly's? That's what I don't understand," Jacob says.

"That's right. And that was John Smith's point as well. He didn't think Dawson had hidden her."

I am staring at my hands.

"You said Molly was in Spain, six years ago. How do you know?" Jacob asks.

"I did all the checks to see if she'd surfaced anywhere, as Molly Forster, but she hadn't. So she was either dead—which is where I'd have placed my bet back then—or she no longer called herself Molly Forster. If that was the case, she probably would have gone to London at some point, and there are only so many networks you can tap into when you're young and without resources. Molly would have been eighteen when I went looking for her, so I put it out there that I was looking to buy a new identity for a young woman, no more than twenty. That's definitely unusual. Girls that age who run away don't fork out tens of thousands of pounds for false papers."

"And you found someone who had recently sold a fake identity to a young woman around that age," Jacobs says, nodding.

"Nope. I found nothing. So I did the next thing, I looked for children who had died young, preferably around Molly's age. Names that Molly might have known about before she went missing. Then I checked to see if they'd suddenly reappeared, and bingo. Susan Bishop had died in Whitbrook and would have been around the same age as Molly. Same Susan Bishop had applied for a driver's licence when she turned eighteen. She travelled together with a small-time criminal and they ended up in Barcelona. I lost her trail, but I found him through a car he hired. He marked me though—he was smart, that one. I told my client I might have found her, that she might be the girl living with that bloke, but we had to move pretty fast. These people know how to disappear, and they know how to do it quickly. Next thing, the client said thanks very much, that'll be all. I got paid in full and some more and that was that."

Gabriel had told me never to get a driver's licence in Susan Bishop's name. When I asked if it would come up, that I—she—was dead, he said not exactly, it's not automatic, but it creates a record out there. When I asked again, what would happen if I got one? He said, probably nothing, unless someone went looking.

I did it anyway. I got myself a driver's licence, and then someone went looking.

"So you don't know if they tracked her down after that?" Jacob asks.

"Nope. But I do know the bloke died shortly after."

I have to look down at my lap again at that. I want to get out of there. I don't want to hear anymore. Back then, I really thought that Gabriel had died because the people he was running away from had caught up with him. It is devastating beyond belief to know for a fact that he had died because of me.

"Do you know how?" Jacob asks.

"Car accident. Ran off a cliff. There were no witnesses but from the state of the car, it was highly possible he got help."

"What are you saying?" I blurt.

"I think he was chased and the car got rammed off the cliff."

"How do you know?"

"I saw it."

"You did? But I thought you said the client finished the contract?"

"Yeah, but the accident happened the next day. I was still in Barcelona. I was packing up to leave, and I saw an item on the news. I recognised the car. So I went to take a look."

"Did the police say it had been deliberate?" Jacob asks.

He shrugs. "I don't think they looked into it too closely. Like I said, there were no witnesses, no one came forward. The guy had been living on his own apparently, which was interesting in itself, because I knew that wasn't true. The car had some damage. It showed there'd been a crash, and it also looked to me like another car had run into the back of it, but who was to say when that happened? But I knew. I'd followed that car, and I knew it hadn't been in an accident before. That damage wasn't there in the days prior."

"What was his name?" Jacob asks.

"He called himself Gabriel Delgado. I knew him as Angelo Cifuente." He shrugs. "I don't think either name was the one he was born with."

The Angel Gabriel. How appropriate.

"You okay, Rachel?" Jacob says.

I look up. "Yeah, sure, why?"

He studies me for just a second. "No reason."

He turns back to Tom. "What happened then?"

"Nothing. I went home, got my money and didn't think about it much after that. Until your podcast."

"And her name was Susan Bishop, you said." Jacob is making a note. "You sure it was Molly?" he asks.

"Yep, I am."

"Why?"

"Like I told you, after I found them the client told me to drop it and paid in full. No explanation. Now why would they have done that if the job wasn't finished?"

We stay silent, mulling over what Tom has just said.

"That with the fact that Delgado was killed, yeah, I'm sure. I'd found Molly. And before you ask," Tom says, "I don't know where she went, or where she is now. Or even if she's still alive."

TWENTY-FOUR

I'm standing in our bedroom, trying to pack.

"I don't understand why you even want to go?" Matt's tone is whiny. Churlish. He's in a foul mood. He's been so weird lately, I can feel an argument building. That's how it is with him. If something is bugging him, he will chip away at it quietly, silently, until it comes out in one big shouting match. We're not quite there yet, but it's coming, and no amount of 'what's the matter' and 'is anything wrong' will make it happen faster. I know that by now. Matt will explode when he's ready and not a moment before.

But I have my own demons to contend with at the moment. I can't stop thinking about what Tom has confirmed. There's another piece to that puzzle, too, one that no one knows about. When Gabriel and I moved to Barcelona, I glimpsed a different life stretch out in front of me. A life with freedom and even joy. We got a small flat by the beach, which sounds more glamorous than it was. We played house. He went to work in the evenings, sometimes I would pop into the bar for a drink, pretend I was a tourist. He'd flirt with me. It was the closest I'd been to having a normal life. I was the housewife. I washed his clothes in the tiny washing machine in the basement, then I hung them outside the window like everyone else did. Our street was so narrow you could almost touch the clothes hanging on the opposite side. Well, not quite. But it was hot and we all kept our windows open, and you could smell what everyone was having for dinner. Children would play downstairs in the narrow street and their squeals and shouts bounced up the facades. It was like living in the midst of a busy, happy village. Susana! They'd call me, the other women in the street. They'd practise their English with me and I'd practice my Spanish. I laughed so much during that summer, there were times when I even forgot about everything else.

I fantasised that I could put it right. I did some research and found out that Edward Hennessy was not the Chief Constable anymore. He was the mayor of Whitbrook then. So I rang the cops at Whitbrook and told them. I am Molly Forster, I said. I'm alive. I'll tell you who did it and who covered it up. I just wanted to live my life with Gabriel, but I now know that this phone call is what killed him.

And now, Jacob and I are going to do some investigating. And I'm terrified. But I'm doing it, I'm going with him, which is amazing, really.

"Are you listening to me, Rach?" Matt snaps.

"Yes, I am." I throw the suitcase on top of the bed and drop a handful of socks into it.

"You've never been away from Gracie for two days before," he says.

"It's one night, love. And I've never been away, full stop, so what? Does it mean I never can?"

He runs a hand through his hair. "I don't get it, that's all."

"It's my job, Matt! What's to get?"

"No, it's not! It's not your job!"

I put a finger on my lips. "Please, you'll wake her up."

"It's almost six o'clock anyway, she'll be up any minute."

"Let her sleep."

"This podcast is not your job, Rach. You only took it on because that guy, that creep, got fired!"

I wince. "Jacob didn't get fired. He left. Then he came back."

"I thought you didn't like him."

"I changed my mind."

"Clearly."

"What's that supposed to mean?"

"You tell me! *You* said there was something not right about him. That he gave you the creeps. Now you're road-tripping with him?"

I had said that. I came home after that first day back from our holiday, where Chris and Jacob made their big announcement about the podcast, and I was terrified. I didn't tell Matt about the podcast at the time, but I did bitch about Jacob over a bottle of wine later that night.

"I just told you. I changed my mind. He's back now and he's doing a good job. Can we not shout at each other, please?" I pull out two tops from the drawer. One of them has a somewhat revealing neckline. I put that one back in and choose a plain white one.

Matt sits on the bed.

"Vivian said she'd help with Gracie. And your mother will too, she loves looking after her."

"I don't need help to look after my own daughter," he says, sullen.

"I know, love," I say gently. I sit next to him and put my arm around his shoulder. His body stiffens under my touch.

"I just want to go because I think this work is important,

and it would be a good experience for me. It's an opportunity to show them at work that I can do more than the website and cook the books. I might get a better pay out of it. You understand, don't you?"

There's something unusually fragile about Matt today. I can't put my finger on it. He's usually so dynamic, highly capable, everything with a smile, nothing is too difficult. He's the perfect boyfriend and father. He enjoys being home looking after his family. He's responsible. He's the guy everybody loves and he's always up. But not lately.

He looks into my eyes.

"Don't stop loving me Rach."

I didn't expect that. "I love you more than ever." Which is the truth. I have loved Matt since the moment I met him. I wanted him to be the father of my children. I wanted him forever. I always did and I always will.

He blinks, but the tear still comes and rolls down his cheek. He brushes it off with the back of his hand. I hold him close.

"Why did you change your hair?" he asks sadly.

I bring my hand up to touch it. I got it cut so short that it doesn't even cover my ears. The colour is different too. Clairol Chestnut is back.

"You know me, slave to fashion," I reply gently.

He rests his head on my shoulder. "I preferred it the way it was."

"I know."

Matt takes my bag to the car. He says it's to save me the trouble, but I know he wants to check it out, both the car and Jacob. Matt might work as an electrician, but he could just as well be a great mechanic. He can figure anything like that out.

He said to me once, "It's all about the signal, Rach. You have to figure out where the current begins, and where it ends. It can only go one way, just follow the trail." I guess cars were the same, just follow the fuel.

Jacob gets out of the car to say hello and Matt eyes him like he's some kind of conman and then grunts. He pushes the bag onto the back seat and then before heading back into our building, he says, "Don't drive over the speed limit. Speeding, that's how most accidents happen." Which is something he's seen on a road safety campaign somewhere.

I watch him go inside, then climb into the grey Hyundai.

"You've changed your hair?" Jacob says. I'm still mortified from what just happened. I reach to touch it, self-consciously.

"That's right. Do you have any music?" I ask. We're only on the Westway but there's some kind of road works ahead and the traffic is moving at a snail's pace.

Jacob pushes a button on the dashboard and the CD starts to play.

"Is that okay?"

"Yeah! What is it?"

He smiles. "It's Zoya's. One of her compilation playlists. I don't know who this is."

It sounds like a happy Bollywood song to me. I turn the volume up a little.

"After we check-in, where do we start?" Jacob asks. "You want to go and see Edward Hennessy first?"

"Have you got a reply from his office yet?"

"No, but we could always do a doorstep. It's not likely to give the same results as an invitation, but it's better than nothing."

I've only met Edward Hennessy once, before I ran away. I look nothing like I did then. No adult does. The hair colouring is just to cover all bases.

"We've got Mrs Dawson this afternoon," he continues.

"Poor Mrs Dawson. It's amazing that she never left this—place," I was going to say 'God forsaken place'. "Her son is known as the local mass murderer and she goes to Church every Sunday."

"She's courageous. She's also adamant that they got the wrong guy, and that she has every right to be here and try to prove it."

"Courageous is the word, yes," I say, wishing I had even half her courage at any point in my life.

I consult my notes, pretending to look up who we are going to interview and when, even though I already know it all by heart. My old teacher Mrs Callaghan won't be interviewed, but to soften the blow, she has put us onto Grace's old teacher and her friend Amanda. I don't remember Amanda, but they're both willing to speak with us.

"We really need to talk to Hugo Hennessy," Jacob says. "He still lives there. He has always refused to speak to reporters, but after all this time, who knows. People change."

I clench my jaw. "Yeah, we should try." I can hear how weak my voice sounds.

"You okay Rachel?" he asks.

"Yeah, why?"

"You look a bit pale there."

"Fighting off car sickness." I reply.

"You winning?"

"I think so."

"Let me know if I need to stop. Whatever you do, don't throw up in the car."

"I'll be fine."

TWENTY-FIVE

I'm told that Whitbrook is a lovely town, but I can't look at it that way. To me it's ugly and heavy. I never think of Whitbrook as *home*. Home is wherever my daughter and Matt are. Whitbrook is the stuff my nightmares are made of.

Once we check-in to our accommodation, which is a perfectly ordinary guesthouse on the edge of town, the kind which you find on the edge of every town in England, I start to relax. I am here and the world hasn't come crashing down. Incredibly, the place isn't even that familiar. I don't recognise the streets at all. I'm almost disappointed. I expected the shock of recognition like a slap in the face. Even when the tower of St Andrew's church comes into view, it's as if someone else is looking at it through my eyes. I recognise it, I know I've seen it before, but it doesn't connect. Maybe that's why I am completely unprepared for the effect the sight of my own house has on me.

I'm looking through documents on my laptop when the car stops, and Jacob says, "Here we are," in a funny tone.

I look up and stare right at my old front door. It's just like my nightmares, only smaller. Then it begins. The narrowing of the vision. The heart palpitations. I manage to open the car door and bend down, taking great big gulps of air.

"Wow, you really do get carsick!" He comes around and stands next to me. His hand is on my back and I wish with all my heart that he would take it off. It feels too heavy. But I can't speak, I can barely breathe.

When it's over, I stand up and lean back against the car. I put a hand on my forehead. It's clammy. I feel hot and cold at the same time. Jacob is looking a little pale himself.

"I think I'm okay now," I manage to say. Then I retch.

He takes me to a coffee shop so I can get some water and recover. I'm fine by now. Just embarrassed. I make up a story about picking up a stomach bug and blame it on Gracie.

"I had something like that last year. It was horrid. You're sure you'll be okay?" I don't tell him I doubt very much he's ever had something like that, ever.

We're sipping hot sweet tea which is exactly what I need. Our table is at the front, right by the windows and I feel exposed. It's grey outside, and a group of children walk past. Shouldn't they be in school? There's a young man on the other side of the street waiting for a bus, and for a second I think it's him and the room tilts. Same build, same hair, but it can't be. Hugo must be in his early thirties now.

"Yeah, thanks, Jacob, it's over now. One of those twenty-four minute bugs I guess."

He laughs.

I need to use the bathroom. There's a woman with a small child sitting at a table and when I walk past, she looks at me strangely and it makes my stomach lurch. In the ladies room, I check my face from every angle. Could anyone possibly recognise me?

I don't look at her on the way back, but I feel her eyes

lingering on the back of my head. It makes me shiver. Jacob is on the phone when I sit down.

"Anything interesting?" I ask after he hangs up.

"Hennessy's office. The father. He doesn't have any time for us. They said he already gave us an extended interview and he has nothing more to add."

"Oh well, it was worth a shot."

"It doesn't matter. It's Mrs Dawson I'm interested about," he says.

I put on my coat and catch the young woman's eye, the one I passed before. She's whispering to the waitress who served us and they're both stealing glances our way. I can't get out of there fast enough.

Emily Dawson lives in a small council house on the outskirts of Whitbrook. She only moved there last year, and I am glad of that. I've been to Dennis's old flat two or three times, with my sister Grace, and I have no desire to revisit.

"Hello dear, come inside, out of the cold. Bring your friend. I'm sorry if the house is a bit dusty. My eyesight isn't good anymore you see. I'm as blind as a bat. It's macular degeneration. Nothing they can do."

She shuffles back from the front door into the living room, feeling her way there by lightly touching the top of various pieces of furniture. An armchair, a sideboard, another chair.

"It's spotless, Mrs Dawson," I tell her.

"Oh good! Thank you! I do worry now that I can't see. It's just me now, so it's all right and I don't get visitors anymore."

She has white hair in short tight curls, and her face is so thin and drawn, her skin is like translucent paper. You can see the veins beneath. I don't remember her, from before, not exactly, but there's something about the lilt in her voice that resonates with a distant memory. I've met her, I know that, but I can't remember when, or how.

"Thank you for seeing us, Mrs Dawson," Jacob says.

"Oh, that's quite all right, Mr Whitelaw. I'm the one who called you."

"I would prefer if you called me Jacob," he adds quickly. Jacob is always so polite, I would have just said, 'call me Rach'.

"Oh, all right, if you like. It's a nice name, Jacob. It means nobleman, I believe. I've made some tea," she says. The low coffee table was set with a tray.

"Thank you, that's kind of you," Jacob says. "Would you like me to serve?"

"If you would, Mr White—Jacob, that would be kind. Thank you."

I feel so sad, watching her. It comes over me out of nowhere. She has gone through a living hell, and yet she is so kind, so thoughtful.

I help things along by taking a cup to Mrs Dawson and making sure she holds it securely.

"A podcast, that's terribly interesting. I'd never heard of such a thing of course. I haven't managed to listen to it yet. But I have a young woman who comes and helps me once a week. From the council services you know. They're very good. Usually I get Sophia, such a lovely name, don't you think? It means wisdom in Greek. Although as lovely as she is, I wouldn't say she's wise, by any means. She's Polish. Not that it has anything to do with it."

She's rambling and I want her to stop. I lean across and take her hand in mine. The skin feels papery, dry. She makes a small gasp.

"Mrs Dawson. Is it all right that we came to see you? If it will upset you, we don't have to stay."

She squeezes my hand. "Thank you dear. It's Rachel, isn't it? Yes. Little lamb."

I freeze. My father used to call me little lamb, or lambkin, sometimes. But then she adds, "It's Hebrew."

She's only talking about the meaning of my name. Rachel means 'ewe' in Hebrew. I pat her hand softly, willing my heart to slow down.

"Are you sure you want to talk to us?"

She nods, very fast, almost frantically, and a single tear pools at the rim of her eyelid, and falls. I squeeze her hand.

"Nothing happened like they said," she says. She pulls her hand away from mine, but not unkindly. She straightens in her seat. "Nothing."

Jacob explained to her over the phone about the podcast, and he asked her permission to record her, which she'd given. But seeing her now, frail and sad, and blind. I can't help feeling like we're taking advantage of her.

Jacob has pulled out his Zoom and is fiddling with buttons. I put a hand on his arm.

"Mrs Dawson, before we continue, I want to make sure you understand that we are recording you. Everything that you say now, anyone can listen to it. Just as if it was on the radio. Do you understand that? Because you don't have to say yes. We can still talk, and we don't have to record you if you don't want us to."

"You record me, young lady, and you Jacob." For the first time I understand what the expression 'a voice with a steely edge' actually means. "You record every single word of what I say, and you put it out there. They didn't want to listen to me back then. They wouldn't let me speak. It's my turn now."

TWENTY-SIX

"They never let me talk. Not at the police station, not at the courts, not at the town hall. They just wouldn't listen to me. I didn't even know that poor family had been killed, or that he'd been arrested, can you believe it? My neighbour, Rosemary, she came to tell me the next morning. She'd heard it on the radio. They didn't even tell me themselves."

"They?"

"The police. They threw him in jail and didn't even bother to call me, his mother."

She pulls out a carefully folded handkerchief from inside the cuff of her sleeve and dabs at her eyes.

"They wouldn't let me see him. I went to the police station, and they were celebrating, can you believe it? They'd come and taken my son and thrown him in prison already, and they were celebrating. They wouldn't help me. He was locked up in Haverigg. I went there right away but they wouldn't let me see him. My own son. They said no visitors. Not even me." She takes a breath, dabs at her eyes again and puts the folded handkerchief back in her sleeve. "I never saw him again."

She's too upset to go on, so we wait, let the moment exist. I look around the room.

"The drawings on your walls," I say gently, "Did you do these?"

They're mostly pencil drawings, delicate and incredibly detailed, of various buildings. I stand up and take a closer look at the drawing of St Andrews' church. Every detail is there, down to the different brick tones.

"No dear. Dennis drew those."

"Really? I didn't know."

Jacob raises an eyebrow at me and I can't believe I just said that. "There was no mention of—" I scramble to come up with something but she interrupts me.

"I always thought he could have been an architect but he could never get into University. He didn't have the traditional learning abilities. But he was going to college, he was going to be a draughtsman," she says.

"They're beautiful," I say.

Jacob nods at me. I've calmed her. And myself.

"Mrs Dawson, can we continue to talk about that day? The day Dennis was arrested?"

"That's why you're here, Jacob, and you, Rachel. Where should we begin?"

"Your son—Dennis, was in the Forster's house when the police arrived."

I return to my seat on the sofa. I watch her face closely.

"He was very distraught," Jacob says.

"Of course he was. He had just walked into a massacre."

"He had blood all over him."

"He was holding Grace, for heaven's sake! She had been bleeding profusely, he was trying to help her! Of course he had blood all over him! They never checked to see whether it was just her blood, or that of her parents as well, did you know that?"

"No, we didn't know that," Jacob says. He makes a note.

"If I could ask about the murder weapon," I say, "The cricket bat was wiped down. There were traces of blood on it, but no prints. Why would Dennis do that? If he was prepared to stick around, and scream, getting himself found at the murder scene. Do you know why he would do that?"

"You know Rachel, the Chief Constable has always dismissed that point as irrelevant. Whenever he was asked about that—and he was once or twice, by journalists who were prepared to do some work, rather than just print the press release—he said Dennis was preparing to leave when Mr Patel walked in." She makes a frustrated sound. "You can't have it both ways. You can't claim Dennis had been caught while on a crazy rampage out of jealousy and hatred, and at the same time paint him as a pragmatic killer, wiping down the murder weapon because he'd forgotten to wear gloves."

"The police said he was upset because she hadn't invited him to her birthday party."

"That was a lie. He had been invited, but he didn't go. I was ill. I had a terrible flu and I had to stay in bed all day. He came to look after me. He cooked some soup in my kitchen. He was at my flat for maybe three hours that afternoon, then he went back to his own flat that evening, and that's when he got the phone call."

I've got so many questions about what she just said I can't get any of them out.

Jacob shoots me a look of disbelief.

"He had an alibi?" he asks.

"That's right."

"And I presume you told the police about this?"

"Of course. They wouldn't listen. They didn't even write it down, can you believe that? They never took my statement. Never. They dismissed me. They thought I was lying to protect him. But I wasn't lying. Dennis wouldn't hurt a fly. He was a gentle young man. And he would never have hurt Grace Forster, or her parents. He wouldn't hurt anyone."

I came in here wanting to get some information from her. Anything that would show that they'd arrested the wrong man. I've got that now, and there's nothing I can do with it. We'll put that in the podcast, I'll insist, but it's true that every-body will believe it's a desperate statement from a desolate mother.

But I got more than I bargained for. I got to see first-hand the horror that was committed, and not just on my family, but on other families too. The Dawson family didn't deserve this, any more than my family did. At least my family aren't treated like monsters.

"Why did you say that before?" I ask, "About a phone call?"

"Dennis cooked some dinner for me, then he went to the chemist to get my prescription filled. He dropped off my medication on his way home. He only lived around the corner from me on Mill Road. It only took five minutes to walk there. He rang when he got back home to ask if I'd be all right if he went out. I said of course I would, I was going to bed. I asked where he was going, he said a friend of Grace's had just rang, asking him over to Grace's party. They were all still there, and she wanted him to be there too."

"Did he say which friend?" Jacob asks quickly.

"I didn't ask. I told him to have a good time and I went to bed. It was the last time I ever spoke to him. And not a day goes by that I don't wish I had asked that question. Whoever the friend was has much to answer for."

I could tell her who made the call. It's not hard to guess, but it wouldn't help now. It's too late. But I always wondered why Dennis was there so soon after they were killed. Now I know.

"Did you tell anyone else?" I ask.

"I told everyone I could. I called the newspapers. They never printed anything I said about where Dennis was that night. Just that his 'distressed mother had expressed disbelief as to his guilt'". She scoffs. "I knew the truth! So of course I expressed disbelief! I called the papers to ask them, why didn't you print what I really said? That he was here with me! You know what they said? That the police had advised it would be prejudicial to Dennis for them to discuss his defence. Can you believe that?" She shakes her head. "But they did print the claim from Chief Constable Hennessy that Dennis had confessed right away, but then he'd recanted. How could he confess to something he didn't do? I never heard anything so ridiculous in my life."

She leans forward, it's like she's looking right at me.

"The police said the family had been killed at least an hour before Mr Patel arrived. At that time, Dennis was at *Boots* on High St. I wrote to the Magistrate to tell him. By then Dennis was already dead."

"I'm so sorry, Mrs Dawson," I say.

"Did you hear back from the Magistrate? After you sent the letter?" Jacob asks.

She pulls the handkerchief out again and presses it against her eyes. I already know what she's going to say.

"Dennis died. Case closed."

"Forgive me if this question upsets you, but the confession. It was his handwriting. But you don't think he wrote it?" Jacob asks gently.

"Oh, I know it was. I believe he wrote it. My Dennis was

autistic. At the extreme end of the spectrum. If you asked him to write a story that he killed these people, he would do it just to please you. He didn't understand the significance of it. It was conveniently reprinted in the papers at the time. They had no problem with that it seems." She shakes her head quickly. "Did you see it? The note? You can see clearly it was written under duress. Anyone can see that."

"I don't think that rules out the authenticity of what he wrote."

"I know. But I know what does rule it out."

"You do?"

She stands up and feels her way out of the room. Jacob doesn't pause the recording so I don't say anything. He makes notes, writing quickly. The clock in the hall chimes four. Emily Dawson returns with what looks like an old prescription. She unfolds it and pulls out a small yellow piece of paper, folded in half. I put my hand out and gently tug at a corner of it. She holds on.

"It's not that I don't trust you, but you have to understand, I'm blind. You could tear it into a million pieces right in front of me and I'd have no way of knowing. I've kept this safe for all these years, waiting for a day just like this."

I release it. "What is it?"

She opens it out gently. "It's a receipt."

"Can we take a look at it?" I ask.

"You can take a look yes, you can take a photo too, you have one of those phones, don't you? But you can't take it away with you, dear. It's not that I don't trust you, but you have to understand, after everything I went through…"

"We understand," I assure her. "If you could explain what we're looking at, and we'll take a photo."

She lets go. Jacob leans across and peers over my shoulder. "It's a printed receipt from Boots Chemist up on High

Street for some cold and flu tablets, some aspirin and other things for twelve pounds fifteen." She has it memorised. It's the VAT receipt, the old-style ones that was printed on paper that doesn't fade so quickly. It's got the date, November fourth two thousand and six, and the time: nineteen thirty-one. Just below 'Thank you for shopping at Boots'.

"Jesus," Jacob says, softly.

"He stopped by the chemist on his way back here, to pick up my medication. Just like I told you. At the time that poor family was killed, Dennis was at the chemist."

"This is incredible. You had this all this time?"

"You have to understand, dear. Everything happened so fast. Dennis was arrested that night and I didn't hear about it until the next day. I didn't even know I had this. Months later I needed a refill from a different prescription, and I found this one, in a drawer of my dresser. It was tacked inside, you see, the prescription was folded in two. By then, what was I going to do? I didn't want to contact the police anymore, I knew they wouldn't do any good. I just put it aside, waiting for the right time, to show the right people, and then I gave up. Now I'm old, I'm blind, and I'm tired. But you, you are the right people."

"I understand what it means to you, Mrs Dawson, but it's not proof, because anyone could have picked them up. It doesn't prove Dennis did."

"But this does, surely." She pushes the old prescription forward on the table. I lift it gently by its corner, barely touching it and turn it around.

It's barely visible, because it's the carbon copy of the prescription, the old style. But It's clear enough. It's Dennis Dawson's name and signature. On the back of it.

Jacob is taking pictures from every angle. I wouldn't have been able to do it. I am shaking so much. This is the most incredible development to happen. It's better than anything I could wish for.

"We'll make sure the right people see these, Mrs Dawson, I give you my word," I say, squeezing her hand hard.

"I know it wasn't my Dennis. You put that on your tape, you hear? You let the world hear all of it."

"Thank you, Mrs Dawson," I say, then I add, "I promise."

"You sound vaguely familiar dear, have we met before?"

TWENTY-SEVEN

"What did I tell you? What did I tell you, Rachel Holloway? Didn't I say this case smells to high heaven? Did I say that? Or didn't I say that?"

We're sitting at the bar of the King's Arms, I'm sipping a gin and tonic and Jacob is having a Perrier. My head is swimming, and I don't think it's from the alcohol.

"You can't bottle it, you know. It's pure instinct." He taps the side of his nose. "Either you have it, or you don't."

I nod. "It's amazing. I can't believe it. No one would believe her. All this time, the poor woman." I drain the rest of my drink and signal the bartender for another.

"It's going to be gold. I'm telling you right now. This podcast will win an award."

I just wish I could be there when Hugo Hennessy hears the episode. I'd love to see his face when he finds out that there is proof that Dennis Dawson couldn't have done it. It's too late for him, but not for his mother. All these years she's been hounded. She'd spawned a monster, they said. She'll be able to spend the rest of her days with her head held high. For the first time since this whole thing started, I can't wait to put this episode out.

"Are you hungry? I have to eat," I tell Jacob, "and I want to call my family."

"Yes, sure, let's get some food into you, Rachel. Sorry, I'm not thinking straight, you must be starving. I know I am."

We sit down at a table and while he orders two hamburgers and chips for us, I call Matt.

"Hi love, how are you?"

"Hi."

I can hear voices in the background.

"Where are you?" I ask.

"At home, where else? Mum's here, and Cathy."

Cathy is Matt's eldest sister. I feel a pang of loneliness that I'm here and they're all together at home, without me. I almost ask if he misses me.

"How's your research going?"

"Good, yeah, I'll tell you all about it when I see you," I say.

He snorts. "Yeah, I'm sure you will."

I ignore that for now.

"Can I talk to Gracie?"

He puts his hand over the phone and calls out to her. I can hear her squealing in the background. She adores her aunt and grandmother. I was worried she would miss me, I've never been away from her overnight before. I'm glad she's enjoying herself but a little jealous too.

"Mummy! Hello Mummy!"

"Hello, my darling, are you having a nice time?"

She tells me that Aunt Cathy is reading her stories and her grannie is there too. She starts talking so fast I can barely follow, and then all of a sudden she says goodbye and drops the phone. I can hear her in the background running and shouting 'Aunt Cathy!'

Matt is laughing when he picks up the phone again, and I wish I was there with them. It dims the glow of the day, that feeling.

Jacob is already having his breakfast when I come downstairs.

"How did you sleep?" I ask. I stare at his scrambled eggs and baked beans. I'm so hungry I could snatch the plate from him and I wouldn't even feel bad about it.

"Better than you, I'd say."

"Why do you say that?"

"I heard you leave last night. Where did you go?" He sips some coffee.

"Let me get some breakfast first."

Our rooms are right next to each other, and you can hear the TV from either side. I thought I was quiet when I left my room. Obviously not.

I get some eggs and toast from the buffet, and a mug of coffee.

"What's on the agenda for today?" I ask, when I return with my breakfast. But it's no use. Jacob won't be so easily distracted.

"I heard you leave your room, and I was worried about you. It was after ten o'clock, I thought maybe you weren't feeling well again."

"I wasn't. So I went for a walk, to get some air."

"It was freezing out."

"I don't mind the cold."

I eat my breakfast without looking at him.

"Did you get any sleep? I waited up for an hour then I went to sleep," he says.

I hold my fork an inch from my lips. "You didn't need to do that. And not much, if I'm honest. Just a lot on my mind."

I might hate being back here, but another part of me longed to experience it again. I wanted to revisit a little of 'before'. I wanted to remember the smells, the tastes, the sights. I was born here. All my memories of my sister, my mother, my father, are from this place. So I went to take another look at my old house. I stood across the road, and watched the lights behind the windows, and pretended it was my family's shadows behind the drapes.

Then I went to the old train station. It was so dark, but I could see how overgrown the ivy was over the wall. If I could climb inside I would have. But there's no way I could have hacked my way through to reach the window. I put my forehead against the cold brick wall and I told my sister in heaven that I was going to get him. *I will be brave from now on, and I will do what needs to be done. I promise. I promise you, Grace, that Hugo Hennessy will go to jail forever for what he did to you.*

"Sorry to hear that," Jacob says now. "And I didn't mean to pry. I was just worried about you."

"Don't be, I'm fine. Have you heard anything from Hugo Hennessy yet?"

"Nothing. We could go by his office. What do you think? After we interview Mr Allen."

"I was going to say the same thing." I can't believe those words came out of my mouth.

Hugo Hennessy has never moved away from the town he grew up in. And why should he? He was the son of the Chief Constable. He could go around and commit the most gruesome murder in the history of the district and get away scot-free. Hennessy the father was now the Mayor of Whitbrook, and Hugo is a property developer now. He heads a large firm called Lakeside Homes, although he pretends he's only an employee. They build ugly houses and even uglier shopping centres. I know this because I looked it up online. But he does own it. I checked the records and it wasn't that hard. I wonder what grubby deals father and son get up to every day.

Mr Allen was Grace's teacher. He still works at the school. He's agreed to be interviewed and we've arranged to visit him this morning.

Outside I pretend to get my bearings. We're not far from the school, so we decide to leave the car parked here and walk.

We turn the corner and walk to the next junction but Jacob thinks we should go the other way. I'm not going to argue. We stand there, stamping our feet, trying to get warm, while he pulls out his mobile to check the map when suddenly the young woman from the cafe yesterday is by my side. She's got her daughter with her in the buggy.

"Hi," she says.

"Hey, hi!" Jacob replies. She's so close to me I can smell her deodorant, and I'm still pretending I haven't seen her. I'm too busy buttoning my coat. Is she here for me? Did she follow me? Does she know me?

"Are you lost? Can I help you?" she asks.

"Thank you, yes. We're looking for St Agnes Secondary School."

"I can walk you there if you like, I'm going that way too."

I give Jacob a look and a very small shake of the head. *Don't.* But he doesn't notice it.

"Thank you, that would be kind of you," he says.

"It's this way," she points her chin. Jacob points a finger at me. "You were right!"

"Are you from the podcast?" she asks.

"Yes, how do you know?"

"We heard you were in town. News travel fast around here."

"Clearly," he says, smiling. He extends his hand and introduces himself, and then me.

"Hello," I say. I leave my own hands deep in my coat pockets. I don't trust them not to shake.

"So you live here, I guess?" Jacob says.

"Born and bred. I'm Cindy McArthur. And Grace Forster was my best friend."

Wow. My heart skips a beat. My gaze cuts back to her, roaming her face. I don't recognise her, and I certainly don't remember anyone called Cindy. Let alone a friend of Grace.

"She was?" Jacob asks.

"Yeah, she was and I can't tell you how much I miss her. Still. She was like my sister. So I thought, if you had any questions about the family, or —"

"That's good of you, Cindy, that'd be great.' He looks at me, excitement clear in his eyes and raises his eyebrows. "Maybe we could do it now?" He means the question for her, but he's looking at me.

I stare at her face and she shoots me a small smile. I remember to send one back, so she doesn't think I'm unfriendly. But I just can't remember her.

Jacob sends a text to Mr Allen that we'll be late, and Cindy McArthur takes us on a detour. Soon we're sitting by the lake, in one of those picnic areas that has wooden tables and seats. It's secluded.

"We were all in love with Hugo Hennessy. He was the ultimate catch around here. Handsome, rich, charming. He excelled at sports, captain of the soccer team. Grace was popular too, so when they started dating in a way it was like we all knew it would have happened eventually. They were both so good-looking, you know?"

Jacob nods, holding his Zoom in place. I remember this too, how they were at first, the two of them, golden and shining with love.

"How long did they date for?" Jacob asks. I have a pen and a notebook so that I can look busy.

"Six months at least. He adored her. He would do anything for her. He helped her with school, so she'd get good grades. He was there for her and she was besotted. We'd be on the phone for hours, I'm not kidding, and she'd go on and on about how in love she was. She wanted to marry him, and she'd talk about how long she should wait."

"I see. He must have taken it hard, when she died."

"You've got no idea. I still see him sometimes, around the place. I don't think he ever recovered, to be honest. He was crushed. That's the word for it."

Jacob is fidgety. We don't have a lot of time, and he must be wondering why we put off Grace's teacher for this. But Cindy is on a roll.

"He was devastated when she died," she goes on. "You should have seen him at the funeral. He was a total write-off. So sad really, they were so in love and everything."

I'm wondering how much longer this will go on before I can't stop myself from hitting her.

"Anyway, I just wanted to tell you, that he was really heart-broken when she died."

Jacob steals a look in my direction. By now, he's as confused as I am. We're waiting for some kind of punchline. Why did Cindy come after us? Surely not to tell us things that were common knowledge?

"Thank you, Cindy, that's good background, we'll be sure to include it," Jacob says.

He's about to put his equipment away when she grabs his

arm and says, "I never said this to anyone, but she was a real slut."

I am speechless. My mouth is gaping and when I turn to Jacob, he's got exactly the same expression.

"What did you just say?" I ask.

"I know she was my friend and everything. But I think you should know, that's all. I'm not judging her or anything."

I want to stand up and I really want to hit her. Hard.

"There were photos," she says. "Naked photos. That she took, of herself."

"Did you see them?" Jacob asks.

Cindy colours. "Well, no—I"

"I didn't think so," he says, nodding to himself. "You heard about that on the podcast, didn't you?"

"No actually—well yeah I heard it on the podcast, but it's true! She gave them to Dennis!"

"It's not—"

I kick Jacob in the shin.

"How do you know she took these photos?" I ask.

"She told me."

"She told you what, exactly?"

"That Dennis liked seeing her naked, okay? That he paid for pictures! He had a crush on her, okay? Like, big time. I'm just saying! I thought you'd be interested, okay?"

She stands up, annoyed now.

"Why wasn't Hugo at the birthday party? If they were so much in love, do you know?" Jacob asks. It's such a good question, I could kiss him.

She gives small shakes of the head. "What?" She says at last.

"Why wasn't he there that night?" Jacob repeats.

She scowls and bites her bottom lip. "I'm not sure, I think they were taking a break. Maybe."

"They were?"

"I don't know, okay?" she says sharply. "Who else have you been talking to anyway? Anyone?"

"We met with Mrs Dawson yesterday, and—"

I put a hand on Jacob's arm.

"I have to go," Cindy says. She stands up and we watch her push the buggy with her sleeping child. She's gone in minutes.

"What on earth was that about?" Jacob says.

"Did you ask Hennessy?" I ask. "About those photos? You said yourself there's no trace of them anywhere. Did he explain that?"

He nods. "Only on email. He replied that the photos were never submitted as evidence. That he wanted to protect the family. I don't buy it."

"Me neither," I say.

TWENTY-EIGHT

Missing Molly - Episode 3 - Transcript

[Intro Music]

(**Vivian**) Today's episode is sponsored by Flowers Everywhere, your flower delivery service, perfect for every
occasion.

*Forsters Killer Commits Suicide - The quiet gardener who
harboured a secret love.*

This was the headline that greeted readers of the Daily Mail
on eighth November two thousand and six. The article went
on to detail why Dawson committed the crime in the first
place.

*"He was obsessed with the oldest daughter Grace. She was
kind, and she always had the time for a nice word, a small
chat on the side of the road with him. He mistook her kind-*

ness for attraction and decided that they should be a couple, that this was love. When his attentions were rebuffed he went to the Forsters' residence and killed them all. 'The murderer confessed right away,' Chief Constable Hennessy declared soon after the arrest. 'He had no choice, we found him at the scene, covered in blood from the victims. Less than six hours later we had a full, written confession.' Dawson's legal representative has claimed that he later recanted on his confession. But as of last night, this is now a moot point. Dawson took his own life in Haverigg Prison a little before midnight. The cause of death was hanging. Chief Constable Hennessy gave a statement this morning, that Dawson had told the guard on duty that he could no longer live with what he'd done. The guard believed that Dawson was distressed enough to be put on suicide watch, however by the time the paperwork was filed, it was too late."

This article closed the case in the eyes of the public. The police had their killer, and the killer had died. There was no crime to solve, no trial required. And just like that, in a little over forty-eight hours, it was over.

But was it?

From the South Hackney Herald, I'm Vivian Brown and you're listening to Missing Molly. If you have any information about the disappearance of Molly Forster, please contact your local police station, or you can leave me a message here on (020) 7946-0318. You can choose to remain anonymous if you wish.

[Music]

(**Teacher**) Grace was very pretty. Blond hair, blue eyed, she was well liked, she didn't have a ton of friends, but she had a handful of close girlfriends, they used to hang out all the time. She was a good student. A bit shy.

(**Friend**) She didn't have a boyfriend for a long time. I think she only ever had one.

(**Jacob**) Did she want one?

(**Friend**) (Laughter) We all wanted one! We were fifteen, sixteen, you know, innocent. We all thought prince charming was out there waiting for us (laughter).

(**Jacob**) What about Dennis Dawson? Did they ever go out on a date?

(**Friend**) Nah. They were friends, that's all. She wasn't interested in him in that way.

(**Teacher**) The story about the photographs? That she sold naked photos of herself? I find it very hard to believe. She wasn't the type at all. She was not shy exactly, but certainly on the conservative side compared to other girls at the school. She was studious, pleasant, I just don't see it. I know with social media these days girls are more at risk, but we're talking twelve years ago. We didn't have the same problems with social media then. No. I just don't see it.

(**Friend**) Yeah, that one made me laugh, to be honest. She was kind of prudish, you know? I mean we all were. She wanted to be a singer. I remember that, a pop singer. Like Katie Perry you know? She had a really nice voice. She played the guitar.

(**Teacher**) It was a terrible few days for our community. The poor Forster family was killed, and little Molly disappeared and then Dennis... just awful. Unbelievable.

(**Jacob**) Did you know Dennis Dawson?

(**Teacher**) I had him in my class year earlier. When he was fifteen.

(**Jacob**) What was he like?

(**Teacher**) Oh dear... he was quiet, but gentle, or so I thought back then. I thought he was a gentle boy. Sensitive. I'd never have pegged him for this kind of violence. Not in a million years. Just goes to show, doesn't it, you never know what lies behind the facade. You just never know.

(**Vivian**) It's no wonder that the community was shocked to discover that a monster lived in their midst, but there was one person who believed in him, and who has been met with obstacles at every turn. Until now. Emily Dawson still lives in Whitbrook, even after her son was arrested and killed himself shortly after. She was dismissed as a delusional mother who couldn't accept that her own son was a monster. But there was more to her unwavering belief than a mother's instinct. In today's episode, you will hear why it's highly likely that the police got the wrong man.

And if Dennis didn't kill them, then who did?

"Everyone! I want to say something, Jenny can you get the glasses please? Come on. Everybody, come on!" Chris is at the large table proudly struggling to open a bottle of champagne.

"Well, this is different," Mike says, rising slowly, "It's not even three o'clock. What are we celebrating here, boss?"

Jenny is separating a stack of cheap plastic glasses. The kind you buy in bulk at the supermarket. "Don't we have real glasses?" Chris asks.

"If we do, I've never seen them," Jenny replies.

"Well put that on the list then. We should have real champagne glasses, for times like these. Never mind. A toast!"

There's a bit of shuffling, we all stand around the table and hold our plastic cup up high. I'm beaming but I try to hide it.

"The latest episode was a cracker. No doubt about it. Congratulations, Rachel and Jacob. You guys did great. All the major news outlets are reporting that there's strong evidence the wrong man was arrested for the murders of the Forster family. And we have passed the half a million download milestone!" he yells.

There are screams and we hug and do high fives and Jacob is shouting "Whoohoo!" and from the corner of my eye I see Vivian staring at me. I'm grinning so hard it hurts my cheeks. For a moment I forget what this podcast is really about, and I feel important, right here, in this job. Like I've really achieved something. I expect her to grin back, but out of all of us, she's the only one who doesn't. She's clapping, even smiling a little, but nothing like the rest of us.

"If Dawson really was innocent of these murders then it's really a tragedy," Chris says. "I feel for his mother. But let justice prevail. That's got to be the more important outcome here."

"So what's next, boss? What's the next podcast then?" Mike asks. "Because I may have an idea or two you know. I think we could do something on horse racing. I hear there's an interest in it."

There's more laughter and then in a more subdued tone, Chris says "and I can't tell you all how proud I am."

"So try!" Jenny says, just as Jacob, glowing, says, "Oh go away!"

"You left out the best part!" Jenny says. "The sponsors are falling over themselves to be a part of the podcast. We're beating them off with a stick!"

"Don't beat them too hard, Jenny, we need their money!" Chris says.

"Yeah, how else are we going to keep Mike here employed doing bugger all?"

"Hear hear!" Mike exclaims.

We're all laughing ourselves silly. Chris raises his hands. "Truly people, I'm delighted. Like Jenny said, that the sponsors are beating at the door. Our little newspaper has earned a reprieve. It's early days, but for now, we can all relax."

There are more whoops and cheers and Jenny refills the plastic glasses.

"Does that mean we should concentrate on finding out who the real killer was then?" I ask, since no one else does.

"Great question, Rach, I suspect that the police department will want to reopen that case soon. They'll be in touch at some point so please make sure all the recordings are stored safely."

"I think we should stick with the Molly angle. We're getting so many leads on the phone lines and on email. Let's get back on that track," Vivian says.

"I agree with Vivian," Jacob says. "We should focus back on Molly."

"I think we should follow up on the boyfriend story," I say.

Everyone has dispersed except Vivian and I. She's standing right next to me. I smile at her.

"We should follow up on the boyfriend story!" She's mimicking me, but not in a nice way. She takes a gulp of her champagne. "You're doing really well for yourself, Rachel, aren't you?"

"What's that supposed to mean?"

"Who would have thought? Shy little Rachel, who went from making sandwiches to producing the hottest podcast in the country. You're killing it, Rach. Well done."

"*We're* killing it."

"Oh, you more than most." She rubs a finger over the top of the table. "It's funny that Chris sent you to Whitbrook, don't you think?"

"Why?"

"You've got Gracie to look after. Surely it would have been easier for me to go."

"I asked to go."

"Ah." She gives me a knowing look before walking off, except I don't even know what it's supposed to mean. I feel awkward all of a sudden, standing there by myself, so I walk over to Jacob's desk.

"I think we should follow up on the relationship between Hugo Hennessy and Grace," I tell him.

The phone rings in the background and I see from the corner of my eye Jenny walking across to answer it. "Especially now that there's doubt over Dennis Dawson as the killer. You said it yourself. Why wasn't Hugo at the party? Why were they having a break?"

There's a shift in the mood. I become aware that no one is saying anything. They're all staring at Jenny who is holding the handset in both hands. She looks pale and wide-eyed.

"You all right there, Jen?" Chris says.

She pauses. It's as if she doesn't know how to say it.

"Who's that on the phone?" he asks.

She blinks. "Detective Mary Halliday, CID. For you." She points the handset towards Chris. He looks at Vivian, Jacob, and me briefly, a small smile playing on his lips, before taking the call.

"They're reopening the case. We did it!" I hiss to Jacob, bumping him on the shoulder, just as Jenny says,

"It's Emily Dawson. She's dead."

TWENTY-NINE

My hand flies to my mouth. "She's dead? Mrs Dawson?"

Jacob looks white. I grab the nearest chair and sit down. "How did she die?"

"At the moment it looks like suicide. They found her hanged in her bedroom."

I close my eyes. A moaning sound comes out of me. An image of Emily Dawson's limp, swaying body flashes against my eyelids. I open them again. Chris is talking on the phone, his back to us.

Jacob sits down next to me. "It doesn't make any sense."

They killed her.

"You spoke to her, before the episode went live, didn't you, Rach?" Jenny asks. "How did she seem?"

"She wasn't there when I called, but I left her a message on her answering machine. To let her know, you know, that we were putting it out, and the interview we had of her, everything. Dennis's alibi. I wanted to tell her there would be ramifications. That she should be prepared. The papers will want to talk to you, I told her."

"Poor Mrs Dawson. What could have possibly driven her to do this? Do you know?" Vivian asks me.

I bristle. "Driven to do this? I don't think anything drove her to it."

"What do you mean? Obviously—"

"I mean that the real killer got her!" I can hear how shrill I sound but I can't help it. "It makes sense! She reveals that she has evidence to prove Dennis's innocence and now she's dead. Convenient, wouldn't you say?"

Jacob's eyes widen and he becomes a shade paler.

"But we don't even know the details yet, Rachel. You can't jump to that," Vivian says, in an overly reasonable tone, I think. "I know it's a shock and it's sad, but let's find out what the police know first, okay?"

"Of course." I nod like that's a sensible request. But I know. I wipe a tear with the tip of my finger. Chris puts the handset back in its cradle.

"So?" Vivian asks.

"They want to ask a few questions."

"Did they say who found her?"

"The home care people from the council. A woman who drops by and helps her with shopping and things. She'd been dead a few days."

"A few days?" Jacob and I both say it at the same time. He's turned grey. I suspect I have too.

"Do they know when exactly?" Jacob asks.

"I don't know," Chris says. "You can ask the police when they get here."

"What do the cops want?" I ask.

"To hear the tapes apparently."

"Why?"

"She wrote a suicide note," Chris looks at me, and then at Jacob. "I'm sorry guys. She wrote that she'd made it all up,

160

about the alibi. Dennis was never with her that day. She lied to you. She made it all up."

"Bullshit," I blurt out. "They should listen to the interview. They'll know then, she didn't make it up. It's pretty obvious she's genuine."

"I think you're overly involved, Rachel," Vivian says. "I understand why you don't want to believe that Mrs Dawson lied to you both."

"She didn't—"

Vivian puts a hand up to stop me speaking.

"The police will have the facts and we should hear them before we decide what's *bullshit*. Maybe you need to step back for a few days."

I turn to Jacob. He's crushed. There's an expression of almost pity on Vivian's face, but I recognise the glint of something in her eyes. Triumph maybe.

What have I done? I've poked the bear, that's what. I have stirred the hornet's nest. My heart weeps for Mrs Dawson. I close my eyes, I can taste the fear that she must have felt. I know a little about that myself.

Jenny is clearing the plastic glasses. The party's over.

"Does it say in the note that she's going to kill herself? Does she specifically say that?" I ask Chris.

"I don't know, Rachel. The detectives will be here shortly. You can ask them yourself," he replies.

I stand up. "Here?"

"They want to talk to you. And Jacob. They have questions to ask you." He shakes his head. "Christ. I'll be in my office, if you need me. I have some calls to make."

I can't have the police take down my details. What if they look me up? I don't know what they'll find. I lean over to Jacob. "Can I talk to you for a sec?"

"Of course."

I bring my chair closer to him. Our knees almost touch. Conspiratorially, I say, "Chris just said that the detectives are going to be here any minute. Do you mind talking to them on your own? It doesn't need the two of us and it's just that I have to go and get my daughter, and—"

"You're sure? I think they'd like to hear from you too. I might overlook something. I think it'd be better if you stayed, if you could."

"Yeah, I know, look, sorry Jacob, it's just that I have to go. I can talk to them another time if they want me to."

"Of course, I understand."

"Ask them about the receipts, and the signed prescription. She kept them in that box, you should describe it to them. They need to find them."

"I'm not stupid."

"Sorry." I put a hand on his shoulder. "Thanks."

I walk off without waiting for a reply. I quickly grab my coat from the back of my chair and hoist my bag onto my shoulder.

"Where are you going?" Vivian asks.

I do a quick turn. "Pick up Gracie."

She flicks her wrist and looks at her watch. It's only a bit after three, which meant technically I still have a good two hours of work to do.

"Is she all right?" she asks, not unreasonably.

"Yeah, fine. I'll call you later." I leave without waiting for a reply from her either.

It's cold. I tighten the scarf around my neck and zip up my coat. Gracie will still be at the preschool for another two hours. I need some time to think.

It's all my fault. I've endangered Mrs Dawson. I put her

straight into the line of fire without thinking about her own safety. I'm so stupid. It never occurred to me that he would go after her. That's because, as I keep reminding myself, I've relaxed too much. Even now, I can't think straight. I'm not thinking ahead. I may as well put up a flag. *Hey I'm here! Come and get me!*

I've come up the stairs and I'm right outside our flat, but something is wrong. A noise, something that shouldn't be there. I strain to listen, then I hear it again. Like a scratching. I put my ear right against the door, at the same time pulling at my glove with my teeth. I fish around in my bag, feeling around for my phone when the door swings open and I stumble inside.

"Jesus, Rach!!" Matt is standing over me, one hand on the doorknob. I scramble to get up.

"You scared the shit out of me!" I shout, trembling. I brush myself down. Straighten my clothes.

"What are you doing listening at the door?"

"I'm not doing anything! I thought someone was inside!"

"Yeah! Me!"

"You scared the crap out of me. Why are you home so early?" I hang my coat on the coat rack. Matt goes in the kitchen and I follow him there. He fills up the kettle. The cupboard underneath the sink is ajar. It doesn't mean anything. So Matt opened the cupboard under the sink, big deal. But it still makes my heart race even faster than it already is.

He pulls two mugs from the drying rack and sets them on the table. "I've been let go, Rach." He says this so quickly that I don't know if I heard him right. He takes two tea bags from the tin and drops one into each mug. He looks at me.

"Let go?"

He nods. The corners of his mouth droop down, and for a

moment I think he's going to cry. I watch him lift the kettle and fill each mug with steaming water. I grab one and drag it across to me.

"I don't understand."

"It's not just me," he says quickly, "two other lads got let go as well. The Fusion contract ended, you know, and they didn't get the tenders they'd gone for. John said he would have liked to keep us on, but there just wasn't enough work, you know? Last in are the first to go, that's what John said."

"Jesus. When did this happen?"

"Two Fridays ago."

"Two weeks ago?"

"Yes! So what? I've been looking for other work, I've been applying for jobs, Rach, I was hoping to have one before I had to tell you, okay?"

I look at his thin face. I knew there was something, but I've been so preoccupied myself that I just pushed it to the back of my mind, filed it under 'later'.

"Oh love, I'm sorry." I stand up and take him in my arms. "It'll be okay, you'll see. You should have told me." I feel him agree. I say words of reassurance, even as it is slowly dawning on me that we barely have any savings, and with the rent and everything else, it's going to be real tight. If Matt doesn't get a job soon we'll be in trouble. But he's a qualified electrician, and they're in demand all the time. We'll be fine, we will.

"Do you think the paper will survive?" he asks. His eyes are filled with anxiety. I can't bear to think what would happen if we both lost our jobs.

"I hope so, it depends on the podcast I guess."

"I heard the podcast," he says softly. I pull out of our embrace and sit back down.

"Did you?"

"Of course!"

"When?" I ask that as a reflex, because I don't want to talk about it yet, after what's happened. I don't have the words.

"Last Friday, when it came out."

"Really?"

Today is Tuesday, and in all that time, Matt has not mentioned anything to me.

"What did you think?" I ask.

He shakes his head in awe. "It was amazing, Rach, how you got the lady to talk about her son like that, and how it couldn't have been him, I can't tell you how proud I am of you. I can see why you're into this so much. It's important, right?"

"Thanks, love." I move my mug around for a bit, then I say, "But something terrible happened."

"Tell me."

So I do. As much as I can. I tell him about Emily Dawson, and what we've heard from the police so far.

Matt grabs a bottle of wine from the sideboard and two tumblers from the shelf. He pours each of us a glass.

"Was it too much for her? The memory maybe, or the frustration?"

"But that makes no sense. It should have been the opposite, don't you see? This was her chance to get justice for Dennis." I bite the side of my thumb in frustration.

"So what do you think happened?"

"You really want to know?"

"Yeah, I do."

"Well, I think that she was killed."

He jerks his head. "Wow! Really? But why?"

"Because if it wasn't Dennis Dawson, then it was someone else. And that someone else probably doesn't like anyone looking too closely at an alternative to Dennis Dawson.

"When did she die?" he asks.

"I don't know yet."

He drains the rest of his glass in one gulp, then immediately pours himself another glass of wine. I've barely touched mine.

"I'm sorry about your job, love," I say. He nods, rubs a finger where a small drop of red wine has spilled onto the table top, then he goes to the sink. I watch the back of him as he rinses a cloth, but as I drop my gaze I notice a small pool of water on the floor beneath the cupboard door. I let out a small, involuntary gasp.

"What's this water doing there?" I ask.

"We had a leak earlier."

I stand up quickly.

"What's wrong?" he asks.

"I'll clean it up," I say.

"No, I'll do it. Sit down."

I sit back down, watch him bend and mop the water with a sponge.

"When did we get a leak?"

My voice sounds unnatural to my ears, but he doesn't seem to notice.

"This morning, just before lunch. Lucky I was here."

"What happened?"

"The joints under the sink, but it's fixed now. Don't worry about it."

I will myself to calm down. I know he would tell me if he'd found the memory book. Wouldn't he?

"Do you think it's the same people that detective was talking about? The one who tracked her down to Barcelona?" he asks.

We included a segment of that interview as well. I wasn't mad about that, I made the argument that at that point it was only guesswork and we should wait for more, but I was overruled.

"I don't know, maybe?"

He nods. "Did you ever hear about it? When you were there? The guy killed in that car accident? You would have been there around the same time, right?"

I reason with myself that he doesn't mean anything by this, but still it feels odd, that he should ask me all these questions. I study his face but see nothing other than curiosity.

Maybe I shouldn't have told Matt about Barcelona. It was early days in our relationship and I wanted to impress him. We'd gone to a Tapas Bar in Soho and like an idiot I decided to order in Spanish, to show off I guess. Oh yeah, I was drunk. So was he. Which was just as well because the waiters didn't speak a word of Spanish, but he was impressed anyway.

The conversation went a bit like this:

"I was an exchange student, in Barcelona."

"Oh yeah? That's amazing, say something in Spanish."

"*Creo que te amo,*" I whispered, shoving my tongue somewhere in the vicinity of his earlobe. I don't remember a whole lot about that night, but unfortunately, it seems Matt does.

"I don't think I was there at the same time," I say, a little abruptly.

I feel ill. It's not the wine, I've barely touched it. It's the fear. It has crept inside my stomach again.

"What time is it?" I ask, even as my phone was right there on the table in front of me. I grab it.

"Shit." We both stand up at the same time and say, "Gracie."

"Will you?" I ask. He hesitates for a moment then he nods.

"Sure," he replies, grabbing his jacket that is dangling off the back of a chair.

I wait five seconds after he gets out the door and dive

under the kitchen sink. I can see a bit of moisture still, and a fresh coating of something white around the joint that meets the tap, but the sheeting looks untouched, thank God. I don't think any water made it down there, from the look of things. I don't move the memory book. I leave it there, in its hiding place. I don't have a better spot for it anyway.

THIRTY

The mood in the office this morning is no longer jubilant, obviously. I make a beeline for Jacob and the first thing he says is, "It's official. The police are not treating her death as suspicious. She killed herself."

"If she killed herself then I'm the queen of England," I say sharply. That gets a small smile out of him.

"The receipts are gone. The prescription, all of it. The cops found burnt fragments in an ashtray."

My jaw drops, and I close my eyes for a moment. When I open them again, Jacob is peering at me.

"That should tell the police something, right? Someone burnt them. That's clear. That dispels the suicide—" But Jacob raises a hand.

"*She* burnt them, because they were fake. That's the theory. Even if they were still there, it means nothing. Anyone can imitate a signature on the back of a prescription. It's not proof. That's what they said."

I pull up the nearest chair and sit down heavily. "What are we going to do now?" I ask.

"I don't know. First, we have to deal with the fallout—"

"What fallout?"

"It's all over the morning news Rachel, haven't you heard? The mother of the convicted killer committed suicide because of our podcast."

"There's more to this, and you know it." I drum my fingers on the desk. "We have to act quickly. We'll say that she had no reason to kill herself. She believed she had proof her son was wrongly accused, so why kill herself now? We'll say that in the next episode, but we have to start looking for the real killer, Jacob. We don't have much time—"

"Chris said to hold off on the next episode."

"What?" I snap around to look at Chris. He's on the phone. He's pressing the heel of his hand against his forehead. His eyes are closed.

"But that's crazy! It's the last thing we should do. Where's Vivian? We need to come up with a plan here."

"She's not in. She's been monstered on social media. She's laying low. Check this out."

Jacob loads up Vivian's Twitter account. Reading the barrage of abuse makes me gasp. They're all addressed directly to her username.

.*@vivianbrown89 Your a murderer I hope your happy now*

.*@vivianbrown89 Your podcast is stupid*

.*@vivianbrown89 What did you do to this old woman*

.*@vivianbrown89 Your a fucking whore and a slag.*

.*@vivianbrown89 She's dead because of you. I hope your proud.*

.*@vivianbrown89 You need a good shag tell me where you live*

"Oh my God. That's awful."

"Facebook's the same, give or take. I didn't talk to her, but Chris said she's taking it in her stride. He suggested she lay low and stay home."

It goes on and on, those messages, but then in the noise

one of them stands out to me. It says, *Grace Forster was a fucking slag and she deserved to die.*

It's him. He's watching. I know it.

I'm back at my desk and I give Vivian a call.

"You're okay?" I ask.

"Yeah," she says, with a sigh, "I will be."

"It's a prank. It's kids."

"How would you know?" I wish I was with her. I wish I could put my arm around her shoulders and hold her.

"We thought things like that might happen, remember?" I reply. "We talked about the trolls and the weirdos out there. You need to block this prick and log out of Twitter. And the rest."

"Done already. That's what Chris said."

"There was a message on the hotline. Right after the first episode. It's the same language. Peppered with 'you fucking slag', and 'Grace Forster got everything she deserved.' I think it's the same person. I think it's just *one* person. It'll blow over Viv, you'll see."

"A message? You never said anything about that?"

"Waste of everyone's time."

She says nothing at first, then finally she replies, "If you say so."

After I hang up, I take another look at Vivian's Twitter feed, and the podcast Twitter feed. Most of the vile tweets are from someone called @iambeserk123. This person created this account two days ago. I don't know where to start to find out who this is. But Chris calls me into his office.

"I'm worried about the direction things are taking. It's a terrible thing, what happened to this poor woman."

I nod. "Look, I know the police say she took her own life. But hear me out for a second."

"Okay."

I tell him about my theory. I watch his face react when I say that I think she was killed because of the podcast. That whoever heard the episode went to see her to get rid of the receipts. I don't say who. He doesn't look convinced anyway.

"We can't just say something like that, Rachel. We'd need proof."

I make a show of considering the options. "Assuming she was telling the truth, then he must think we're getting close to this guy, the person who killed the family. I think we should keep the pressure on. Let him make a mistake, hopefully. Something else could happen."

"I don't know. I'll hear what you have but I can't make any promises."

I do my best to keep the eagerness out of my voice. "We should focus our efforts on showing that because of his suicide, and the short amount of time he was in jail after his arrest, there had been very little investigative work. His death had stopped everything in its track and as a result, his guilt had been assumed, but not proven."

"What about his confession?"

"We covered that in the interview with Mrs Dawson. She says he didn't understand what he was doing. Who knows what promises, or threats, were made? Maybe the Chief Constable said he'd go free afterwards. And there's the small detail that Dennis was autistic. Did he understand what he was signing? I doubt it."

"Okay, put something together and I'll have a listen. But don't waste too much time on it. At the very least, we should get back to finding Molly."

I make promises I have no intention of keeping.

I go to check in on Vivian after work. I miss her. We can find a way to be friends again, surely. Friends have fights, and then they make up. Or so I'm told. I've never had many friends.

"Was Gracie okay?" she asks.

"Yes, sure, why?"

"Just that you left in a hurry yesterday, I thought maybe she was ill."

I shake my head. "She's fine."

She grabs two beers from the fridge, which I take as a good sign, and we go into the living room.

"You said some things too, yesterday, about me going to Whitbrook with Jacob. You didn't seem very happy about it."

I sit cross-legged on the floor with my back against the couch. She hands me a beer.

"It's just, I'm surprised, that's all. For someone who didn't like the idea, you seem to be all over this podcast. It's like you want to get all the credit."

"That's ridiculous."

"Is it? Why would you put your hand up to go to Whitbrook? We never discussed it. By the time I'd heard of it, it was a done deal."

I swirl my drink for a couple of seconds. "Jacob told me about the call he got, from Mrs Dawson."

"So?"

"So it sounded like a breakthrough, I guess."

She snorts. "A breakthrough? What are you? A detective now?"

I scowl at her. "It's not like that."

"It didn't quite work out the way you wanted though, did it," she says.

I sigh. "I think there's a lot more to it. I don't think Mrs Dawson—"

"Yeah I know, you told me. She was murdered by the real

killer. There's another possibility though, one that you haven't thought of."

"What's that?"

"That she killed herself."

I shake my head. "I don't believe it."

"It's very likely that you're in over your head there, Rachel."

"Vivian, stop. I don't want to argue with you anymore."

She shakes her head, but then her face softens.

"I should go," I say, standing up. I knock back the rest of my beer, then I blurt, "Matt's lost his job."

"Oh no, what happened?"

"He was working on a big commercial contract and that ended, basically. They hired a bunch of tradesmen for that contract, and now they can't keep them all employed. Last in, first out, so he had to go."

"That sucks," she looks at me gently, and gives me a small smile. "I'm really sorry. Is Matt very upset?"

"He's been applying for jobs, electricians are always in demand, it won't take him long. Might not be the same pay though, that was a good contract."

She leans over and hugs me. We're both a little stiff, but it's a start. I stay like this, sad and deflated. I have rarely felt so lonely as I do now, so physically close and yet I can't tell her the thing that is scaring the hell out of me. *They're getting close, I'm scared they're going to find me. I'm scared they're going to hurt you.*

"I miss you," I tell her.

She hugs me again, tightly this time. The way she used to.

"I miss you too. I miss the way things were. You're my friend. My best friend."

"How did we come to this?" I ask.

She releases me. Her face looks sad. "I wish I knew," she says.

On impulse I say, "Matt organised for his mum to look after Gracie on Friday, we're going out to that club, in Camden Town. Why don't you come with us? We'll make a night of it. I'm sure Matt would love you to come along."

Which I think will be true, once I tell him.

I gently punch her shoulder. "Hey why don't you bring someone? One of your Tinder guys. We could go on a double date. What do you say?"

She doesn't say anything but there's a smile lifting one corner of her lips.

"There might be someone," she says, coyly.

"What?" I laugh and suddenly I don't want to leave anymore. It's almost like old times, between us. I get us another beer.

"Tell me everything. What's his name?"

"Peter," she says, and smiles, then she adds, "It's a nice name, don't you think?"

I let out a short laugh. "Wow, you really are smitten!" We clink our bottles together.

"You're sure Matt won't mind if we crash your date?" she asks.

"He'll love it."

Matt and I are both fairly social people, and when you have a child, as wonderful as that is, the thing you miss is hanging out with your friends. The idea of going out just the two of us is nice, but the idea of going out *with other people* is even better.

Or at least that's what I thought, but Matt isn't jumping with joy at the news.

"I thought you wanted it to be just us. Isn't that what we said?"

"I know, I did, I do. I'm sorry, love, I kind of made a mistake I think. I spoke too soon."

"So undo it, Rach, how hard can it be?"

"You know I can't." As if I would tell Vivian that no, actually, she's not invited, I made a mistake. This would snap our friendship in half.

He groans loudly. "You can, but you won't."

"Don't be like that please." I reach out to touch his arm, but he jerks it away.

And now it's Friday, and Matt and I find ourselves mingling through the crowd of people who had the same idea.

Vivian texted that she'd be late, and Matt and I stand together by the bar, barely speaking to each other, waiting to be noticed by the bartender. It takes so long to get a G&T, I almost wish he'd ordered two at the same time. But the band sounds great and I feel like dancing. Maybe Vivian will bail. Maybe she changed her mind. I can't help wishing she would. Just as I think that, I feel a tap on my shoulder.

"Hey, hon!" she says, planting a kiss on my cheek. Then she throws her arms around Matt who can't help but grin. Maybe it will be all right after all.

"We got a booth, come with me," she yells in my ear. She beckons to Matt and we grab our glasses and follow her, elbowing our way across the room.

The table she makes a beeline for has a guy seated already, who smiles warmly at her and even puts his hand on her arse when she reaches him. For some reason, the gesture annoys me.

Vivian introduces me to Peter, who shakes my hand and brings his lips close to my ear, and says, "Hi Rachel, it's nice to meet you."

I don't feel well. I go from too hot to too cold and back again. My skin is clammy to the touch and my heart is beating too fast. The problem with a panic attack, is that you start to panic about having one. But I don't understand why this is happening to me here, now.

Except that when he pulls back, smiling at me, the room tilts around me. I know I've finally gone crazy as I stare right at Hugo Hennessy.

THIRTY-ONE

I have wondered many times what I would do if I came face-to-face with Hugo Hennessy. Each time it went like this: *Run*. I am a coward. I have always been and always will be, and today is no different so I bolt to the ladies room before he has time to finish saying, *I'm Peter*.

I lock myself in a cubicle, close the toilet seat and sit. I'm shaking, wringing my hands together, my thoughts jumbled together. I can't think, I can't breathe, I couldn't run even if I wanted to.

There are girls at the basins chatting and swapping lipstick, then I hear "Rach, you're in here, hon?" as Vivian crosses the length of the room banging on the cubicle doors one by one.

"Rach? It's me, hon! You're in here?"

I consider ignoring her, but I can't bring myself to do it. I lean over and pull the latch so the door opens just as she bangs on it.

"Oh there you are." She crouches down at my feet, which

is not easy considering how cramped it is in there. I start to cry.

"Oh Rach. What's the matter? It was a mistake, this place. Matt should have known better. It's too crowded on a Friday night."

She pulls me close, and I lay my forehead on her shoulder while she pats my back with a series of 'there there' and 'oh hon.'

"I'm so scared, Viv, I'm just so fucking scared." I sob.

"I know, hon, there there. Remember to breathe, hon, it'll pass, you'll see."

I sniffle. Then she says, "You want me to get Matt?"

"No, it's okay," I manage to say. I pull away from her embrace, grab some toilet paper and blow my nose. Maybe I've imagined it. I never thought I'd find myself hoping I've merely been having a panic attack, but this time I do. Maybe it wasn't Hugo Hennessy but I got myself all confused. It wouldn't be the first time.

"I'm okay, I think. We should go back."

"'Scuse my French but you look like shit, Rach, let's get you cleaned up a bit." We stand up awkwardly and she takes me by the elbow and guides me across to the sinks.

"'Scuse me! 'Scuse me but we have an emergency here!"

The girls that are already positioned at the mirror come apart just enough for the two of us to slip in, with a chorus of 'Aw, you okay babe? He's not worth it, you know, they never are'.

"What have you got in there?" Vivian asks, pointing at the small bag hanging from my shoulder.

My fingers shake as I try to open it. She moves my hands out of the way and pulls out my make-up case. She pats some foundation under my eyes with a small sponge. I stare at my reflection in the mirror. *What if it's him? Stop it. You're being paranoid. How can it be him?*

I smile an apology at her. "Sorry. Your friend must think I'm crazy."

"No, he won't." She shrugs. "He might think you've got the runs though." In spite of myself I burst out laughing. I pull a crumpled tissue from my pocket and dab at my nose. Vivian applies a spot of rouge on my cheeks.

"There. All better now," she says in a sing-song voice.

"Thanks, Viv." She smiles and winks at me. "Let's go, the boys will be wondering where we went."

But the boys are doing no such thing, instead they're deep in conversation, both leaning across the table to discuss the merits of vinyl versus digital. I slide next to Matt. He looks at me, with a question in his eye that says, 'you okay?' I blink my acquiescence.

"You girls want some sparkling?" Peter asks. There's a plastic champagne bucket, filled with ice and a bottle. Next to it are four tumblers. "They ran out of champagne glasses apparently," he adds.

Matt and I don't usually drink sparkling but I see that Matt has a glass filled already, so I say "yes please". Peter pulls the bottle out and fills up the remaining two glasses. Matt puts his hand on my leg. "Peter knows a hell of a lot about sound," he says to me.

"Does he?" I say, plastering a smile on my face to pretend that I care.

"Yes, I'm a bit of an audiophile," Peter says.

"It's all about the signal," he and Matt say in unison, and toast their shared passion.

I take a gulp of the sparkling wine. I see from the corner of my eye Vivian tickling the back of Peter's neck. He whispers something in her ear.

I make myself look at him, and immediately get the same anxiety in the pit of my stomach. He and Vivian are cooing sweet nothings to each other, and I take the opportunity to study him. He doesn't have any hair. Hugo Hennessy had thick blond hair but that means sod all. It was a long time ago, and I wasn't born a brunette either. He could have shaved it off. I can't make out the colour of his eyes from here, but I'm sure they're blue from what I saw moments earlier. Hugo Hennessy's eyes are also blue. The shape of his jaw matches too. But beyond that it's hard to tell.

I close my eyes. I can see him now, the bloody cricket bat raised high. The only other way out of the house was through the kitchen, and out the back but I couldn't bear to go in there. I remember the blood. My mother's body sprawled... I ran into the bathroom at the back of the house, screaming, and I locked the door.

Open the door, Molly!

He started to hit it with the bat, over and over.

Open the fucking door!

I stood on the top of the cistern to reach the small window and I got out that way. He was still trying to knock the door down. He probably didn't know about the window. I ran as fast as I could to the old station and hid there.

And now, all these years later, sitting here, with Matt's hand on my thigh, I know, in the pit of my stomach, that it's him.

Maybe I could pretend I'm ill and I have to go home. Peter keeps buying bottles of wine and I keep drinking what's put in front of me. We all do. Then Vivian and I dance together and we're both so pissed, we have to prop each other up.

"What do you think of him," she slurs in my ear.

"Who?" I say, because I think that makes me sound more natural.

She punches my shoulder, but not very hard.

"Peter!" she says, dragging each vowel so it comes out like "Peeeteeer!!!"

I make a face, pretending to think about it. She looks at me with her big eyes, her face an inch from mine.

"Sooo?"

"He's a bit old, isn't he?" I shout into her ear.

"What? No!! Crap!! And what if he is anyway?"

"How old is he?"

"I don't know! Why?"

I shrug, then I grin.

She laughs. "You're funny," she says.

"He's got nice eyes," I say, and without vomiting too. She smiles. "Yeah, he does. He's sexy, yeah?"

She grins so I make a thumbs up gesture.

I am so drunk by the time we get home that I can't stand without help anymore. I throw up twice before I get to bed.

"I think you overdid it there, babe," Matt says, uselessly I think.

"No, I'm fine I'm fine," I slur for the tenth time. He laughs as he helps me take my clothes off. "Where's Gracie?" I ask, sitting up so quickly it makes the room spin.

"She's asleep, where else?"

I lay back down. "Where's your mum?"

"She's asleep, with her."

"Oh. She doesn't want to go home now?"

"It's after three in the morning, Rach."

"Oh yeah." I close my eyes as Matt helps me get under the covers.

"How did we get home?" I ask.

"You don't remember?"

"Hum …"

"We got a cab."

"Ah."

"You were so funny."

"Was I?"

"You thought the fare was two pounds fifty—"

"Did I?"

"—and he kept saying, 'no ma'am, that's the time.'" He laughs.

I don't get it, but I laugh too. "Ah, that's funny," I say.

"Yeah, you go to sleep now, Rach. You're going to get a heck of a hangover tomorrow."

"Will I?"

"I'd say so."

I open my eyes. "What did you think of Hugo?" I asked.

"Who?"

I close them again. "Hugo."

"Vivian's friend?"

"Yeah, him."

"His name's Peter. Go to sleep."

"Oh yeah, Peter," I giggle. "What did you think of *Peter*?" I say his name in a deeper voice, like I'm making fun of him. Matt doesn't seem to notice.

"I liked him. He's a nice guy. It's nice to see Vivian with a nice bloke."

"Mmm."

"Poor bloke," he chuckles.

Matt's voice sounds further and further away, so I'm not sure I hear him correctly when he says, from a great distance, "He might be able to help me get a job."

I am slipping into darkness, and it's almost a relief.

"I'm going to die," I murmur, matter-of-factly.

"No, you're not. You'll have a heck of a hangover, that's all."

THIRTY-TWO

I don't die that night, but the way I feel the next morning, I may as well have. I wake up with the worst headache in history, but it's more than that.

I've been so stupid. I should have made him talk. I should have asked questions, I should have done plenty of things to try and assess why he was here now, and whether or not he knows who I am. I should have figured out if he was just after Vivian to find out how much we know. I should have asked how he met Vivian. But no, instead of using my brain, I've got myself completely drunk and spent hours dancing. If that's what it was called, whatever I was doing on the dance floor. Maybe I should be running away from myself.

We spend the morning as a family. Matt makes fun of me, but in a nice, teasing way. The three of us go to the park, we watch Gracie squeal with joy at the ponies on display. I don't know why there are ponies in the park.

"You okay now, babe?" Matt asks. I put my hand in the crook of his arm and hold tight.

"I'm good. Don't you believe me?"

"You're miles away, that's all."

I squeeze his arm tighter.

I need to come up with a plan. I am shocked at the realisation that I haven't planned for anything like this. It's all very well to use the podcast to expose the real killer, flush him out, but then what? I almost want to laugh at my own stupidity. The killer is flushed out and he's dating your best mate. Well done.

He's going to hurt her. The very thought makes my stomach lurch. I let go of Matt and fish around in my bag for my mobile. "What are you looking for?" he asks.

"My phone. I just want to make sure Vivian got home okay," I say, by way of explanation. I send her a text that says exactly that.

Did you get home okay? How you feeling?

I stare at the screen after pressing send, then I chide myself for thinking she'd be holding the phone waiting for a message from me. I keep it in my hand, but at least I stop staring at it. Then it buzzes.

Thanks hon, all good, chat later ok x

I let out the breath I'd forgotten I was holding. Gracie comes running back to us and rushes into Matt's arms. We wander off to the other side of the park, where the playground is. I am filled with dread.

"Did you have fun last night?" I ask Matt.

"Yeah, it was good," he replies, in typical Matt fashion: economically. I nod gravely as if I had to think about what he just said, then I change my mind. It hurt my head too much.

"What did you think of Peter?" I ask instead.

"Grace! Come down please! Now!" I turn to look. She's climbing up a tree, all joy and no fear. She makes a face at us but comes back down easily and jumps to the ground, then she runs to the sand pit.

"That's more like it," Matt mutters. We sit down on the wooden bench. He puts his arm around my shoulders. I wait a moment then I ask again.

"So? What did you think?"

"Yeah, he's a nice guy I thought. I hope it works out."

"Yeah, me too," I say, after a pause.

Some of Matt's friends are coming over this afternoon to watch a game at our place. The group includes Fred and Milly, a nice couple who have a child just a few weeks older than Gracie, so the two of them can enjoy the afternoon together.

"Why don't we ask Vivian and Peter to come over too? Watch the game with us?" I suggest. The pitch of my voice has gone up an octave.

"I don't know, depends," he replies.

"On what?"

"On what side he's on," he turns to me and smiles. I laugh, or I try to. It comes out like a cackle.

I text Vivian again:

You and Peter want to come over and keep me company this afternoon? Matt + mates watching the game.

I don't need to wait long for a reply.

Peter left for weekend now. Im free tho! :) Xx

Great! See you later x

Vivian's idea of fun is no more watching a soccer game than, say, watching grass grow. She and I are like-minded on that front. So while Milly and the boys shout and whoop in the living room, we retreat to the kitchen, with two tumblers and that nice bottle of red she's brought along. Hair of the dog, she said.

"I won't mention it again I swear, but you okay now?" she asks. There is pity in her eyes.

I look away. "Of course. I'm totally fine. Crowded clubs, you know."

"You should tell that boyfriend of yours to take you out to better places."

"I thought the exact same thing," I say and smile.

"You should tell your shrink though, she could prescribe something I'm sure," she continues, scratching an invisible mark from the top of the kitchen table.

"That part where you don't mention it again, when does that start?" I mean to say it lightly, but it comes out more aggressively than that. She flicks her eyes up at me.

"Sorry," she says.

"No, it's me. I'm embarrassed, that's all. You're totally right, I should tell Barb when I see her next time. And I will."

"And you'll ask her about some meds?"

"I promise." I squeeze her hand. What else can I say? *Meds won't help, Viv, it's your new boyfriend that's the problem.*

I top up our glasses. "Tell me about this new man of yours, that's much more fun."

She grins, lifts her shoulders. "He's hot, right?!" she laughs.

"Yeah, definitely."

"He's different from the guys I normally date. He's more, I don't know. Mature."

"That's great!" I say too brightly. "How did you meet him? You said he's a friend of Jenny's?"

She frowns in confusion. "Did I?"

"Or you met him through Jenny, I think you said."

"Ah, no I meant, Jenny and I were together. We went to the Cat & Mutton last Friday night and by the time I got our drinks, the two of them were chatting. When she introduced me, I thought he was a friend of hers, but they'd only just met, right there and then. Lucky she's already taken, hey?"

"Wait, you've only known him a week?"

"I know, right? Feels like I've known him since forever!"

I feel the chill down my spine. He must have waited for her outside the building where we work, and followed them to the pub.

She tells me about that day, that they stayed out most of the night together, and ended up walking the streets at 3 a.m. laughing and holding hands. She tells me he texts her all the time, just a kiss sometimes, to show her he's thinking about her and isn't that the sweetest thing? Of course Vivian always falls head over heels within five minutes of kissing a guy. Tommy had been no different. And when she tells me that he's going to help her with her troll, because 'he's good with computers, he says he can probably find out who's harassing me', I know, without a shadow of a doubt, that it's him, sending Vivian these creepy messages.

"So you've seen a lot of him?"

"He's been at my place most nights, put it that way." She grins.

"What's his place like?" I ask, thinking it's a smarter question than 'where does he live?'

"Don't know, he prefers to come stay with me. He lives in a flat in Peckham I think."

"Peckham's nice."

"Is it? I don't think I've ever been there."

I smile.

"Anyway, it's only temporary, he's only just moved to London, so at some point he'll get a more long-term place."

"Huh. Where did he move from?" I ask, replenishing our tumblers. There's an explosion of noise coming from the living room. Someone must have scored a goal, on the wrong side.

"Birmingham. Do you have any crisps or something?"

I rummage through the cupboards until I find an unopened packet of pretzels.

"What about this? I've also got some crackers and some nice cheese to go with them."

"Perfect."

I open the fridge, and ask, "What does he do?" before pulling some cheddar from the cheese compartment. I set it onto a wooden cutting board, along with a couple of knives while Vivian opens the packet of crackers.

"He's in finance, something, not sure."

I grab a knife and cut a small piece of cheese.

"Finance? That's good, right? Which company, do you know?" I pop the cheese into my mouth.

She cocks her head at me. "What's with all the questions, Rach?"

"What do you mean?"

"You're supposed to ask me what the sex is like, not his job title."

"Sorry. Just want to make sure he's a good catch."

She stares at me for a second longer than necessary. "What is it? Come on, out with it!"

"Nothing! I don't know him enough to like him, or not like him!" But I can see I've hurt her feelings. I put my hand on top of hers and squeeze. "I'm sure he's wonderful. I'm just looking after you, that's all."

She purses her lips and bites the side of her mouth, then she says, "He's twenty-eight."

I cut up another piece of cheese, thinking that he's not twenty-eight. He's a liar.

"I asked him," she continues. "This morning. So you see, he's not *that* much older than me."

"I didn't say he was."

"Yes Rach, you did! Last night!"

I don't remember saying that, but then again, a lot of the night had ended up on the blurry end of my memory.

"Has he been married before?" I ask, thinking that, at least, is more of an expected question, but Vivian's had enough.

"Jeez, Rachel! I don't know. Give it a rest, okay?" She shakes her head in annoyance, knocks her drink back and finishes it in one gulp. I look at her straight on.

"I'm looking after you. I want to make sure he's a good guy."

"You've never done this with anyone else I've dated. Why now? I just met him! We're getting to know each other! What's the problem?"

"He's come out of nowhere, and you hardly know him."

"It's called dating in the twenty-first century. And anyway, you hardly knew Matt but that didn't stop you from spending every waking moment with him the minute you met! You're not making any sense!"

She's right of course. I'm doing this all wrong.

"I won't mention it again, okay? But I have a bad feeling

about this guy. There. I said it. I'm sorry, Viv, I love you, you know that. But be careful, okay? That's all I'm saying."

"Can we get to the part where you don't mention it again?"

I chuckle, but she doesn't. Fred bursts into the room laughing. He stops abruptly when he sees us, as if he'd forgotten we were there.

"Hey, what are you two doing in here? You should come and join us!" He opens the fridge and pulls out a six pack of beer. Vivian gets up.

"Come on, Rach, let's go and watch the game."

THIRTY-THREE

I told Matt we needed some groceries. He was writing emails and making calls. He didn't ask anything, just waved. And now I'm back at the Internet place near my flat. I'm desperate. I have to find a link between Peter and Hugo Hennessy, somehow, so I'm thinking that if I can get hold of a current photograph, I might be able to convince her. It feels like a stupid idea, but it's the only one I've got.

"Can I get fifteen minutes of Internet?" I ask, handing the money over. I need to be quick. I hope fifteen minutes is enough.

"Sure." The young woman behind the counter hands me a ticket with a number on it and something on her hand sparks a memory in me. It's her tattoo. I follow the ink up her arm, which is partly covered in an intricate garden of flowers.

I've seen this arm before. I look up into her face. There's a flash of recognition for both of us.

I was about fourteen, we were both living in the same shelter, a big ramshackle of a house that had something like twenty homeless kids at any one time, where someone was always looking to steal your stuff and the locks were always broken.

She barely acknowledges me, and I do the same, but we both have that look on our faces. Somewhere in between pride and pleasure. That's what it's like to find that another one of us has escaped the fate that living on the streets holds. She's got a job in a convenience store. It might not seem like much of an achievement to most people, but to people like us, it's the path to independence, and the freedom that comes with it. I'm so proud of her I could hug her.

She gives me a ticket and doesn't charge me.

I take the ticket and go out the back. I pick the computer that faces away from the front window, open a browser and type 'Hugo Hennessy, Whitbrook'.

The first relevant entry I find is a small news item from five years ago, about his father having been elected Mayor of Whitbrook. He's standing on the steps of the town hall, flanked by his wife and son. The caption reads: *Newly minted Mayor Hennessy with his wife Margot and son Hugo.*

The photo is in black and white and it's been scanned from the original, as has the entire article. I peer at the picture. Even in its blurry state it makes me ill to look at him. Why is he preening about the place when my entire family is dead because of him? What kind of a sick parent would protect someone like him? I close my jaw, biting down so hard that my teeth hurt.

I check that the printer behind me is working and not in use, then I send the page to it. There's another item from around the same time that makes me gag.

Edward and Margot Hennessy are pleased to announce the engagement of their son, Hugo, of Whitbrook, to Heather Donohue, daughter of Phil and Penelope Donohue, also of Whitbrook.

I want to throw something heavy at the computer screen. I go back to the search results and keep looking for recent photos of him. There's an older picture and I already have that one in my memory book. It's a snapshot from my family's funeral. Hugo is looking sombre and sad for the cameras. He is standing near my sister's open grave, a hand over his chest, as if he's making a silent prayer. I added that printout to my memory book not because I want to remember, but because I don't want to forget.

The other entries I've seen before, but I take a closer look at them now. They're all about big scale developments in the area. There was some grumbling in the news because he's the son of the mayor, but the mayor categorically denied any impropriety. All council transactions happen at arm's length, etc. There's an especially big land grab coming up for a shopping centre. There's a picture of a man in a hardhat outside the old railway station and something nags at my memory, but I can't catch it. Anyway, it's not him. None of these entries have the photo I'm looking for: a clear, recent picture of Hugo Hennessy. It's almost like he's doing it on purpose, always turning away from the camera.

On my way out, I catch sight of the newspaper headline. I backtrack two steps and look at the stack.

Emily Dawson's suicide, who is responsible?

I snatch a copy of the *Mail* from the rack and begin to read.

The podcast trend started with the hugely successful Serial. We all gushed over it. 'The podcast we've been waiting for, the greatest podcast ever made.' At over a million downloads and counting, it fast became one of the most popular podcasts in the country.

"Are you going to buy that?"

I turn around. The young woman, the one with the tattoo, the one I'm so proud of, she's staring pointedly at me. I fish out the right change and drop it on the counter, leave the store with my purchase and walk out. I turn the first corner and lean against a brick wall.

Ever since, true crime podcasts have become the preferred pastime for armchair detectives. Everyone's a sleuth and all that's required is a smart phone and an iTunes account. Checks and balances? Who needs them?

Missing Molly is no different. The new kid on the podcast block is fast becoming the topic du jour around water coolers everywhere, and while its production value is not without merit, its morals are. Whose idea was it to prod and poke and broadcast an interview with the mother of one of England's most evil murderers? Mrs Dawson, mother of Dennis Dawson who was arrested for the murder of the Forster Family, and who confessed, unequivocally, to the killings, was found dead at her home last Saturday evening. A community worker charged with regular visits to Mrs Dawson became concerned when no one answered at her flat, and after a second attempt, returned with a locksmith.

Mrs Dawson was found hanging from the light fitting of her bedroom ceiling. She left a note behind, speaking of her shame at being "England's most hated mother" and explained how she took the opportunity of the podcast to rewrite history.

A few days earlier, she had received a visit from the makers of Missing Molly, eager to interview her. And why not? The podcast is tasked with retracing the steps of the only member of the Forster family that wasn't found that night. There has been plenty of conjecture in the past that Dennis Dawson killed Molly Forster as she ran away from the house and hid her body. Because Dawson committed suicide soon after being arrested, there was no opportunity to interrogate him in that regard. Extensive searches of the area failed to produce a body.

What seemed to have happened here is that, given the opportunity to defend her son, Mrs Dawson concocted a story. She claimed that Dennis Dawson was in fact busy caring for her, his sick mother, while the family was murdered. But once that story reached the million listeners, the enormity of what she had done was too much for Mrs Dawson.

It's not for us to judge the morality of Mrs Dawson's behaviour, and the lengths a mother will go to, to exonerate her child is nothing new.

But is it right of the producers to trawl through a family's grief, even offer hope of redemption because it makes for good listening? We believe that the South Hackney Herald has a lot to answer for. Maybe they should have stuck to what they do best: community bulletins.

My chest is tight with anger as I shove the paper in the nearest bin. I quickly walk across to the supermarket and buy a handful of items, the groceries I've promised to get. How could they write this stuff? They didn't even mention the receipts we photographed. We uploaded them on our website too, so that anyone could check them out.

I need to talk to Jacob.

But when I get home, Chris calls and says, "I know it's Sunday today, Rachel, but can you come in anyway? We need to discuss our next move." I tell him I don't mind. I was expecting it.

"I'll be there shortly."

Before he hangs up he sighs. "What a mess."

A mess. That's one way of putting it. The story is being picked up by every news outlet around the country. The Twitter-sphere is up in arms. We've gone from '*Molly's last chance, the little newspaper that could*' to '*shamelessly exploitative, how the South Hackney Herald killed the podcast*'.

There's talk of 'regulating the podcasting space' and the 'lack of journalistic rigour' which is bad enough, but the chatter now has turned to 'Vivian Brown's credentials as an investigative journalist'. Vivian is getting the brunt of it. Jacob and I are also mentioned as producers, but other than the odd reproach—*the liability rests with the producers*—no one seems to care about us. They also don't bring up the fact that Vivian wasn't even there when we interviewed Mrs Dawson.

We have to put out a statement and defend ourselves. Immediately. We've come this far, and we can't get shy now. We have to press on. We have to identify the real killer.

And at the same time, I have to protect Vivian, and my family, somehow.

"I need to go to the office. Can you look after Gracie for a bit?" I ask Matt.

"Really? Now? Can't they get on with it without you? It's your day off, Rach."

"Come on. You've seen the Internet, you've heard the news. We all need to put our heads together and try and fix this mess." I cock my head sideways. "I need to be there. Please. It's just for an hour."

"Tell them it will have to wait until tomorrow."

"I can't. I told you. It's my job."

"Bullshit," he mutters. "It's this podcast. You're obsessed, that's what it is."

"Don't say that. It's not true."

We stare at each other and he blinks first. He drops his shoulders, and adds, in a softer voice. "I try to talk to you, about anything, about Gracie even, and all I get is a vacant stare. It's like you're not here. If I walk into a room, you jump. You're talking in your sleep—"

"That doesn't count, I had too much to drink," I joke.

He takes my hand into his own and turns it over. "Your nails," he says. "You've started biting them again."

I snatch my hand away and push both fists down into my jeans pockets.

"No I'm not."

"I'm worried about you, Rachel."

"So don't be!" I snap. I know exactly what he means. *I'm worried you'll do it again. I'm worried you're losing the plot, just like last time.*

Sometimes I wonder if he will ever let me forget it. My *episode.*

"I have to go," I say quickly. What I really want to say is, *don't be an asshole.*

I gather my things without looking at him, but before I leave I say quietly, "Keep an eye on Gracie, Matt. Don't let her out of your sight."

"Why would you say that?"

"Just—please. Keep an eye on her. I'm asking."

THIRTY-FOUR

When I get to work, I go straight to Chris's office and give the door a quick rap of the knuckles. Then I enter without waiting to be asked and almost bump into Jacob.

"Rachel, good. Thanks for coming in," Chris says.

"No problem."

I feel like I've interrupted something but for some reason, they're not bringing me into that conversation.

"Okay, here's what we're going to do," Chris says. "We need to record an extra episode, today," he looks at his watch. "Rachel, if you could do it this afternoon, please."

Shit. I told Matt it would only be an hour.

"But since we're here, I think we should talk about what happened," he continues, "and where to go from here."

"What about Vivian?" I ask.

"She's at home. She's taking a couple of days off."

My heart skips a beat and I stand up quickly. "Is she okay?" I ask.

"Yes, of course!" Chris replies. He makes a gesture with his hand for me to sit down again. "She's staying away until the social media trolls find their next victim. She's fine." He puts his elbows on the desk and crosses his hands.

"Okay, great." I jump right in. "I know you wanted me to keep on the Molly angle, but I really think we need to concentrate our efforts on who really killed the Forster family. We need to look at anyone who had a relationship with the family, especially Grace. I think—"

"Whoa, stop right there!" Chris has his hands up as if to stem the flow of my words. "We're suspending the podcast completely, *that's* what we're doing."

"What? No!"

"Yes! We're recording a short episode this afternoon to say that the podcast is suspended until further notice. That's why you're here."

"But why?!" I whine.

"Have you not been paying attention, Rachel? Everyone hates us!"

"But we haven't done anything wrong!"

"The optics are not great," Jacob says, shaking his head.

"Fuck the optics," I blurt out.

"You think we're going to survive this?" He throws the *Mail on Sunday* across the desk. "You think the sponsors are going to stick around? We're putting the brakes on right now."

"Sponsors? This is about sponsors to you?"

"Damn right! And it's about sponsors to you too, Rachel, don't kid yourself. I've made the decision. We're shutting it down."

It's like I've been punched in the gut. I look at Jacob. He's staring at the floor.

"But we know, Jacob and I, that she was telling the truth. Don't we, Jacob? What about the receipts? The prescription? We photographed them! They're on the website!"

"We took them down."

"Why? It's the proof!"

"They're fake, Rachel!" Chris snaps.

"No, they're not, Jacob—"

"They may as well be! It's not possible to say if the signature was genuine or not," Chris says. "Not without the originals. It might have been Mrs Dawson who bought the medication, then tried to make it look like it was Dennis."

I look at Jacob, expecting him to jump in, to argue, but he just nods and looks uncomfortable.

"Bullshit!" I snap.

"That's enough, Rachel. If you don't want to record the extra episode, Jacob can do it." He throws a pen on the desk. I'm waiting for Jacob to say something, anything. To back me up, but he's too busy looking at his shoes.

"I still think it's worth pursuing—"

"Rachel, I swear, if you don't give it a rest I'm going to do something I won't regret."

"Okay, fine! Give me the script." I get up and put my hand out. "Please," I add, belatedly. Chris pauses, then he rummages through the papers in front of him until he finds it, and hands it to me. There's not a lot to it. It consists of one single paragraph and the generic closing line:

The South Hackney Herald is deeply shocked at the suicide of Mrs Dawson. Though the fate of Molly Forster remains very much in our minds, we have resolved to suspend the production of Missing Molly until new evidence warrants its return. We want to assure our listeners and the community of the integrity of our efforts at all times.

My name is Vivian Brown and you're listening to Missing Molly.

"Say your own name, not Vivian's," Chris says, pointing at the script.

"Thanks Chris, I'd never have thought of it," I snap before walking out. Jacob follows me. "Do you think she faked them?" I ask him once we're out of earshot.

"No."

I stop in my tracks.

"What do you mean, no?"

"It's possible, but I don't think so."

"So why didn't you back me up in there, to Chris?"

"Because it won't make any difference. He doesn't want to fight this battle."

I sigh. "Fine. Can I have a copy of the photos?"

"Chris doesn't want anyone to have a copy."

"Really?"

He doesn't reply. I wonder where's the 'I knew there was something' bravado? 'I could smell it!' attitude.

"I'll go and record this—" I lift the script, "—piece of flash fiction, then we need to have a talk, you and me. There's got to be something we can do. You fancy a coffee? My treat."

"Rachel, I'm not going to have a coffee with you. And we're not going to talk or do anything. I'm in deep shit enough as it is. Don't you get it? The podcast was my idea, remember? I need this job. I'm going to put my head down and wait for it all to blow over. And you should do the same."

He steps away from me, but I take hold of his sleeve, I grab it, close my fist tight around the fabric and lean close.

"Doesn't it strike you as odd that Hugo Hennessy was never interviewed by the police? He was the boyfriend, and according to Cindy McArthur, he was like a knight in shining armour. Couldn't do enough for her. So why wasn't he at the birthday party? And he happens to be the son of the then Chief Constable. And yet, he's never made a statement. He's never been asked." I tap the side of my nose. "How's your sense of smell, Jacob? Because there's something there, I'm telling you."

I don't mention Mrs Dawson, because I have yet to explain a way that the killer knew about the episode before it was available to the public. I'm wondering if Vivian told Peter what we got from Mrs Dawson.

"We need to look at this guy," I continue. "You and I know that Emily Dawson was telling the truth. It couldn't have been Dennis, because he didn't have the time. Think about it Jacob, someone's out there." I put my lips right next to his ear and whisper, "We're getting close, and he knows it. The question is, are *we* going to let him get away with it?"

I pull away, waiting for the penny to drop, but all I get for my troubles is a puzzled look. Then he shakes his head and walks away, leaving me standing there. I go to the makeshift recording studio, making a mental note to insert the word 'alleged' before the word 'suicide'.

In the darkened room, I pull my mobile from my pocket and call Vivian again. Something lifts inside me when I hear her voice. It's the relief. After all, she's spending a whole lot of time with a murderer, and she doesn't have a clue.

"Hey," she says.

"Hey you, you're okay?"

She sighs. "Yes, I'm fine. Just, you know—"

"Has anyone been bothering you?"

"If you mean, has anyone been trolling me, then yes, resoundingly. Funny, three weeks ago I only had a dozen followers on Twitter, now half the world wants to come to my house and have sex with me."

I laugh softly but my heart is breaking. "Good to hear you haven't lost your sense of humour."

"Yeah well, fuck 'em."

"That's the spirit. Fuck 'em. Trolls."

"I was talking about my parents, actually."

I really laugh. "Have they been in touch?"

"Apparently they're terribly embarrassed."

"Good," I say.

"Where are you anyway?"

"In the office. We're putting the podcast on hold, I'm just recording the announcement now."

"Oh yeah, I heard."

"You want me to come over after?"

"No, don't worry, I'm totally fine."

"You're on your own?"

She pauses. "Peter is coming over later," she says finally.

"Okay, good," I say. What I really want to say is, *Run, Vivian. He's not real. He's a killer. He's going to hurt you. Please, trust me, and run.*

"I know you don't like him, Rach," and for a moment I wonder if I've spoken out loud, "but you know what?" she goes on, "You don't know him. You barely spent enough time with him."

Neither of us speak. Finally, I say, "So come over for dinner, tomorrow night. With Peter."

There's a short silence, then she says, "You sure?"

"Yes, I'm sure. I can make sure you're—" I was about to say *safe*, "—okay and I can get to know Peter at the same time."

"You're going to love him." I can hear the smile in her voice.

"I'm sure I will."

After we hang up I quickly record the podcast announcement, upload it to the feed and schedule it for 6 a.m. tomorrow morning, as per Chris's instructions. Then I check our social media. As expected, there's a fair number of accusatory comments, although not as many as I'd feared. There are even a couple of posts that suggest there was more to the story, and some of them even ask why would Mrs Dawson go to such lengths to exonerate her son, and then having been heard, recant and kill herself.

But it's the ones directed at Vivian that make my heart stop.

I know where you live, you fucking bitch. I'm coming for you.

THIRTY-FIVE

When I left work yesterday Chris said to take the morning off, and Matt let me sleep. It's almost nine when I wake up, and the silence in our flat is heavy, like an accusation. I make my coffee and spot it on the kitchen table, the note, scrawled quickly on the pad we keep to jot down groceries.

Gone to the park.

He wants me to feel guilty. It's working. Actually, I just feel left out. I can picture them, Gracie on the swing, squealing, wanting Matt to push her higher, *Push me to the stars, Daddy!* The other mothers looking on smiling.

Has Matt even been looking for a job? If I said that, he would narrow his eyes at me, and ask me how he could possibly do that when I keep taking off, going to the office, making everything and everyone more important than him.

Until this stupid podcast, I'd just about forgotten my name was Molly Forster. I got used to being Rachel Holloway, partner, mother, loved, safe. Now, I'm not just trying to save my own life, I'm trying to save everyone else as well.

I pour my coffee into my favourite mug, which isn't really

my favourite, just the one I always use. My habitual mug. I fantasise about the truth coming out, about Hugo and his father getting arrested, about the headline in all the papers, *Molly found, safe and sound.* The police in our flat, a nice woman constable maybe, explaining to Matt who I really am, and that every lie I ever told him was to protect us.

The printouts from yesterday morning are still in the inside pocket of my jacket. I pull them out and lay them flat on the table, smoothing the creases away. I peer at the grainy photo, trying to find Peter in Hugo's face. I know it's there. I just don't know if anyone else will see it.

I train my ear to the front door, just to make sure Matt and Gracie aren't about to burst in the door. Then I grab my mobile, switch off my caller ID setting and call the offices of Lakeside Homes, where he works, supposedly. As if he didn't own the place. In my best brisk, professional voice, I ask to speak to Hugo Hennessy.

"May I ask who's calling?" the equally brisk receptionist asks, and my heart skips a beat. Could he be there? Because if he is, then I may have been completely wrong about Peter. I'm pretty sure Vivian said he was in London today.

"Mel Dutton, returning his call," I say. Easier that way. I don't have to explain where I'm calling from. If he comes on the line, I'll just hang up.

"Mr Hennessy is out on site today. Did you want to leave a message?" she asks.

I breathe out, slowly.

"No that's fine, I'm on the road myself. Do you have a mobile number for him?"

"Sorry, I can't give out Mr Hennessy's mobile number. I can take a message."

"No problem. I can try again later, when will he be back?"

"I'm not sure."

"I'll call back later." I hang up.

I call the other number I got, from an online directory this time. His home. I close my eyes, wishing the phone to just ring, maybe go to voicemail.

"Hello?"

She's not brisk at all, she sounds bright, friendly even. So this must be Heather. The way she answered, confident and relaxed, I don't think she's not the hired help.

"Is this Mrs Hennessy?"

"Yes." I hear a burst of young children's voices in the background. Someone has taken something from somebody and a war has broken out.

Hugo has children. A wave of fury engulfs me and I grip the phone hard. It's never occurred to me that he might have children now, but it feels so very unfair.

"One moment please," she says, then in a muffled voice. "I'll take this outside, Alison." The cries recede and I hear footsteps, heels on a hard floor. I force myself to breathe, the way Barb taught me, feeling the breath beneath my nostrils.

I try to picture her, an elegant wrap dress knotted at the waist. What colour is her hair? Blond, styled straight, a pony tail against the back of her neck? Or auburn hair cascading in waves on her shoulder?

"Sorry about that," she says. "How can I help you?"

"This is Mel Dutton, from the Property News. We're hoping to do an article on your husband's firm and we had arranged a time to speak this evening."

"Oh? You should call his office then, this is his home."

"Yes, I know, I apologise for disturbing you at home, it's just that Mr Hennessy isn't at his office and I can't reach him on his mobile. We have a phone conference scheduled, but I need to change the time."

"Hum, Hugo's away on business right now, he won't be

back until Friday. You need to speak to his secretary. She'll have his diary. Or try his mobile again. He might've been in a meeting."

"I'll do that, thank you for your time, Mrs Hennessy."

It doesn't prove anything. But it doesn't disprove it either. But I really want Hugo's mobile number, because then I could call him.

When Peter's here.

I listen closely again for noises in the stairwell, and satisfied, I retrieve the memory book from under the sink and carefully file the pages away. Then I put it back, and I've just finished putting up the metal sheeting when my mobile rings. I freeze. I was sure I blocked my number on both calls, but now I can't remember. Did I make a mistake? I reach for the phone and breathe a sigh of relief.

It's Chris.

"Bloody hell, Rachel! What's the matter with you?" he bellows.

THIRTY-SIX

The Bolognese sauce is simmering on the stove. It's my staple 'dinner for more than two people' dish. Everybody loves a good Bolognese and mine is better than most. The trick is in the olive oil. I learned that from the chef at the pub where I worked for a year, taking orders from customers, washing glasses and stacking plates. Simon, was his name, and he insisted we refer to him as the chef, not the cook. As part of our pay conditions, we, being the staff, got dinner, and I asked him once what made his Bolognese so good.

"You have to use the best quality virgin olive oil, if you can, and plenty of it." He showed me the bottom of the pan where the garlic and herbs were literally swimming in it. Cooking this sauce is one of the things that I do when I need to feel centred because it reminds me of kind people.

I give Gracie her bath. I'm so nervous that I've timed it so that I'll be elbow deep in shampoo suds when they ring the doorbell. Then I won't have to hug him or kiss him hello. Or maybe it's just that I didn't trust myself not to strangle him right there and then. Hearing his children in the background today has awoken inside me a kind of fury I haven't felt in a very, very long time. I've been so busy being scared lately, I forgot to be angry.

In the end, they arrived late, of course, because Vivian is always late. I don't know how I didn't think of that. As a result, I'm trying to get Gracie to eat some steamed fish when they come in.

"Hello!" Vivian's arms are wide open, waiting to be hugged. Gracie runs to her and Vivian picks her up, settling her on her hip. Behind her, Peter is smiling, a bunch of flowers wrapped in colourful paper in one hand.

"These are for you," he says, pointing the bouquet in my direction, and with that, even the tiniest lingering doubt vanishes. It's him all right. I take the flowers with an overly loud 'how lovely!' and turn away before he has time to do anything else.

Vivian grabs my hand and pulls me close to kiss my cheek. My palms are sweaty and I quickly pull my hand back and wipe them on the sides of my hips.

"Your cheeks are cold," I say, taking her face in my hands.

"It's freezing out there!"

Matt offers everyone drinks and it's going to be all right. From the corner of my eye I watch Matt greet Peter, and when Peter puts a hand on Matt's shoulder and squeezes it, as if they were *buddies*, it's all I can do not to slap it away.

Vivian and Peter sit on the sofa, with Gracie on Vivian's lap, playing with a bracelet Vivian has just given her. Peter has one hand next to Vivian's thigh and is rubbing his fingertips against the fabric of her dress. I can't bear his proximity to Gracie, so I whisk her up in my arms with a quick "Come on, bed for you, young lady!" She's about to cry in disappointment but Vivian offers to put her to bed and read her a story. I wait until she's out of earshot.

"So, Peter, Vivian said you moved to London recently, where were you before?"

He leans forward and picks up a handful of peanuts from the bowl.

"Birmingham. Have you been there?"

"I don't think so. Is it nice?"

"It's all right, but I was ready for a change."

"Oh?"

He looks away, shifty eyes, "I like London. And there's more opportunities for advancement in the London office, at my firm, so when the position came up, I thought why not?"

"Good for you. And what firm would that be?" I ask.

"I'm in finance, investments," he replies, not answering my question.

"And you travel quite a bit, Vivian said you're never around on weekends. I didn't know finance required extensive weekend travel." Matt shoots me a funny look that says, 'what's the matter with you'. Peter looks at me with a small smile, but if he finds me rude, he doesn't show it.

I want to ask more but Vivian has returned with a "Fast asleep. Is that a reflection of my story telling skills, I wonder?" and we all laugh. She sits back on the sofa and nestles herself against Peter as he puts his arm around her shoulders.

"I am—was—the primary carer for my elderly parents," Peter says. "They've moved into assisted care now, which is a relief to be honest. Not because I minded looking after them, far from it, but because I have to work. I always worried about them during the day."

"And they're in a good place, aren't they," Vivian says. It's not a question. Peter has obviously spun this touching, bullshit story before. A perfect excuse to explain why he's never in London on weekends.

"It's great. Excellent facilities. Great people. I wouldn't

mind being there myself, truth be told." We all laugh, or rather they all laugh, and I pull my lips away from my teeth.

"They still have to sell the house and I'm helping with that. And getting everything organised. It's all very recent. I'm looking forward to it being over, to be honest. It would be nice to be here and get a chance to settle in."

They look so comfortable, the two of them. Like they've been dating for months, rather than barely a couple of weeks. She rests her head against his shoulder, tickling his hand with the tip of her fingers.

"Are your parents in good health?" he asks me.

I feel a crimson wave rise up my neck. I shake my head. "My mother has passed away. My father and I aren't close, but I think if he was ill he would tell me."

"I'm sorry. That's tough, losing your mother, when did it happen?" he asks.

I flick my eyes up at him, ambers burning. There's a funny look in his eyes, like a question. I catch myself and say, "About ten years ago." Then I turn to Matt and add, "But I have my own family now, and I'm close to Matt's mum." Matt smiles at me and a current of tenderness passes between us.

"Well, cheers to that then," Peter says. He raises his glass at me, then squeezes Vivian's shoulders with his other arm. I can't stop myself from watching his every move and while that gesture is meant to be affectionate, it creeps me out. I want to slap his arm away from her.

I try to remember what he was like with my sister. Did I ever see them like this? I stare at my hands in my lap and catch sight of the raw skin around my nails. I quickly pull my sleeves over them.

"I should put the pasta on," I announce, and leave the room.

. . .

When we are all seated at the dinner table, I contemplate making a prayer. Just to see his face. *Lord, thank You for the food before us, the family and friends beside us and the love between us. Keep us safe and let our enemies die a horrible death. Amen.*

Everyone has helped themselves to some pasta and now I am serving the sauce from the heavy pan.

"If you pass me your plate," I say, to no one in particular.

"Let me do it," Peter says. "You've done all the work, Rachel, you relax."

"Oh, that's so kind of you, Pete," Vivian gushes.

Pete.

I have the ladle in my hand, poised to serve. Peter is sitting on my right and he leans across, and takes the spoon from me, brushing his fingers against mine for just a little longer than necessary. I want to vomit. He lifts Vivian's steaming plate. "Say when, Viv."

Matt laughs, Vivian chuckles, but I saw the look she gave me.

When Peter comes to serve me and I hold out my plate, he looks straight into my eyes and says, "This smells divine, Rachel."

I shoot him a fake smile and pull my plate back.

"Rach has been telling me about all the trouble you've had online," Matt says to Vivian. "Are you okay?"

I watch his reaction, Peter slash Hugo, because I've been poring over our social media accounts and Vivian's too. It's always one person who's doing the bulk of the abuse, and there's almost always a mention of Grace. *She was a fucking slag, a fucking whore.* Something like that.

I know it's him. He's screwing Vivian and trying to terrorise her at the same time, while pretending to protect her.

She shrugs, gives a small smile. She wants to pretend she's taking it in her stride, but I can see it's upsetting her.

"I just ignore it. I stopped looking to be honest. Jacob at work is monitoring it for me now."

This is news to me. "Is he?"

"He suggested it. I didn't want to look at any messages on social media, but he said in case there's something we need to report, someone should keep an eye on it. I spoke to him just before I came here, he said that the messages were dwindling anyway. Seems the troll caravan has moved on."

"I'm glad you guys are taking a break from the podcast," Matt says.

"I agree," Peter adds. "With all the press lately, it feels like you're embarking on dangerous territory. Don't get me wrong, it's very impressive, what you've been doing, Vivian. I'm in awe of your talent. But I think a break is a good idea."

"How old are you?" I blurt out.

Matt frowns at me and Vivian sighs, audibly.

"Twenty-eight, why?"

I shrug. "No reason. I don't know why I asked." I would have loved to catch him out in the lie, but he's ahead of me.

He runs his hand over his head. "Is it the hair?" he asks to polite titters of laughter. "I had hair just like yours once, Rachel, thick and dark, same colour in fact," he says. Then with a sigh, "Unfortunately every male in my family lose their hair in their twenties. What can you do?"

I stand, praying, willing Matt and Vivian to say nothing. "Does anyone want more of this before I take this away?" I ask quickly.

"Rachel's hair isn't really that colour, actually," Vivian says.

Well, fuck.

"I don't know why she colours it. She has the most beautiful natural colour. Kind of like copper," Matt adds.

I reach for the heavy pot. I don't need to look at Peter to

know he's staring at me. "Why would you colour it, Rachel? Not that's in any of my business, but it sounds nice," he says.

I catch a flicker of irritation pass over Vivian's face.

"It is," Matt says, taking the pot from me and setting it down on the stove. He must have sensed something in me because he reaches out to touch my waist. "But she's beautiful, either way."

"There's dessert," I say.

"I'll get it." Matt walks across to the fridge. I want to stop him. I wanted to get it because I need a moment to steady myself.

Peter picks up the plates from the table, stacks them up and takes them to the worktop by the sink. Matt hands out bowls of vanilla ice cream all around.

"What is it you do on the podcast again, Rachel?" Peter asks, with a fake nonchalance that makes the hair on my arm stand up.

"Rachel works on the production side," Vivian says quickly.

"And she's obsessed with it," Matt mumbles.

And just like that, I understand what a phenomenally stupid idea this dinner had been.

Peter cocks his head at Matt. Then out of nowhere, Vivian bursts out in a peel of laugher and puts her hand on Peter's arm. "Obsessed is right! In the closing segment we put out this morning," she begins, trying to stop laughing.

No don't, please don't say it.

"In today's episode, announcement, whatever," she continues, still chuckling, "Rachel slipped up, and do you know what she said?"

Matt and Peter are both laughing, anticipating the joke, I'm staring at Vivian, making small shakes of my head. She's laughing hard, one hand on her chest. I know exactly what she's doing. She's been watching Peter pay too much attention to me all evening. She wants to make me look foolish. It's a putdown in front of him, and maybe it's innocent enough, maybe, in any other circumstances it would have been fine. But not now. Not this.

"Don't," I say, quietly.

"In the closing segment," Vivian repeats, breathless. "Normally I say, *Thank you for listening blah blah blah, I'm Vivian Brown and this is Missing Molly.*"

"Okay, so?" Matt says, smiling.

"Don't," I repeat, trying to keep the urgency out of my voice, and telegraphing it at the same time. Vivian is laughing so much she's hiccupping.

"In the recording, Rachel said 'Thank you for listening, I am Molly Forster, and this is Missing Molly!'"

Now she's laughing so hard she's screaming.

"'I am Molly Forster!'" she says again, slapping her palm on the table.

I close my eyes.

"What?" Matt asks. He's not laughing anymore. Up until then both Peter and Matt had a big smile on their face, ready for the joke. But Matt's smile has vanished and he turns to me.

"You did? Why?"

I shake my head. "I just messed up."

"You sure did!" Vivian almost yells, pointing her finger at me. She erupts in a fresh round of laughter that brings tears to her eyes. "Chris nearly killed her for posting it!"

"I got my words muddled! We had to get it out fast. I made a mistake, that's all! It happens to everyone!" I speak really quickly, feeling the corners of my mouth drooping.

"Jacob had to fix it, he told me," Vivian says, wiping tears of laugher from her eyes. "I swear, people were freaking out on the Internet."

"It wasn't like that," I say lamely.

But now, even Matt is laughing. "I told you you're getting obsessed, Rach!"

I look at Peter. He stares at me. He doesn't laugh, but a small smirk dances on his lips. He pats my hand, and with a wink he says, "Don't worry, Rachel, your secret's safe with me."

THIRTY-SEVEN

If I had wanted to put myself in the line of fire, I couldn't have done a better job. I finish the evening pretending everything is fine and dandy and what a nice time we are all having. Matt and Peter even get into a conversation about some job Peter knows about, supposedly. A big commercial contract and they are urgently looking for electricians. It's a total lie, of course. Peter is just trying to insinuate himself among us. And by the time the two of them come to their senses it will be too late. By then he will have reached inside our group and plucked me up.

After they're gone, I tell Matt that I'll clean up. He likes to watch the late news sometimes so I encourage him, "Why don't you? I can do it, love. I don't mind."

As I dry plates, I can no longer stop the tears. The enormity of what just happened finally sinks in, and all I can think about is my daughter. What will happen to her? What will he do to her? To us?

I never pray. I know first-hand that praying means sod all, but I have nothing left, so if there is some kind of god, I beg him not to let me die. I beg him to protect my child. I feel so powerless that I drop to the floor and put my hands in prayer and whisper to myself, tears wetting my cheeks.

Please Lord. Please don't let anything happen to me or my family. Not again. Please protect us.

"What are you doing?"

I scramble back up quickly. I don't know how long Matt has been standing there, but it's certainly long enough to make the lie futile.

"Nothing. I'm going to bed." I throw the tea towel on the back of a chair. He doesn't say a word, just watches me walk out of the room.

It's early, so early that when I drop Gracie off at preschool this morning she's the first one there, which never happens. I haven't slept at all. It's like my limbs won't work properly. My reflexes are too slow or just wrong. I'm not looking forward to what I'm about to do, but I don't think I have a choice anymore. Because he knows. I'm sure of it.

When I get to Vivian's building, I wait just across the road, in the cafe. I know he's upstairs with her and I don't care how long it takes. Finally, he walks out, preening like a peacock. Even from here I can see the smug look on his face. He checks his watch, then looks up and down both sides of the street and hails a cab.

As soon as the taxi turns the corner I run across the road and press the buzzer. I leave my finger on it the whole time I wait for her, until her voice comes on with, "Miss me already?"

"It's me, Viv. Let me in please."

I think I hear a 'oh' of disappointment, but I hear the familiar click and push against the door.

"Everything all right?"

She's wearing her dressing gown, knotted at the waist, a cup of coffee in her hand. She hugs me awkwardly with one arm.

I pull away and take her free hand in both of mine and lead her inside the living room.

"You have to listen to me, okay? Listen to what I have to tell you."

She frowns at me. I know I'm probably shaking a little, and my eyes are wide and darting everywhere. "What is it?" she asks.

"Let's sit down, okay?"

I notice the bit of silky fabric on the sofa. I pick it up to make space. It's her knickers. I blush furiously but she just takes them from me and lets them flop to the floor over the back of the sofa. She's not even embarrassed, she's downright cocky in fact. She raises one eyebrow, as if to say, *so what?*

I take both her hands in mine again.

"Peter is not who he says he is."

"Is this a joke?"

I lean into her, I'm almost talking into her face and she pulls away from me. "You have to believe me, Viv. I can't explain everything, and maybe one day I will, I hope I do. But you need to trust me, darling. His name is Hugo Hennessy, and he's a dangerous man."

"What?"

"Hugo Hennessy. Grace's old boyfriend. He killed them all, Vivian."

She recoils, pulls her hand from my grasp. She thinks I'm crazy, it's written all over her face.

"What are you talking about?"

"You have to break it off with him, now, today. Tell him something, anything. You've already got a boyfriend, and you're really sorry, but you wanted to make him jealous, I don't know. But break it off, okay? I'm begging you."

Now that I've let it out, I can't stop. I'm grasping her arm like she's the raft that is stopping me from drowning. And yet I'm the one who is supposed to save her.

"He's not a good man, Vivian, I swear. He'll hurt you."

"I'm worried about you, Rach, I really am. I think you should go and see Barbara."

"What? No! It's nothing like that!" I take hold of her arm again and dig my fingertips into the skin. "Please listen. Hugo Hennessy killed them all, except Molly who ran away. He set up Dennis to take the fall. I'm telling you Viv, I swear, he's very, very dangerous. He's a liar, and he's a killer, and he's—"

"Rachel! Stop!" She yells, pulling her arm away. "You're scaring me! You've gone completely mad!"

"No, don't say that. Don't choose him over me. You have to believe me. He's just using you to get to M—"

"I'm calling Matt."

"No, no, no don't call Matt. Please Viv, listen to me. One day, I will be able to explain, I swear. I'm doing everything I can to make that happen."

"Go home, Rachel. Go get some rest. Go and be with your family."

"Just listen to me. Peter is not a good man!"

She's rubbing her arm where I gripped her just before. "You're confused, hon."

"I am not confused—"

"Yes, you are. Rachel, please, hon, listen to me. You're confused, but it's okay. We can get ahead of this one, okay? Just listen to me. We are not in danger. Peter is not Hugo. Peter is Peter. And Peter is a good man."

Why doesn't anyone ever believe me when I say the truth?

"Rachel?"

"Yes?"

"You need to call Barbara."

I shake my head. She's rubbing my back while I bite at the side of my thumb. I've lost. I know it. The tears well up, they're already on my cheeks. I need to get out of here.

"You really think that?" I ask, brushing my cheek with the back of my hand.

A flicker of relief passes across her face. "Yes, I do. Can you see why?"

I pretend to consider it. "Because Peter is just Peter?"

She nods and smiles. "That's it, Rach."

"You aren't in danger?"

"No, hon. I'm not."

A long silence stretches. "Okay, I think I will call Barbara," I say.

She feels for my phone in my pocket, pulls it out, and hands it to me. I pretend to leave a voicemail about some emergency appointment, then I hang up.

"I should go home."

She walks me all the way to my front door.

"You will tell Matt, won't you? When you get home?"

I nod.

"Do you want me to tell him for you?"

"No! I'll do it."

"Okay."

"Do you mind not telling Peter about this?" I ask.

"Of course not," she says, but I can tell she will. *You'll never believe what Rachel said!* She'll say. And it occurs to me that I've just put my family in the most dangerous situation I possibly could. If he didn't know who I am, he will now.

And that I'm telling everyone who he really is.

THIRTY-EIGHT

Matt is seated at the kitchen table when I get back, and I know that something is very wrong. It's his posture. I bend forward a little and stare into his handsome face. He's pale. His eyes are red, like he's been crying. He doesn't speak, just stares at me with a look filled with such sadness it makes my heart ache.

"What have you done, babe?" he says, his voice raspy from tears.

At first, I think that Vivian did call him after all, but then I see the book, the memory book. It's opened flat on the table, its protective plastic wrapping on the floor at his feet. The cupboard beneath the sink is wide open, the flat metal sheeting hanging by a single screw.

"We had another leak," he says softly. "The plumber came, he checked behind the panel."

I nod slowly, I have no words. But maybe that's not so bad. Maybe it's time to grab the truth and be brave. I picture my daughter climbing up trees, jumping from walls. I take strength in her courage and make myself do the same. It's time.

"My name is Molly Forster."

I have waited twelve years to say that out loud. The words sound so right, and so wrong, all at the same time. I pull up a chair and sit down.

"I couldn't tell you before, I never wanted to tell you. I never wanted to tell anyone. Ever." I reach out and lay my hand in the middle of the table, hoping for him to do the same. But he's shaking his head slowly, from side to side, his mouth distorted with pain.

"I love you, Matt, I love you more than my own life. I couldn't tell you because I didn't want to put you in danger, you understand?"

I grab his hand and squeeze it hard.

"I am Molly Forster, and there are people looking for me. These people want to kill me because I saw—"

A strange thing happens to me. I don't panic, my breath is a little shallow, but not too bad, I don't cry, I just tell it like it is.

"I saw a man murder my family."

The page I printed the other day is on top of the messy pile, the one with a grainy photo of Hugo.

I put the tip of my finger on the photo. "Him. His name is Hugo Hennessy. Can you see?" I tap it hard. "Do you see that's Peter? It's not, it's Hugo Hennessy. But look, it's Peter. He found me."

I turn the paper around so it's facing him. I lift it up and bring it close to his face.

"Can you see?" I ask.

I reach into my jacket pocket and pull out my mobile. I snatch the page from him and point at the number I've scribbled on the margin.

"That's Hugo Hennessy's number." I punch the digits. "But he won't be there, because he's here, you see? He's pretending to be Peter, but it's him—yes hello, it's Margaret Smith, can you put Hugo Hennessy on the phone please? It's urgent. I'm returning his call. Yes, it's urgent."

I shove the phone at Matt, hitting his torso. "Quick!" he almost drops it, then puts the phone against his ear.

"Hello? Is this Hugo Hennessy? Right, my name is Matthew Kenny, I don't understand why I'm calling you but—"

I snatch the phone back from him and hang up.

"Did it sound like Peter? What do you think? They might have linked the number to his mobile somehow. Was he surprised when you said your name?"

"Rachel—"

"I called the other day," I slap my forehead with the palm of my hand. Hard, over and over. "That was stupid. I called his house, I spoke to his wife. Shit."

"Rachel, love, please—"

Matt is crouched next to me, looking up at me, pleading. I swivel in the chair and take his face in my hands.

"You believe me, don't you?"

His mouth is distorted from the strength of my grip, I release him.

"Don't you?"

"I—I don't know, babe, you're scaring me." He wipes his face, then takes both my hands in his. His palms are moist from the tears.

"Oh Matt, honey, don't cry."

"It's happening again, don't you see?" he says, in a small voice. "You're doing it again, like the last time."

"No, I'm not."

"You are. You remember last time? You said people were looking for you, they were trying to kill you. You remember, baby?"

He's crying. He's moved onto his knees and puts his hands on my lap.

"It's not the same," I say. "It's nothing like that."

"You were terrified. You took Gracie, and you disappeared. I didn't know where you were. We looked for you. The police. Everyone. Remember, Rach?"

"It's not like that, I swear to you. I *am* Molly Forster." I take his face in my hands again, urgently. Desperately.

"You took her away, and you hid in that filthy place, that horrible, disgusting flat—"

"Don't, Matt."

"You kept here there, filthy and hungry and—"

"Don't, please."

"—And when we found you, God, Rachel. She was dehydrated, filthy, in your arms and you were cowering in the corner. You hadn't eaten anything in days. You were rambling. You didn't know where you were, and—"

I stand up so fast the chair tumbles back behind me. "Enough! Stop! It's not like that! My name is Molly Forster, and these people, they're coming after me, you understand?"

"Please stop, Rach, please!"

I sit back down, closing my hands into fists.

"Matt, listen to me. You have to trust me, that's all I ask. I know it's hard. But the memory book, everything in it, it's true. It's me. It's my life. And that's why I panicked that other time, when Gracie was a baby. That's why I always look over my shoulder. It's why I'm like I am. Broken."

"I'm scared, Rachel."

"I know, love. Me too."

"I don't want to lose you."

I rest my forehead against his. "You won't. But I need you to believe me. Promise me, you believe me."

"I'm trying. I don't understand, but I'm trying."

"Matt?"

"What, babe?"

"I'm sorry honey, but we have to run."

"Why?"

"Because otherwise, we're all going to die."

THIRTY-NINE

Matt wants us to go to the police. He says if what I'm saying is true, then the police can interrogate Peter. I almost laugh in his face. "You have no idea who we're dealing with."

I rush through the flat, giving instructions the entire time. "Your passport. Driver's licence." We're in the bedroom. I've pulled the drawer so hard it's fallen out. Matt's passport is on the floor, along with all our important stuff. He picks it up.

"We'll have to change them later, but for now it'll do."

His hands are shaking, everything about him is shaking, but he gathers his papers, our papers, things we think we cannot live without, because as I explain to him, anything we leave behind will be gone forever. We are never coming back. I put my hand on his shoulder and look into his face.

"I promise you it's going to be okay."

He shakes his head. I pull down the suitcase from the top of the wardrobe and throw it on the bed.

"You call the preschool. Tell them we're going to pick up Gracie on the way, okay? We have to get out of here. Before he gets to us. He knows now, that his cover is blown. We have to move fast, okay, love?"

I've pulled out clothes at random from various drawers and shoved them in the case. I run into Gracie's room and empty drawers, wardrobes, throwing everything I don't want or need onto the floor, and scoop the rest in my arms. First aid kit. Clothes. Her favourite stuffed animal—a baby jaguar she calls 'cutey'—I shove all of it on top of the stuff already in the case. Matt comes back, holding the phone in his hand.

"We can't take the phones. We'll have to leave them behind," I say. I snatch it from him and turn it off.

"I just called. They've gone on an excursion." Matt's face is white.

"Who?"

"The kids, Gracie."

"An excursion? Where?"

"To the zoo."

"What? Now?"

"I forgot to tell you, and I forgot it was today. I had to sign for it the other day. It's a birthday breakfast thing. But they're on their way back now."

I pause. "Okay."

"What do you want to do?" he asks. "Should we wait here?"

"We'll have to go to them," I say. "Did you say they're at the zoo?"

"They've left already. They're on their way back."

"Okay. That's fine. We have to leave anyway. We'll meet them at the preschool."

Matt swings back into action, checking the room for things we might need, putting more things in the case.

"What else?" I do a quick scan of every room and grab a couple of things from the bathroom.

"That's enough," I say, pushing the lid down. Matt lifts the case from the bed. In the kitchen I gather the loose pages and scraps of paper from the table and fold them inside the memory book. Taped against the back cover, on the inside flap, is an envelope. It contains two thousand pounds, a driver's licence and a never-used credit card, both in the name of Sophia Durrante. I check that everything is intact and slip it in the inside pocket of my coat. I unzip a corner of the case and push the memory book inside. Matt stares at me, astonished.

"You really prepared for this day."

"I had to."

I check my watch. "How long before they're back?"

"Fifteen, maybe twenty. We should wait ten minutes."

"No, we'll leave now. We'll wait near the preschool. After we pick her up we'll go to the car rental place, using this," I pat my pocket, "and then—"

I heard it moments earlier but it was far enough away to be irrelevant. But now the siren is intruding on my brain, because it sounds as if it's right outside. I look at Matt and watch his face crumble in misery.

"Oh, Matt."

FORTY

I wake up in a room with white walls and cheap beige curtains
drawn across a high window. I don't know where I am exactly,
but from the smell, I am in no doubt it's some kind of
hospital.

I rub my hands on my face. Why can't I remember? It's as
if my brain is swimming in fog. Snatches of memory make
their way through. Matt crying. Me screaming that he needs
to protect Gracie. I sit up. Where's Gracie?

It all comes flooding back in a rush of agony. Barb had
been there at our flat. She was asking me to sit down.

"Leave me alone!" I yelled, pushing her away. I kept
screaming over and over: "I am Molly Forster! Why won't you
believe me? I am Molly Forster!"

"No, you're not. You're Rachel Holloway." Her voice was
soft, she meant it to soothe me, but all it did was enrage me.
"That's not me! I stole that name! I took it from the real
Rachel Holloway! My name is Molly Forster, take some
DNA!" I implored with them all to believe me. Matt, Barbara,
the male nurses who were holding me down, one on each side,

"Take a blood test, it's a DNA match to my family!" I saw the needle go into my arm.

I don't know if I ever felt such despair, even with everything that has happened to me. I watched the agony on Matt's face as they lay me down on a gurney, Barbara whispering to him, probably words of comfort. *It's going to be okay.*

It's not, Matt, it's not going to be okay, not now. Not anymore.

"You're awake!"

Her name-tag says Dr Cavanagh. She's smiling at me, both hands in the pockets of her white coat.

"How long have I been here?" My tongue feels thick. My eyes dart around the room, and she hands me the plastic cup of water from the side table. I snatch it from her and greedily gulp the cool water.

"Your psychiatrist is here. She'll see you in a minute, I'll just take a look at you first. How are you feeling?" She takes my wrist, presses two fingers against the veins.

"How do you think?"

"Confused, I know. Your pulse is a bit slow but that's to be expected." She checks the drip next to the bed and makes a couple of adjustments.

I stare at the ceiling. "Where am I?"

"St Vincent's Psychiatrist Hospital. You've been here before?"

"No. How long have I been here?"

"Since yesterday."

"Where's my daughter?"

"I'm not sure. I'll find out."

I sit up. "Where is she? Is she all right?"

The door swings open and Barbara walks into the room.

"Hello, Rachel." She sounds more cheery than she looks. Dr Cavanagh puts the chart back at the bottom of the bed and after a brief, "Call me if you need me," she leaves the room.

"Where's Grace?"

"She's fine, she's with Matt. They're staying with Matt's mother."

I take a breath and feel an ache in my chest, like a stitch. I exhale slowly. I put my palm on my face, but the sobs come anyway.

"What's happening to me?"

"You're going to need some rest, you've had an extreme psychotic episode."

She sits next to me. I stare at the ceiling.

"Why am I here?"

She takes a moment to consider, then she says, "It seems like the podcast you've been working on triggered the extreme reaction you've been experiencing. You've become afflicted with a dissociative personality disorder."

"How long do I have to stay here?"

"I don't know, Rachel. It depends on your progress."

"You think I'm crazy?"

"We don't use that word anymore."

I wipe the tears off my cheek with one hand. "What's my name?" I ask.

"Your name is Rachel Holloway."

"Are you sure?"

"Positive."

"How do you know?"

"You mean, apart from your birth certificate? Your husband's word?" She smiles. "We spoke to your father."

"My father?"

"Yes."

"Where is he?"

"In Australia. Matt tracked him down. He's living in Sydney. He's going to come over to see you."

"My father."

"He hasn't heard from you in years," she says, smiling. "He's very relieved, let me tell you. He thought you were dead, Rachel. Now he finds out not just that his daughter is alive, but he has a grandchild."

"Oh God. How is it possible? That I would believe I'm someone else?"

"If I knew the answer to that, I'd be a very rich woman. It's a psychotic disorder. A person starts to believe they're someone else, sometimes more than one person."

"But a real person? Like I did?"

"There was a German woman by the name of Ana Anderson. She's probably the most famous case of an identity dissociation disorder. She woke up in a hospital believing she was Anastasia Romanova, the sole survivor of the ruling family murdered in Russia."

"That sounds familiar," I quip, thinking of my own murdered family, but she misunderstands since it means nothing to her.

"It's a famous story," she goes on, "she managed to convince distant relatives, she claimed she could speak Russian, and that she remembered her life up to the massacre in vivid detail."

"But it wasn't her."

"No, after her death the bodies of two Romanovs were exhumed, and tests proved that she wasn't related. But there's no doubt she believed that she *was* Anastasia Romanova. Technically, she wasn't lying."

I nod. "So how do I know so much about Molly? I thought I could remember in horrific detail everything that happened to that family."

She shrugs. "It's not as difficult as you'd think. It was all over the news for months. You've had some degree of fascination for that case for a long time. That's clear from the amount of information you've collected. You have newspaper clippings in your possession that date back years. After Grace was born, you experienced extreme postpartum depression. Again, your case is not unique. But when you took Grace—"

I flinch, and she notices.

"It was a long time ago," I say.

"I know. Postnatal depression can be so serious that mothers become convinced their baby is going to be taken away, or that some harm will come to them. This is what happened to you, Rachel. But every case is different and with your psychosis, you convinced yourself that you and Grace were both in danger. You remember that, don't you?"

I nod. I trust Barbara. She's my psychiatrist and it's true that I screwed up when Gracie was born. I became paranoid. I started getting anxiety attacks, and Barbara has helped me, she still does. But it's not the truth exactly, and there's no point in trying to explain. She'll never understand. She'll have me locked up if she believes that potentially, the danger to myself and my child *was, is,* real.

"When you began working on the podcast, it must have triggered another episode. A shift in your psyche. You'd been very engaged with these events."

"Obsessed. That's what Matt says."

"Words are difficult to choose sometimes." She pauses. "I believe that the podcast is what caused the schism to open in your psyche. As if you were split in two. The coincidence was too much for you."

"The coincidence?"

"You've been consumed by this tragedy, for years. Then out of the blue the very paper you work for decides to investigate the case. You thought it was a divine sign maybe, but it was just a coincidence. You took it upon yourself to get involved with the podcast at every level. We may never know when you *became* Molly Forster, but it was probably a gradual process. A fantasy at first. Then over time, a suspicion. Then images came that you mistook for memories. But they weren't yours, they were just your brain filling the blanks of what you'd been hearing. When the podcast happened, it's also possible that at some subconscious level, you were frightened that the podcast would reveal you're not Molly Forster. So you had to have complete control."

I really am, and have always been, Rachel Holloway. I say this to myself, to see how it fits.

"You're fragile, Rachel, and no wonder. Life wasn't always kind to you, was it? The death of your mother would have been terribly hard on you."

I nod. "I'm starting to remember. About me, I mean, the real me, Rachel Holloway."

"Good. And I have every confidence that you will recover all those memories, yes. And that you will realise that Molly Forster is a person separate from you."

I bring the sheet to dry my cheeks this time. It feels rough against my skin, dry.

"Rachel..."

I look at Barb.

"Can you tell me about how it was to be Molly? Where you went? What you did?"

"What do you mean? In my head?"

She brings her chair closer to the bed. "Why don't we start with the day you found out about the podcast."

So I do. I tell her everything I can think of about those last few weeks, from the day Chris told us about the bloody podcast until now. It takes ages. I don't think I leave anything out. Well, maybe one or two details.

She doesn't write anything down, mostly she nods, asks a pointed question, mulls over the answer.

"And here we are. I woke up in this bed an hour ago and, you're here."

"Thank you, Rachel. I'm grateful for your candour." She hesitates and then adds, "Your friend told me about your visit."

"Vivian?"

"Yes. I know that you were convinced her friend…"

"Peter."

"That's right. That's a big jump into acute paranoia."

"What do you mean?"

"Feeling that people around you are pretending to be someone else, that they want to harm you, it's a big shift for you. We need to understand what may have triggered it."

I shake my head, look away. "I have no idea."

"You must be tired, I'll let you get some rest."

"When is my father coming?"

"He couldn't get a flight until tomorrow, but Matt has all the details." She checks her watch. "I'm sure Matt will be here soon. He can tell you himself."

She has one hand on the doorknob, almost out the door, and I call out to her. "Barb… what do you think my prognosis is?"

"We'll be doing an evaluation shortly, but there's no need to worry."

"How do you know?" I ask.

"I'm your doctor," she replies, smiling, before closing the door after her.

And not a very good one after all, Barb.

FORTY-ONE

If Barbara really wants to believe that the name I was born with is Rachel Holloway, that's her choice, I guess. But then what's the point of these professions? Barbara is a psychiatrist. Isn't she supposed to spot the difference between the truth and a lie? I spent my entire life hiding my true identity and now I don't know why I bothered. It's taken me twelve years to drum up the courage to tell someone, *my name is Molly Forster*, and for what?

Maybe it's better for me that way. Let them all believe I'm Rachel Holloway. The only problem will be when Mr Holloway shows up, all the way from Sydney, Australia. He may not have been in touch with Rachel for the past nine years, but he'll know I'm not Rachel when he sees me.

She almost got to me though, Barbara. There was a moment there, where I was contemplating the reality that I really am Rachel Holloway, complete fruit cake. When enough people tell you that you're crazy, you start to wonder if you are. But I know I'm not Rachel Holloway.

I met the real Rachel Holloway when I returned from

Barcelona. I was in London, homeless, again. I zeroed in on the same places I used to hang around before, like a homing pigeon. It had only been a year since I'd left, or not much more, but most of the old faces were gone. That's the thing with the abandoned. You either find a path for yourself, or someone finds one for you. But you rarely stay still.

I was almost nineteen and I looked young for my age. She may have been only a couple of years older, but she looked like she was a hundred. That's what crystal meth will do to you. And the rest. The things you do to get the money to buy it, for one.

I was asleep in the doorway of a building. I didn't mean to fall asleep but I'd been up for three days and it just happened. Until she nudged me awake with her toe.

"You want to come up?"

That's how naive I was, I thought she was being nice to me. I was desperate for a bed, so I said yes. She flicked her cigarette butt on the ground without bothering to put it out. I scrambled to get my things together, which was only a coat and a backpack.

We went up the three flights of stairs to her room. It stank. The whole building reeked of urine and stale cigarettes. And something else, like vomit, maybe. The smell you get sometimes in an old pub where they never bother to clean the carpet.

"What brought you here, then?" she asked.

I shrugged. I told her a tale of abuse, of a father who beat me, and of a mother who died too soon, while she rolled cigarettes and drank red wine from a cardboard box.

"Yeah, my mother's dead too. I've been on the street for a year, I reckon. I don't know what day it is anymore." She tucked a strand of greasy hair behind her ear. It was bleached blond, but it showed at least an inch of dark roots. Like everyone else around here.

"What about your dad?" I asked.

"He found some other bitch who didn't know what she was getting herself into, right after my mum died, like days, I'm not kidding. He said he couldn't help me anymore, that I'd brought it upon myself by my behaviour, but that was bull-shit. He just wanted to be rid of me so he could fuck off with his new squeeze. The prick."

I didn't want any wine and she didn't offer. But she said she had to go out and if I wanted, I could lay down on her bed for a while. It was just a mattress on the floor, with some cheap bedcovers on top of it. But I didn't care. I was happy to be safe.

"You can stay over tonight, but it'll have to be the floor. I'll want my bed back when I return."

I was so grateful I could have wept.

I was awoken by the sensation of a foot pressing down on my shin. I opened my eyes. There was a large man, looking down on me. I still remember the pungent smell of aftershave.

"What's your name?" he asked. He was wearing a shiny dark jacket. He hooked his thumbs in his jeans' pockets and I caught the spark of a gold chain around his wrist.

I sat up.

"Sorry, I'll go. I shouldn't be here," I said.

I stood but he put a hand on my shoulder and pushed me back down. I lost my balance, stumbled backwards and my head hit the wall.

"What's the rush, pretty girl? I just got here!"

I rubbed the back of my head. Behind him I could see her, sitting at the table. I wanted to call out to her but didn't even know her name. She was counting money, licking her index finger, making a little pile.

The big guy smirked. "I'll go first, shall I?" He undid the belt of his trousers, licking his lips. I sprung forward, screaming, and rammed my head into his stomach as hard as I could. He stumbled backwards onto the floor.

"What the fuck!?" she yelled, my Good Samaritan, but I was already out the door, running down those steps two by two, my hand flying down the bannister, and I was all the way down the street by the time I realised I didn't have my backpack.

All I had was me, running.

Run, Molly!

FORTY-TWO

"Hey, hon."

I open my eyes, knowing already it's Vivian.

"Hey, you too." I sit up, making a show of how gingerly the effort is. I don't know why. Because I'm in a hospital maybe, it makes me behave like I've been in an accident.

"How are you feeling?" she asks sweetly. I pat the bed beside me for her to sit down.

"Like shit. You?"

She laughs and pats my hand. "I'm sorry, about yesterday."

"Was it only yesterday?"

"'I'm afraid so."

"Oh. Well, there's nothing for you to be sorry for."

"Matt called me. I didn't know, Rach. That you'd been so..."

"Sucked into another reality?"

"Yeah."

"Well, if it's any consolation, neither did I." I pluck imaginary lint from the thin cotton blanket. "You tried to help me. I know that."

"I should have gone home with you. Talked to Matt with you, it would have been easier."

"I wouldn't have let you."

"You don't still think…"

"No."

"I didn't make the connection, you know, with the other time. I knew you were confused over Peter, but I thought you were just seeing danger and plucking the scariest name you could from your head. I didn't know you thought then too, that you were, you know."

"Molly Forster?"

"Yeah. Shit. That's full-on. Do you still think that?"

I heave myself up a bit more and I put my hand behind her neck, gently pull her head close to me. Then I whisper in her ear, "I *am* Molly Forster."

She recoils, and I laugh. "Sorry! Sorry, I was kidding."

"It's not funny."

"I know. Sorry. Is Matt coming soon?"

"I don't think he's coming yet."

"Why?"

"He's pretty upset."

"Did you talk to him?"

"Of course."

"What is he upset about?"

"It might not make sense to you, but he's in shock about Gracie."

I pull back the covers to get out of bed, but she puts a hand out to stop me. "About her name. He said that you insisted on calling her Grace. Because she was a miracle you said. Now he finds out she's named after that dead girl in Whitbrook."

I wince.

She shrugs. "You have to admit, it's kinda sick."

"I have something called dissociative personality disorder. Haven't you heard?"

"Matt loves you, Rach, you know that. But he has to think about himself, and Grace."

My heart starts beating faster. "Think about what?"

"About what's best for Grace, for her to be safe."

"What? Are you kidding? I'm not a danger to my daughter! Did he say that?"

"You have to understand, you need to get well."

"I am well!"

"No, you're not, honey. It's not just that you called your daughter after some dead kid, it's also, you know, that other time."

I don't need to ask what she's talking about. It seems no one will let me forget it for as long as I live.

"Do you remember, Rachel? What happened then?"

I nod. "Of course I remember."

"But do you remember how it started?" she asks.

I sigh. I'd taken Gracie out, in the pram. It was a lovely sunny day, warm and bright after what felt like weeks of rain. Matt was at work, Gracie was six weeks old.

There's a small park down our street. It doesn't have swings or a sandpit, nothing like that, which didn't matter since she was so small. I bought a coffee and sat on the bench. I took her out of the pram and I was holding her, enjoying the feel of my baby in my arm, the smell of her skin as I nuzzled her cheek.

"Is it a girl?" a voice beside me asked. Everyone loves babies. It's what we all have in common. Humanity. People who wouldn't give you the time of day in normal circumstances will spend half an hour cooing over how pretty your baby's face is. I turned, a smile already on my lips, and came face-to-face with Hugo Hennessy.

Or so I thought. It wasn't him, I know that now. But back then, some strange chemical reaction made me think it was.

I ran away, clutching my screaming baby. I left the pram behind and ran all day. I don't think the word *terrified* could do justice to my feelings. I sat in the gutter in a small alleyway and rocked her until she went to sleep, then I rented a cheap room in a hostel.

I wish I could explain to Vivian that I was, and still am, in a way, a little bit crazy, a little bit broken. Being hunted for so long will do that to you. But I can't, obviously.

That poor man was stunned at what happened and he went to the police to explain. He even brought the pram with him.

"It took almost a week for them to find you."

I nod, wiping my tears.

"She almost died, Rach."

"No she didn't!"

"Shh, don't get upset."

"I was trying to protect her!"

"She hadn't been washed, or fed. She was dehydrated, if they hadn't found you when they did, who knows what might have happened."

"Don't say that, please."

"I'm just—"

"I know, okay? I was there! But there's a lot you don't understand."

She stands, straightens her skirt.

"You're leaving?"

"Peter is waiting for me. And I think you should get some sleep."

"Don't be angry with me," I plead.

"Oh Rach, I'm not angry. I'm just really worried about you."

"I know. I'll be okay. I just—I made a mistake."

"Just get some rest, hon." She turns to leave. "Oh, you haven't heard the news."

"What news?"

"The cops have reopened the case against Dennis Dawson!"

"You're kidding?"

"Nope, all thanks to you and Jacob, too."

"Oh my God, that's fantastic!"

"I know! Apparently, the woman who worked at the chemist has come forward. She remembered the case of course, because she'd heard that night that the family had been killed, and then the next morning she heard that Dennis had been arrested. She thought it was odd, since he was at the chemist at the time of the murders. But she assumed the police knew what they were doing, as most people do. So there you go! You were right!"

It's the most incredible news, but I'm sad for Emily Dawson, who achieved what she wanted, but died anyway.

I swing my legs out of the bed. "I need to get out of here, Viv. I have to go home."

She puts a hand on my shoulder.

"I don't think you're ready, have some rest, okay? Enjoy it while you can."

After she's gone I close my eyes. Maybe I should get some rest, but that's impossible right now. My brain is spinning with the news. I want to talk to Chris. And Jacob.

"How are you feeling?"

Reluctantly, I open my eyes again. The nurse checks something on her clipboard and hands me a small cup that holds two white pills. The badge on her blouse says 'Jackie'. She has a nice smile. Dimpled.

"I don't know. Okay I think." I take the small pills from her, pop them in my mouth and take a sip of water from the cup she hands me.

"These will help you sleep."

"Jackie?"

"Yes?"

"Can I leave here? If I want to?"

She shakes her head. "Not yet. You're under our care."

"Do you know how long?"

"Dr Morrison will come by tomorrow morning, he's our resident psychiatrist. He'll do an assessment and manage your treatment." She pats the bottom of the bed. "You'll be out of here in no time. You'll see."

My eyelids are heavy. I want to ask what she's given me but she's already gone. I should have checked. I close my eyes again and a sensation of falling washes over me. I really need to sleep.

I hear the door click softly. I think someone is in the room. I don't want to open my eyes. I don't have the strength. I figure Jackie will do her thing and leave again. There's a smell of flowers. I feel a breath on my cheek. A soft puff of air.

"Hello, Molly."

FORTY-THREE

My eyes fly open. Peter—no—Hugo is standing over me.

"You can't be here," I mumble.

"Wow. It really is you."

"Haven't you heard? I'm Rachel Holloway," I slur.

"I think we both know that's not true."

He sits down on the chair by the bed. "I can't believe this day has come, finally. I have been looking for you for a very long time, Molly Forster."

His voice resonates with me in a way I hadn't noticed before. But now it does. It's like something deep in my core has woken up. He's speaking differently—entirely differently —than when he was *Peter*. Even through my haze, I can see that his mannerisms and posture have completely changed.

"Are you cold, Molly? You're shaking."

"What do you want?"

"That's no way to treat an old friend, *Molly*. You know, I wasn't completely sure it was you. When Matt said you coloured your hair I thought, yeah, probably, it's probably you. But I needed more, to be absolutely certain. Calling my house? Thank you, Molly. Your little slip up on the podcast was gold, by the way. *I am Molly Foster.* Gold! Then getting your boyfriend to call my house? Cherry on top. Pity you never heard of call forwarding. When Matt called, I was a few blocks away from you. Don't you love technology?"

"I'm going to scream and someone will come."

"Oh, Molly, don't do that. At least wait until I finish my piece. I've come all this way to see you!"

I hold my breath.

"It was nice to meet your daughter, by the way. And I thought it was very sweet of you to name her after your slut sister. Touching even. I almost felt a tinge of nostalgia when I heard her name. Is your daughter a slut, too? Oh, wait, she's three years old. Early days. Oh well, maybe I can teach her a thing or two."

I open my mouth to scream, but before I manage to let out a sound, his hand has muffled the breath.

He puts his lips very close to my ear and whispers, "I don't think you understand. You're in a lot of trouble, little Molly."

I look into his eyes. It's like I'm twelve again. I feel the warm sensation between my legs that turns cold and wet in an instant. The smell of urine is pungent. He releases me and steps back, wrinkling his nose.

"Oh gross! Get a hold of yourself, girl!"

I'm losing consciousness. I have to speak very slowly.

"The police are going to come. I'm going to tell them everything. They will come after you, *Hugo.*"

"I don't think so."

"You killed Emily Dawson, you burnt the receipts, but there's still the photos. And our testimony, and our recordings. And the lady from *Boots.* The police will be able to piece it all together. That's one murder you won't get away with."

"But Molly, I didn't kill Mrs Dawson! Don't you remember? *You* did."

"What?" I can't breathe.

"You're going to get caught, Molly Forster."

"I don't understand what you're saying," I finally manage.

"You shouldn't have gone poking around, Molly. You should have let dogs lie. Now, Mrs Dawson is dead, and it's all because of you."

"How did you know? The podcast wasn't out yet?"

"I didn't. But I followed you and your little mate. I didn't even know you were Molly then, I thought you were some stupid bitch from the podcast. Dad told me the podcast people were in town, poking around. Everyone knew you guys were there. I sent that moron Cindy McFuckme, to see who you were talking to. That girl will do anything for me, seriously. She thinks I love her and she sure loves me. Anyway, when she told me you went to see Dennis's mother, well I just had to go and ask good old Mrs Dawson what the three of you chatted about. And now, thanks to you, she's dead."

"They'll catch you, Hugo."

"No, Molly, they'll catch *you*. Oh wait, I didn't tell you. When that stupid bitch from *Boots* piped up, 'I remember Dennis at the chemist that night'," he says in a high-pitched, stupid voice, "and the cops announced they were looking at the case again, what did you expect me to do? Sit on my hands?" He tutted. "I called the cops, and lied about who I was, and said that they might want to take a closer look at Rachel Holloway, who is so fucked up she thinks she's Molly Forster reincarnated or something. And she's the one who interviewed Emily Dawson. And now that poor Mrs Dawson is dead," he slaps his palms on either side of his face, like he's pretending to be shocked, "I wonder if she's had anything to do with it. She *is* crazy after all, ask her boyfriend."

"Why would I want to kill Mrs Dawson?"

"Because she just revealed, on record, that it's unlikely her son committed the murders, so it follows that it must have been somebody else, wouldn't you agree? I thought long and hard about this, you know. And I've come to the conclusion, that it must have been hard to grow up in the shadow of your perfect sister. That's what they'll say. I'll make sure of it, once it occurs to everyone that they did indeed put the wrong man in jail for those terrible crimes. Poor little Molly. It's no wonder you went crazy, after what you did. You grabbed a cricket bat and smashed your father's skull, then you ran to your mother and smashed her skull too! Or was that it the other way around?" he shrugged. "I can't remember. It's such a long time ago."

I can't breathe. My chest hurts so much, like it's in a vice. "You killed them, Hugo," I managed to say. I want to scream but he's so close, almost on top of me.

"Maybe I did," he says, "but you're the one who's crazy. That's why you're here. One day, you're Rachel Holloway, the next you're Molly Forster, one thing everyone agrees on though: you're crazy."

"I was twelve years old. They'll never believe you."

"Of course, they will. You know, I think maybe my memory failed me, back then. The shock, you know. But all these years later, something will come back to me. Some detail that will open Pandora's Box. I have it all worked out. The tales of your jealousy, of you being in love with me. I'll say that Grace broke up with me because she was afraid of you. I'll say that I never wanted to make that public, out of respect for your family. But you were becoming a monster. You were going insane and nothing could stop you. I'll cry when I say that if I'd known back then, that you were the killer, I would have spoken up."

He leans forward and speaks softly right into my ear.

"Why don't you end it all now, Molly. It's the best way. Think about it. You won't win this fight. It would be very easy for me to prove to the police that you really are Molly Forster, and that you killed your family. I have relatives in high places, haven't you heard? They'll find you guilty of murdering your family because we now know it wasn't Dennis. Then they'll put you in a psychiatric hospital, and trust me, it won't be as nice as this. Or you could save yourself all this grief and kill yourself right now. What do you say, Mol?"

It happens too fast. With two fingers he pinches my nose so I have to breathe through my mouth. I begin to scream but he has dropped the pills on my tongue and he pushes my chin up hard. I can't get away from his grip. The medication Jackie gave me earlier has sapped all the strength from me.

I'm going to die.

"Knock, knock! Visitors' hours are over, I'm afraid. Your friend needs to go now."

I inhale and cough at the same time, my hand on my mouth. Hugo is already upright and doing half a turn.

"Sorry, I was just leaving," he says sweetly.

Jackie stands against the door, keeping it open for him to get through. "Tomorrow is another day, Rachel. You'll have plenty of visitors then, I'm sure."

She thinks I'm disappointed. I don't have the time to tell her otherwise. As soon as she shuts the door I pull back the covers and run to the bathroom. I stick two fingers down my throat and throw up the pills.

When I wake up later, it's dark. An image flashes inside my mind, Hugo had been in the room. It was horrible. For a second, I am awash with relief that it was only a nightmare, and then I see the small bouquet of flowers on the side table.

I move slightly, and my legs feel cold. I know then. I throw the covers back. I remember. I've wet the bed.

There's a wardrobe in the room, and inside are the clothes I was wearing when I got here. I go to the bathroom and clean myself as quickly as I can. Once I'm dressed I peek out the door of my room. It's funny, but what I notice is that the corridor is surprisingly lovely, the way they decorated the place. Not your horror movie white tile corridor at all. Instead it's all pastels and warm and surprisingly comforting. It makes me feel that, had I really been crazy, this would have been a fine place to heal.

But I'm not crazy, so I stick my head out and look both ways. Everything is deadly quiet. Holding my shoes in my hand, I tiptoe out softly in my bare feet. There's carpet everywhere. I walk slowly in the direction of the Exit sign.

"You all right?"

I was just about to turn the corner. I turn around. There's a small, elderly woman staring at me. She's dressed in a nightgown, slippers on. She asks again, "You all right?"

"Yes! Thank you!" I walk quickly, purposefully down the hall but she follows me at a distance.

"Are you here to see someone?"

I stop, close my eyes. She's talking too loudly, she'll wake the whole place up.

I turn around. She's frowning at me.

"Everyone is asleep," she says sternly. "It's night time. You should come back tomorrow,"

"Ah. Thank you, I'll do that. I'll just find my way out and be gone."

"Okay then."

I hurry down the corridor, which leads into a small foyer,

with a comfortable seating area. I'm again surprised at how pretty it is here, with its pastel colours and fluffy cushions. Matt and I don't have private insurance. Can we really do this on the NHS?

There's a counter that separates the nurses' station from the foyer, but it's unattended. The Exit doors have a pane of glass and I can see beyond, into what looks like another corridor. I hurry across and press my palm against the door, but it doesn't budge. Then I notice the keypad, just to the left of it.

"You can't go out this way. You have to put the number in first."

I stare at her.

"Sorry, what's your name?"

"Maureen."

"Okay, Maureen. Do you know the way out of here?"

"There's a way out the back."

"There is?"

"This way."

She shuffles away, and I follow her along. "How do you know?"

"I work here."

"You do?"

"I serve the morning tea. You'll see me tomorrow, I'll be the one behind the trolley."

Not if I can help it.

"And they let you stay here? You don't seem dressed for it."

"I'm supposed to be asleep. But I don't need to. I only need four hours a night, and I already had those."

"Four hours?"

"Yep."

"Okay." We've walked down the corridor and into some

kind of communal room. There are tables for four scattered around like card tables. I don't see any exits.

"Where's the way out, Maureen?"

"This way."

She turns around and takes me back the way we came. We walk past a sign for the ladies room. I really need to pee. "Would you mind waiting for me here for a minute? I won't be long."

"All right. I'll be here."

I check my face in the mirror. I look terrible. My skin is pasty, my eyes are red. *I am Molly Forster* I tell myself, to check that it rings true. It does.

When I come out, there's no sign of Maureen. What kind of a place is this where no one is around? I don't want to call out for her, so I continue the way I thought she might have gone, which takes me down a dead end. I backtrack and turn down another corner and there it is. A door. Big double swing doors with glass and a lawn beyond it. Freedom.

I push against the heavy horizontal bars, but nothing happens. They're locked. I have to find Maureen, maybe she has a key.

"Are you all right?"

I'm back in the foyer, and she's sitting in the same armchair as before.

"Maureen! There you are. I thought I lost you. I found the door but it's locked, do you have the key?"

"Are you here to see someone? Because they're all asleep you know. You'll have to come back in the morning."

That's how desperate and confused I am. How could I not know right away that Maureen is a patient? Why didn't I ask her for the keypad code that would have let me out of here?

"Rachel? What's wrong?"

My heart sinks. Jackie stands behind the counter at the nurses' station. She comes out through the side door.

"You should go back to bed. Why are you dressed?" She takes my elbow and gently turns me around. "Do you need something to help you sleep?"

"I only need four hours sleep," Maureen says behind me, "I work here. I serve breakfast."

"That's right, Maureen," Jackie says, winking at me. "Rachel, you should go back to bed."

I let myself be guided back to my room. "What time is it?"

"Four a.m."

We're at the door to my room. She holds it open and I step inside.

"I—"

"What is it?"

I feel myself go red from embarrassment. I look down. "I need the bed linen changed."

She pulls the bed covers back. "Ah, that's why you're wandering around. That's all right. It happens. Don't worry, I'll go and get some clean sheets and another nightie for you. You sit down here, okay?"

When Jackie returns, she hands me a plain cotton nightie. I help her make the bed, tucking the corner of the sheet under the mattress.

"Did you hear me, Rachel?"

"Sorry, I was miles away."

"Do you want something to help you sleep?"

"No, thank you."

"All right. Buzz me if you change your mind."

"Jackie? That man who was here before."

"Your friend? What about him?"

"If he comes back, I don't want to see him, okay?"

"I'll leave a note."

FORTY-FOUR

"Wake up, Rachel. Dr Morrison is here to see you."

I must have dozed off. The words pull me out of my dreams—or was it a nightmare? I don't know anymore. It's slipping away too fast for me to hold on, and all I'm left with is an image of me running and crowds of people behind me. My heart is still pounding. I think I woke up too fast.

"How are you, Rachel?" he asks. He pushes his thin-rimmed glasses further up his nose. Dr Morrison is maybe in his late fifties, he has white hair. He doesn't smile but his face is gentle. He looks at me with concern.

"I'm fine, I'm very sorry I fell asleep." I'm flustered, annoyed with myself. I get up quickly and straighten my clothes. I'd already had breakfast, I was showered and dressed. I should have sat in the armchair by the window, but instead I decided to lay down just for a moment. Just to rest my head a bit on the pillow.

"You don't need to be sorry," he says kindly.

"I wanted to be up and ready." An image of Hugo

standing over me flashes through my mind. I'm going to cry. I tilt my head back a little to stop the tears.

"There's no need to apologise. You can sleep as much you want. Sit down, please."

He indicates the armchair. He settles on the other chair, the hard one. The one without armrests. Jackie gives me a little nod of encouragement before leaving the room. She leaves the door open.

Dr Morrison reads something in the folder, then he says, "I'm going to ask you some questions. It's not a test, and there are no right or wrong answers. It's to help us determine what you need to get better, do you understand?"

"Yes."

"Would you like some water?"

I don't answer, I just grab the water cup by the bed and sit back down. I take a sip.

"What is your name?"

"Rachel Holloway."

"How old are you?"

"I'm twenty-six."

"Where were you born?"

"Newcastle."

"Do you have any siblings?"

"No." I have to rush the word to get it out. Otherwise I fear it would get stuck in my throat.

"Okay. I'm going to ask you whether you've had certain experiences, and you just need to tell me if you have, and approximately how often. Can you do that?"

He must think I'm a complete idiot.

"Yes."

"Have you ever been in a car or public transport, like a bus, and you don't remember what has happened during all or part of the journey?"

"Sometimes."

"How does it feel when it happens?"

"I don't know, I was deep in thought and I was on autopilot I guess."

"In percentages, how often does it happen, fifty percent of the time? Eighty percent?"

"Twenty percent, I guess."

He makes a note.

"Do you ever find that someone was talking to you, and you don't recall what they just said?"

"Sometimes, if I'm distracted or if I have something on my mind."

"How often?"

I shrug. "Not often. Ten percent maybe."

In spite of what he said earlier, I really do want to 'pass' this test. It's the difference between me getting out of here and being stuck here indefinitely. I figured some of these things happen to everyone so I'm reluctant to say "never" in case it flags the fact that I'm lying. I just have to not be crazy, essentially.

"Have you ever found yourself wearing clothes that you don't remember putting on?"

"No."

"Do you hear voices inside your head?"

"Other than my own internal monologue? No."

"Does your internal monologue tell you what to do?"

"It might tell me to get a move on when it's time to go to work in the mornings." I smile.

"Do you ever find drawings or scribblings that you know are yours, but you don't remember doing?"

I shake my head. "No. Never."

We go through this for quite a while. I don't tell Dr Morrison that I've already taken this test. After what happened with Gracie when she was a baby.

After the test, Dr Morrison wants to talk about what happened to get me in here.

"I had some kind of nervous breakdown," I say. "It made me believe I was someone else."

"Who are you now?"

"Rachel Holloway."

"Who were you when you arrived here?"

He makes it sound like there's a number of us, and we take turns.

"I thought I was Molly Forster."

"But you don't think that now?"

"No. I was ill."

"How long did you think you were Molly Forster?"

"I don't know exactly. I think it started when I was pregnant with my daughter. Or maybe after she was born."

I throw that one in, firstly to remind him that I have a child waiting for me at home, and also because we're educated now. Everyone knows there are mothers who have suffered from postnatal depression to the point where they did something they shouldn't have. Giving birth is no picnic, either on your body or your mind. I hope he will be understanding.

"Do you know why you chose this person? Molly Forster?"

I turn to look out the window. "I think something about her story resonated with me. Something about being on your own, having to fend for yourself. My mother, Katherine, died when I was young. My father remarried and moved to the other side of the world. He has a new family now. I think, in a way, it's as if he was dead, too. Maybe I wanted to be like Molly: someone people wanted to find, you know?"

The last part brings unexpected tears to my eyes. I quickly rub them off with the back of my hand.

Dr Morrison nods, looks at me kindly and writes things down.

"Do you think you're better?"

"Yes. I think so. I hope so."

"How can you tell?"

"Because I know who I really am."

"Who are you?"

"I'm Molly Forster."

FORTY-FIVE

"Hey."

"Matt!"

He has one hand on the doorknob, the other dangling limply by his side. My heart swells at the sight of him. I'm sitting in my chair, and spring up at the sight of him and throw my arms around his neck.

But he doesn't react in the way I expect. He doesn't envelop me in his arms or look at me with water in his eyes. He doesn't tell me how much he's missed me. He just stands there as I embrace him, until he gently steps away.

"How are you?" he asks.

I shake my head. "Not great. I made a mistake. It's this stupid test. They try and trick you, you know? He was asking so many questions, so quickly, I got confused but it's not my fault." I realise I'm biting the side of my thumb and quickly put my hands behind my back.

"How's Gracie?" I ask.

"She's fine. She's good."

"You didn't bring her."

"I don't think this is the place for her. Seeing you in here."

"You're right, of course. Thanks."

He sits on the side of the bed. "The cops have been to see me," he says. There's a strange look on his face.

"Why?"

"They asked me about your trip to Whitbrook."

"Why would they ask you? You weren't there."

"They wanted to know if you'd said anything to me, about Mrs Dawson."

"Like what?"

"Like whether you were upset by something she might have said."

"That's ridiculous."

"They asked me about Barcelona. About what you were doing there."

"What?"

"They said you were connected with someone who died in suspicious circumstances. They wanted to know if you'd ever talked about that."

I'm biting the inside of my mouth and now I can taste my blood. My heart is pounding in my chest. Has Hugo already started acting on his threats? He's setting me up? I stare at Matt, trying to come up with the right words to make him understand. He's lost weight. I see that now. His face looks pale and dry. The skin under his eyes is bluish. It makes my heart weep.

"Have you done something, Rachel? Something you shouldn't have done?"

"No. Matt, I swear. No."

"Do you know what you said to me the day before you came here?"

Came here. As if I had a choice.

"No. I don't remember."

"You said, keep an eye on Gracie, Matt. Don't let her out of your sight."

I look at him. "So?"

"Weren't you trying to tell me something?"

"Other than please watch our daughter?"

"I think you were saying you might do something. You were telling me to protect Gracie from you. That's what you said, 'don't let her out of your sight.'"

"Oh, fuck you for that. I would never hurt our daughter and you fucking know it, you piece of shit. There. Does that help?"

We sit in silence. All I want is for him to come and put his arms around me. He doesn't have to say anything, just to hold me. But he sits there like a limp bit of lettuce and I can't look at him anymore.

"Rach?"

"What?"

"Hugo Hennessy called me back."

I close my eyes.

"I mean, he called *your* mobile back, after you left, you know…"

He looks pained when he says it. I can see myself in my mind's eye, punching the numbers to call Hugo's house. I was frantic. I hadn't changed the setting on my phone. I didn't hide my number. I forgot, didn't I. I am a stupid, hopeless, worthless person that put everyone in danger. It doesn't matter anyway, he already knew.

I pinch the bridge of my nose hard. I want the pain to take over, so that I don't have to endure the one in my stomach.

"Rachel?"

"I heard you, Matt."

"He didn't sound like Peter."

"When did he call?"

"The day before yesterday. That night."

"What did he say?"

"He wanted to know who I was and why I called. I explained, about you, the podcast you know, all that."

I look up at that. "About me? What about me?"

He looks sheepish. "Does it matter?"

"It does to me."

"I told him you were ill, and that you were working on the podcast and that you thought someone we met recently was him, I mean Hugo Hennessy."

"Why would you say that? I had a breakdown, but I know who I am Matt. I'm Rachel Holloway, okay?"

He frowns. His head gives a little jerk, like he does when he's confused about something. I used to find it endearing.

I sigh. "What did he say?"

"Not much, he listened mostly. He said he'd heard about the podcast but he hadn't listened to it. He said he knew nothing about this Peter. He also said beside being happily married, that he's in construction and hasn't been able to leave the site in months. They're about to tear down the old railway station in Whitbrook and he—"

I snap my eyes to him. "The railway station?"

"Yeah. But the point is, Rachel, that Peter has nothing to do with this man, and the real Hugo has been on a construction site for weeks. I just thought you'd like to know, that's all."

He comes closer finally and kneels on the floor. He takes my hand and puts it over his cheek.

"Are we going to be all right?" he asks.

"I wish you'd brought Gracie with you."

"I told you, I didn't—"

"I know, I just wish she was here, with us, you know?"

"I wish you hadn't insisted on calling her Grace. I'll never know now, if you did that because she was a miracle, or because you were… unwell."

I lean down and put my forehead against his and say, "I did it because she's perfect."

Just like Grace.

I don't have my phone with me. It's at home, with Matt. If it was here, they would have taken it away from me. But when I tell Matt that I feel really unwell, and that he needs to go and get the nurse at the station, he doesn't ask questions, he just goes.

They come back together, today's nurse and Matt. By now I've got his mobile from his jacket pocket, turned it on silent, and I've safely hidden it in the drawer of my night table.

"I'm having stomach cramps, I don't understand."

She checks how much medication I've been given. Am I allergic to anything? Matt wants to stay and look after me, but I tell him to go, to come back tomorrow, and to give Gracie a kiss from mummy.

Tell her I love her, and I miss her so much I'm going to hug her till Christmas, I say.

"I'm all right now, thank you—" I check her name tag, "—Susan. I'm fine. I have a sensitive stomach. Always have. It's from my mother's side of the family."

Matt and I hug tightly. I inhale the scent of him so I can bottle it up and keep it close. I promise myself that I will find a way to make him see that I'm telling the truth.

"Will you keep an eye on Vivian please?"

"Why?"

"Because."

"Okay."

As soon as he leaves I retrieve Matt's mobile from the

bedside table. I have phone reception. I open the web browser and search for the number. I find one, but it's a landline. I just hope it's the right one, and that someone's there.

But I recognise Jacob's voice when he picks up.

"Help me," I say.

FORTY-SIX

He came, thank God. He's sitting close to me because I insisted. We may be in a private room but what if someone walks in announced just as I say, *get me out of here*, they won't let me have any visitors again.

"What do you want me to do?" he asks.

"Get me out of here," I whisper. Jacob looks away, like he's thinking about it.

"Rachel—"

"Molly. The name is Molly Forster."

"Ra—Molly, look, I don't know. Look around you. See where you are? You're in a psychiatric hospital. Sorry, but there's no way I can get you out of here. Even if I wanted to. And I don't want to because you're not well. You're supposed to be here."

"Jacob, right now, you are the only person in the world who can help me. I need to get out of here. I know how, you just need to do what I ask you."

"Why are you telling me this? It's the reason you're here, that you think you are—"

"I am."

"Why tell me?"

"Because I have to tell someone the truth. We don't have a history. But you were more invested in finding Molly than anyone. It's the reason I got you fired."

"I didn't get fired, I just—"

"Whatever. I thought you were in on it, with the Hennessys, I know that's not the case now—have known for a long while. But you know so much about Molly, you've researched the case, you told me so. If I can convince you—and I know I can—then I have a chance."

"And if not?"

"Then I'm either going to be in a psych hospital forever, or at least until someone kills me in here."

He drops his head, like it's all too much. I bring my chair even closer, so close that our knees are touching. I keep my voice low.

"You remember when we got to Whitbrook and you parked the car outside my house? I threw up. Right on the grassy knoll outside the front gate."

"I remember."

"Let me tell you about that house. In the middle of the front door is a door knocker. It serves no purpose because the house has an electric doorbell, but my mum picked it up from an antique shop. It's shaped like a swan and she loved them. It's made of brass. She got my dad to put it up. No one ever used it. I wonder if it's still there? You push the door and you're in the hall. There's a dent in the skirting board on the left where I rammed my tricycle. My mother, whose name was Mary by the way, told me not to ride my tricycle in the house, but I thought I could go faster on those black and white tiles than I did on the grass outside or on the gravel path in the garden. That's at the back of the house, the garden. It backs onto the river and it's huge. Inside, in the kitchen are cupboards handcrafted by a friend of my dad's called Tony Buckhouse. They have pretty door handles, round and white with a pink flower painted under a clear laminate. But one of them broke and was replaced by a plain white handle. That's the cupboard to the far right, near the window.

There's a walnut tree near the house at the back and on the trunk are Grace's initials, carved. Just below those are mine. Also carved. It's not a big tree, or at least it wasn't when I was a kid, and you can climb it and sit on the branch that shoots out to the left. When my sister Grace turned thirteen, she was given a small toolset, they were real tools but smaller. That day we took them and punched small holes in the west wall of the garage until my mother came and took them away from us. But the holes were small and never got filled in. You can probably check that too. The French doors at the back of the house open onto a paved patio. The tiles are light grey, almost beige, with a pattern that looks like marble. One of them is cracked, it's on the edge, almost at the far corner, and it's a hairline crack from when my dad dropped—"

"Stop." He sits up straight and looks at me. I say nothing. "What does it prove, Rach?"

"Molly."

He puts his hand up, palm facing me, and says, "I'll listen, fine, but it's going to be Rachel okay? If that's a deal-breaker, then tell me now and I'm out of here."

I nod. "How could I know those things unless I was—"

He keeps shaking his head, as if he can flick off the frustration. "What, that there's a tree at the back of the house with initials on it? Or that the paving is grey?"

"Didn't you listen to all that I just said? There's a bit more than the colour of the paving."

"But all that you could have found out from newspapers!

272

Magazines! The telly! The press were all over this for months! They had photos of everything! Including the gardens! And yes! Including the paving!"

"You can't be serious."

"Maybe you went in the house! How would I know? Maybe you went there after they were killed because you're like, obsessed with them!"

He must have caught the incredulous look on my face because then he says, "People do that, you know. You'd be amazed at the fanatics out there, the kind of stuff people will do to get a closer look."

"So how can I prove it to you? There has to be a way."

"If you could prove it to me then you would prove it to everyone else. That's the idea, isn't it?"

The door bursts opened, startling us. A different nurse walks in, someone I haven't met yet, and frowns at us, as if we're doing something wrong. She hands me a small pill container with two tablets. I take it and put it on the nightstand.

"You need to take these now," she says.

"Could I have some water then?" I hand her my water cup, shake it to show it's empty. She takes it from me with a frown and while she fills it with water from the bathroom tap, I slip the pills under my pillow. She hands me the water cup and I make a show of emptying the container into my mouth.

"Shouldn't you be taking those?" Jacob asks after she's gone.

"No."

"Rachel," he begins, "if you really are Molly Forster—"

"I am."

"Then why are you going around pretending your name is Rachel Holloway? People have been looking for you for years.

Why not walk into the first police station you see and tell them who you are?"

"Because I didn't want to be found."

"Why not?"

"Because there are people out there who want to kill me."

"So what's changed?"

"The podcast, that's what. It's brought these people closer to finding me—they did find me. And now I need to get out of here because I'm a sitting duck."

"Which people?"

"You know when I told you the other day, about Hugo Hennessy, that he is dangerous, that there's more to the story—"

"Whoa, wait a sec here, I heard all this from Vivian already. You're not still saying that Peter—"

He won't believe me if I tell him the truth about Peter. So I don't.

"I need to get out of here, right now. Hugo Hennessy, the real one, he's going to come after me. Because I'm Molly Forster, and I was there when he killed them."

"It's a lot to process, Rach."

"I was there, Jacob," I say, my voice shaking. "I was there and I saw it, I saw him do it. I ran away and I hid in the old railway station but he found me. I managed to get to the police, and Edward Hennessy put me in this room and called his son. I heard him, on the phone, talking to Hugo, telling him that I was sitting right here and he needed to come right now and sort this out. That it was his mess and he needed to come and fix it. So I ran, and I've never been back until I went with you."

He's pale now. He stares at me with his mouth open, and with my index finger I push his chin up to close it, saying, "You'll catch a fly. That's what my dad used to say."

"Have you ever told anyone?"

"No, never. I've spent every waking hour since making sure no one knew. Until a few days ago that is, when I tried to tell Matt and I ended up here."

"Jesus."

"They don't believe me. No one believes me. You have to believe me. You're my last hope, Jacob."

FORTY-SEVEN

Technically, the only way to leave is through the foyer door, the one with the keypad. If you're allowed to leave, a nurse presses a button from the nurses' station that unlocks it. From there you simply walk out to the main hospital reception, and then out of the building. The other way is through the glass doors that lead to the garden. They're open during the day since the garden is for the residents, as they call us. It's a large garden, and there's a tall metal fence around the perimeter, and at two different points there are gates, both of which are locked. I figured out all this before Jacob arrived.

It's possible to climb over the fence, at a spot where you are least likely to be seen. It's too high to climb on your own, but if you happen to have someone tall, like Jacob, by your side who could give you a leg up, you could do it.

We walk out into the garden as if going for a stroll. I take Jacob to the most secluded spot I can find. You could be seen climbing the fence if someone inside happened to walk past the windowed corridor, so we have to be quick. He gives me his hooded parka to wear, and with a quick lift and a push I

276

am on the other side. I scan the parking lot and quickly move next to a parked car that gives me some cover. Then I crouch next to it and wait, while Jacob walks out of the building the normal way, without his parka.

My heart is thumping in my ears. I'm suddenly scared he'll just leave but when I see him come out, he walks briskly to his car, turns on the ignition, and waits. Seconds later I'm in the passenger seat.

"Go go go!" I urge him. I don't think the 'pillow under the blanket' trick will give me cover for very long, and if I could I would reach out with my foot to push down on the accelerator.

Jacob is shaking. "I can't believe you made me do that. I've never done anything like that before. Never," he says.

"Thank you. I mean it," I say. But he just shakes his head.

Whitbrook is a couple of hours away from London. That's enough time for a lot of questions. He wants to know every-thing. He bombards me with questions. Where did I go? Did I try to contact someone? Anyone? How did I survive?

"I slept in doorways and in back alleys. I stole stuff. The first thing I stole was a pair of garden clippers that had been left near a hedge. I used them to cut my hair as short as I possibly could. I found a beanie. I looked like a boy. I took a train and no one stopped me. I ended up in London. I figured that it would be easier to be invisible in a crowd. I joined the hundreds of homeless children who live on the street because they can't go home, sometimes, because they're neglected, sometimes because they have parents who simply don't want them."

"Jesus."

"But mostly because they've been abused and it's got too dangerous for them to stay at home."

"How did you eat?"

"I met a girl not much older than me. Homeless kids can pick each other out, and I'd only just arrived, but they look after each other. Especially young girls. She took me to a shelter. There are a few, as well as hostels, for homeless children. They don't ask you for ID; they don't ask for explanations either."

"Didn't people figure out who you were?"

"I became adept at hiding who I was. I coloured my hair. I even used make-up sometimes. I wore hats as much as possible. I lost a lot of weight very quickly. Street kids always do. It doesn't take long before we look nothing like our former selves. Going without sleep or food will do that to you."

"Did you go to school?"

"Eventually."

"How did you do that?"

"I stole someone's identity."

"That's when you became Rachel Holloway?"

"No. That's when I became Susan Bishop."

"Oh. Wait. So Sneddon did find you."

"Yup."

"Why Susan Bishop?"

"It was my friend Gabriel's advice. Pick someone real, someone dead, someone around your own age."

"I didn't think that worked anymore. The tombstone thing."

"It doesn't, I almost got caught."

"How did you get into school?"

"There's an organisation called Railwaykids that help street children get into school. They helped me. They really thought my name was Susan Bishop. They vouched for me."

I have never told that story to anyone before. It feels liberating, cleansing even. Like peeling away years of dirt and grime from my skin.

The phone rings in my pocket. I've been expecting it but it still makes me jump. It's Matt.

"Where are you?"

"I'm sorry, love, I can't tell you. But I promise you that I'll be back tonight. I just need to do something and then I'll be back, okay? I love you."

I hang up. "Can I have your mobile please?"

"Why?"

"Because this one is Matt's and I'm going to turn it off."

"It's in my bag, in the back seat."

I pull the sim card out of Matt's mobile. I'm about to do the same with Jacob's but he reaches across and snatches it from me. "Don't take my sim card out of my phone! What's the matter with you?"

I struggle to get the phone back but he drops it under his seat, on the door side. "I can't risk it, Jacob. They can track our location with those sim cards."

"So let them!"

"I'll get you another one. I promise."

"I'm not giving you my phone, Rachel. Deal with it."

I let out a huff, but I don't argue.

"Do you think you could go faster?" I ask.

"I'm driving at the speed limit."

"You call that the speed limit?"

"Rachel!"

"Okay. Sorry."

"Why are we going back to Whitbrook anyway?"

"I need to get something. Something that belongs to my sister. I just assumed it was in the house, but something Matt said made me realise that it couldn't have been."

"Why?"

"Because if that had been the case, Hugo Hennessy would have been caught."

"Where is it?"

I don't answer the question exactly.

"I think I'm right. I never had the guts to go and check before, and if I don't do it now, it will be gone forever."

We drive in silence for a little while, then he asks, "What prompted these people to hire Sneddon?"

I look out the window and think for a moment. "I had such a normal life, by my standards, you see? I was happy, I wanted it to last forever. Gabriel was talking about us moving back to London. I wanted to be free, not to have to look over my shoulder all the time. So I did something incredibly stupid."

"What did you do?"

I take a breath. "I called the Whitbrook police station from a payphone. I spoke to a policewoman and I told her who I was, that Hugo Hennessy had murdered my family and his father had covered it up."

"What did she say?"

I shrug. "What could she say? She asked me for my name, my phone number, as if. She said it had been a long time since anyone had called to say they'd seen Molly Forster. I told her, I *am* Molly Forster. She said I was welcome to come in and make a statement. She said that Hennessy was the Mayor of Whitbrook now, and as it happened he was right there. I hung up."

"Do you know if she did anything about it?"

"She didn't believe me. I could tell. All I know, as I found out a few short weeks ago, a private detective was hired to track me down right after I made that call. They got very close, and Gabriel died."

"But why? If they could find you through Gabriel, why would they kill him?"

280

"He tried to warn me. He called me, he told me to run. I guess they wanted to stop him."

Jacob gives me an odd look. It's almost a look of pity. Maybe he's beginning to believe me.

"After that," I continue, "I was more careful. I had to change identities, and let's say I chose more carefully."

"How did you do that?"

"That's a long story, Jacob. I'll keep it for another time."

I don't want to tell him about Rachel Holloway. Not so much because of what she tried to do to me, sell me like a piece of meat to the highest bidder, but because of what I did. I'm afraid that Jacob won't help me if he knew.

After running away from her place, I huddled into another, different doorway, and spent the next few hours feeling sorry for myself. I was cold, I didn't have a coat anymore, but I didn't even care. I could always steal another one. There was only one thing I wanted from that backpack I left behind: my memory book. I'd just lost Gabriel at that point, and I had a photo of us in there, that we took in a Photo Booth in a train station. The goofing off kind. It flashed four times and the strip of four photos came out from the slot. We cut it in half, he got the two snaps where we were laughing, goofing. I got the one where he kissed the side of my face and I look at the camera straight on, a smile on my face that told of my happiness. The other one I had, our lips were locked and our faces in profile.

I didn't care what happened to me, I just wanted those photos back.

When I returned, it was without a plan. I was going to tell her she could keep it all if she wanted, but I was taking my memory book with me.

I banged on the door and she yelled from the other side, "Go away!" But I kept at it, anger making my teeth gnaw and my pulse race, until she opened the door.

"What the—?" She looked over my shoulder, as if she couldn't believe I'd come alone back to this dump.

"What do you want?" she slurred.

"My things."

"Your things?" She laughed an ugly laugh. "You see this?" she pointed at the red mark on her cheek that was already turning blue around her left eye. "That's what he did to me after you pushed him. So you can fuck off, I'm keeping your junk. Not that there's much to look at there by the way, but if it pisses you off, then I'm glad."

She closed the door but I had my foot wedged in already. It wasn't hard to push the door open. She was completely stoned.

Inside she had a little setup going. You could smell something burning. I'd been around plenty of drug addicts. I knew what the paraphernalia looked like.

"What's this?" I asked anyway.

"Don't fucking touch it, you hear me? Get the fuck out of here!!"

Her eyes were darting all over the room, wild and scared. I could have taken my things, they were right there, on the floor. She had turned my backpack inside out, looking for something I didn't have by the look of it. Drugs, probably.

"Don't worry. Whatever you're taking, I don't want any part of it."

"Oh, miss goody goody, are you?" she cackled. "Enjoy it while you can babe, one day you'll get a taste and trust me, you won't be so uppity then!" Then she burst into tears. "I was like you once, you know. Before … before all this!"

It all came out of her like a river of pain. She told me

more stories of hardship, and how nobody cared for her, nobody was looking for her, and this, she added with a sweeping gesture toward the drugs on the table, was all she had. All the while I just picked up my belongings and put them back in my bag, as if it was the most natural thing for me to do. She watched me, and she rambled on.

"Don't you have any friends? There must be someone who misses you." I almost added, *what about that man who was here before? He seems nice.*

She cried some more, about the unfairness of it all and I was thinking that if she didn't shut up soon I was going to slap her. What did she know about 'unfair'? I watched her with mounting disgust until I couldn't bear it anymore. She was trying to knot the rubber tourniquet around her arm. Her veins were so damaged she couldn't get hold of a good one to shoot up in.

"Don't just stand there, help me!" she hissed.

I tied the knot for her and watched her fill the syringe. I guided her hand until the needle found a vein, and she immediately went into a kind of a slump. Like the air had been let out of a balloon. Her eyelids closed, and she let out a sigh. She looked disgusting.

I didn't know she would die. She was slumped back in her chair and I didn't check to see if she was still breathing.

I saw her handbag on the floor and I took a peek inside. Among the assortments of make-up, condoms, keys, and tissues, was her wallet. A cheap plastic thing with fairies drawn on it that would look more at home with a ten-year-old than a grown woman. I checked her ID.

Rachel Holloway.

I didn't know how long I could use her cards before they got cancelled, but then I saw her photo a few days later, with a small item in the *Daily Mail*. They had described her as a prostitute who had died of an overdose, and police were trying to identify her. She had gone by the name of 'Lilly' but so far police had been unable to make a positive identification. If no one came forward she would be buried as Jane Doe.

I could have told them who she really was, but I didn't. I needed a name, so I claimed hers as my own.

Memories, unpleasant ones, are like a scab. You hate them but you pick at them anyway, and when Jacob says, "Do you think Matt will call the cops?" I almost resent him for interrupting.

"Because I've left the hospital? I don't know. I hope he waits until tomorrow, like I asked."

I fiddle around with the buttons on the dashboard until I find a working radio station.

"—Mayor of Whitbrook where the Forster family was murdered twelve years ago, has made shocking claims at a press conference earlier today. Our correspondent Suresh Chaudhary was in Whitbrook: 'Today, Edward Hennessy is the Mayor of Whitbrook, but back then his title was Chief Constable Edward Hennessy. As such, he was in charge of the investigation into the terrible murders of the Forster family. Dennis Dawson was arrested at the scene and remanded in custody, but he committed suicide the next day and the case was closed. As we now know, thanks to the hugely popular podcast Missing Molly, it's now highly likely that Dennis Dawson was not the murderer after all, in spite of his alleged confession."

Jacob looks at me. He's smiling, and he expects me to do the same, because *we did it! Didn't we.* But I just look at my hands on my lap and listen to the thump of my heart, and I already know what's coming next. Edward Hennessy's voice fills the car.

"—Justice was denied, in this case, because of the suicide of Dennis Dawson. His culpability or innocence was never tested in court, and we had every reason, and I stress this here, back then we had every reason to believe that Dennis Dawson had murdered Jack and Mary Forster, and their daughter Grace Forster, in a fit of jealous rage.

"There was however another person of interest at the time, someone who has remained a person of interest and frankly we never put that theory forward to the public because of the ramifications. But we have in our possession some credible evidence that Molly Forster may have brutally murdered her entire family."

FORTY-EIGHT

Jacob has stopped the car, opened the door and now he's standing outside, banging on the roof.

"What the hell? What the hell is going on here!" he yells.

Bang! Bang! With every one of his thumps I flinch further into my seat. I unfasten my seat belt and slowly get out of the car. The traffic whizzes past us.

"You can't believe him," I say, "They're trying to discredit what we're doing on the podcast, don't you see that? They're trying to pin it on me."

"All I can *see* is that everywhere I turn, there are dead bodies and you're in the middle of it!"

"I will prove it to you, if you could just trust me a bit longer!"

"Trust you? You must be joking. I don't even know who you are! One minute you're Rachel Holloway, nut job, escaped from the asylum thanks to yours truly, the next you're Molly Forster, professional identity thief and accused murderer!! Which one is it?"

I've come this far. We are maybe half an hour away from

Whitbrook and I'm frightened that I won't get there. I won't be able to finish what I started, and I won't be able to bring justice to my family because everybody is against me. I'm not giving up without a fight.

"My name is Molly Forster and Hugo Hennessy killed my family. That's why his father is putting out these lies. He is trying to distract any investigation away from the real killer. He will stop at nothing. Get back in the car, Jacob, please."

"What if you really are a crazy killer? Why should I get in the car with you?"

"Jacob, if there was any possibility that I was the monster he says I am, don't you think he would have mentioned it before? Why keep it quiet until today?"

"How should I know? Maybe the cops thought they had the right guy with Dawson!"

"But you don't suddenly come up with a new suspect out of thin air, all these years later? Either they had some evidence, or they didn't!"

He bangs on the roof of the car again. "I don't know what to think!" he yells.

"I was a kid! Do you really think I could physically bludgeon my father, my mother, and my sister? Without any of them stopping me? Think about it!"

"How would I know? Maybe they were asleep!"

"You know that's not true. You know everything about the case. No one was asleep. Hennessy is going to try and pin it on me because we've come too close. We're about to expose them."

He keeps shaking his head and making frustrated sounds. I'm still wearing his parka. I make a move to take it off and give it back to him but he gets back in the car.

The radio is still on. Hennessy's voice still spinning its ugly tales.

"We also have reasons to believe that Molly Forster returned to Whitbrook on the night that Mrs Dawson died. She may be implicated in Emily Dawson's death."

I reach across and turn it off. We both stare straight ahead. I want to speak but nothing comes out.

"Where did you go?" he asks. He's not yelling this time, but his voice is cold.

"When?"

"The night Emily Dawson died?"

"I went to look at my house again. I walked around the roads we used to walk together, my sister and I. Then I went to the old railway station."

"Why?"

"Because it was the first time I'd been back since I left that night."

"I meant, why the old railway station? What's there?"

"It's where we're going now."

Seeing the old railway station in daylight makes my heart weep. I spent my childhood years—the few I had—playing here with my sister. When we were little, we'd bring along a pot of lukewarm tea and some cake, and lay a pretty table-cloth on the floor for our feast. We thought of it as our secret home. We decorated it with drawings taped to the walls and small bouquets of primroses from our garden. Once, when we found an old tin of lavender paint in our garage, we armed ourselves with brushes and rollers and tried to give the inside a coat of paint, but it wouldn't stick on the old flaky surface. I can still smell it sometimes.

She hadn't been coming with me much those last few weeks. It was as if overnight she'd grown into a teenager, and I was left behind. If I tried to play our old games, tempt her to come with me to the old station, she'd shoo me off. I annoyed her, she'd say. I should go and make some friends, instead of latching onto her all the time. Even our mother, who thought Grace walked on water, chided her for being so hard on me. Now, I think she did it to protect me. I think she was scared, and she was shielding me.

I went to the old station by myself the day before her sixteenth birthday, and I climbed up the ivy at the back. I could just peer over the windowsill, and I was surprised to see her inside. She was writing in her memory book. I knew instinctively that I shouldn't make myself known, so I just watched. She was crying. After a while she put the book away, under one of the floorboards. I came back down and hid in the bushes until she left.

My mother asked me what was wrong when I came home, and I didn't tell her. I thought if I kept it secret, then later on when I told Grace that I knew, and that I'd never told anyone, she would love me again. It was a way for me to prove to her that I was grown up too, and that I could be trusted.

The next night, she was dead. They all were.

I should have told my mother.

There are two trucks parked down the street. Both say "Lakeside Homes" on the side, in a nice big curly font. There's already some tall temporary fencing down the road on the other side of the tracks, but by the look of things, they only just started. I'm just relieved there's no one here right now. I'll have to be quick.

The ivy is so thick and dense that even if I could climb it, I'd have to hack my way to the window. It doesn't stop me from trying.

"What are you doing?" Jacob says. He's leaning against the car, his arms crossed. His tone is still cold and dripping with suspicion.

"What does it look like I'm doing?" I say, trying to get hold of a solid bit of ivy.

"I have no idea."

"I'm trying to get to that window, can you come over and give me a hand please?"

"Why don't you use the door? Just a thought."

I rush around to the other side, the tracks side, and stare at the wide open door. Jacob has followed me, and I turn and grin at him, but he doesn't grin back.

"You're going to be long?"

"No, why?"

"I'm not parked legally, I have to move the car."

"We're in Whitbrook. No one gives a shit."

But he leaves anyway, and seconds later I hear him drive off.

Inside it's dusty and damp and the smell hits me like a punch in the face. I can almost feel her in here, right now. I want to put my arms around her and tell her that I'm sorry that I didn't tell our mother, that I didn't know any better.

The floor is hidden under half an inch of dust. I scrub it away with my foot, where I think the loose floorboard is. I try and pry it loose with the tips of my fingers, but it doesn't budge. I feel the next one along, my fingers quickly blackened with grime, and I feel a jolt when that one moves. I hold my breath. Gently, slowly, I manage to loosen it. And there is it. The sight of it brings tears that immediately roll down my cheeks. The memory book. It's mouldy and dusty, but otherwise intact.

I wipe my fingers on my jeans and I open it. The sight of her handwriting makes my heart ache. I brush a finger against the surface of the page. Then I turn to the last entry, the one I know she wrote the last time she was here.

I went to see Mr Hennessy this morning. I stood inside the hallway of his house and told him everything. I'm sorry, I said, but your son, he's not well, Sir. He's evil. He likes to hurt people. You have to do something, I said. Then I told him about the time he cut my thigh with his pen knife, but then later he said he was sorry, he would never hurt me again. Hugo says terrible things about me, then he cries and says that he loves me like he's never loved anyone. He says he can't live without me. I showed Mr Hennessy my bruises, and I told him that I never wanted to see Hugo again, but that he won't let me go. I told Mr Hennessy that I broke it off with his son but he won't listen. I told him Hugo threatened me. That he said he would kill me if I left him. I told Hugo I didn't want him to come to my birthday party, and he said I would be sorry. I told Mr Hennessy that Hugo had sworn he would hurt us. Molly, mum and dad. He said he would never let me go. He'd watch me die first. He said—"

"Who the fuck are you?"

There's a man behind me. I turn around. He's wearing a hard hat and a high-visibility vest.

"I just came to have a look," I say.

"I know who you are. You're from the podcast, aren't you? You nosy cow. You've got no business being here. You're trespassing."

I'm about to leave—I'm not going to argue—but he takes my arm and roughly pulls me towards the door.

I flinch my arm away. "Take your hands off me. I'm going."

There's a crackle on the handheld radio at his belt.

"We've got an unauthorised visitor at the station. She's from the podcast," he says into it.

"I'll go, no need to call for backup," I say, snarling, as he clips it back onto his belt.

"What's this?" He points to the dusty memory book that I've wedged under my arm.

The two-way radio crackles again. "The boss is on his way," it says.

"It's mine," I tell him.

"No, it's not. I saw you, you took it from over there," he points to the hole in the floor.

"Jacob?" I call out. I move towards the door, but in an instant the man has his hand on my shoulder. "Not so fast, lady."

"I'm leaving. Let me go."

"Give this back." He reaches for the memory book and I kick him hard in the shin. He yelps in pain. I quickly move towards the door, but it's blocked by a tall, dark shadow.

Edward Hennessy.

"I'll take over from here," Edward Hennessy says to high-vis man. "You can go."

The man's face is still distorted in pain. He limps out the door, shooting me an angry scowl in the process.

"Well well well, if it isn't little Molly Forster."

"My name is Rachel Holloway," I say. I can't get out. He's in the way. Again. I can feel the shortness of breath coming on. My legs start to give, but I lock my knees. I will not go down. I won't be running. *Not this time.*

"I know who you are, Molly."

"Let me go," I say.

"Why are you here, little Molly?" he asks. "And what have you got there?"

I back away from him. I can hear my breath, thick and pained, pushing through my chest. I clutch the book in my arms.

"Get out of my way," I say again, but I don't feel so sure of myself anymore. In a flash, I'm a child and frightened and alone, and I am looking into the face of the only person who can help me. Chief Constable Hennessy.

I can see myself, a child, sobbing, as Edward Hennessy closed the door behind me.

"I'm so scared, he's coming for me." I had managed to say.

"There's nothing to be scared about anymore, Molly. I'm here now."

He sat me down in front of his big desk and told me that everything was going to be fine now because Dennis had been arrested and couldn't hurt me anymore. Through desperate sobs I told him it wasn't Dennis, it was Hugo. I saw him. I was there. I was hiding. It was Hugo and he ran after me but I got away.

He said he understood, and he was going to fix it, that I should wait right there, and he went out the side door into a different office. I got up and watched him from the doorway. He had his back to me. He was standing but huddled at the same time. At first, I couldn't see what he was doing but then I saw his fingers gripping the phone, holding it tight against his ear.

"I told you. She's here," he whispered, "Come over now. Right now... No, I'm not going to take care of it, you can take care of it yourself. I've cleaned up enough of your shit, Hugo. You come here right now and find a way out of this, do you hear me?"

In the end, I never heard the rest of the conversation Edward Hennessy was having with Hugo. I just ran out the front door into the street and I've never stopped running.

The dark spots are dancing around the edges of my vision. I can feel the blood drain away. My back hits the brick wall. I shake my head to clear it. I'm not alone, not anymore. I'm not a child, I'm a mother. And I'm angry.

"Get out of my way," I say to him now, with false bravado.

"Poor little Molly. What's the matter, little girl? No one will feel sorry for you now, not after they hear what we have to say. I'm going to find reams of witness statements that will paint you as a sick, jealous, hateful, dangerous *freak*. By the time I'm done with you, they will be braying for your head. That will teach you to go after my son."

White hot fury shoots through me at his words. I can feel the book in my arms. Slowly, I brush off the mould and dust from it. Under a clear plastic cover, there is a collage of photos, some of them from magazines, but there's one photo of Grace and I, our cheeks touch, we are grinning at the camera. She has drawn a heart around it.

I think of my daughter, and how brave she is when she faces the world—just like her aunt. I draw strength from them both. I squeeze my eyes shut once, twice, then I open them and lift my head to look at Hennessy. He has his mobile in his hand and is tapping on the screen. I feel my breath on my top lip.

"She came to see you," I say.

"What?"

"My sister, she came to see you, to tell you about Hugo. She told you that he was sick, that he was dangerous."

He scoffs. "So what? She only had herself to blame. Your sister shouldn't have seduced him like that. She made her bed, I didn't see why she couldn't lie in it, I told her as much."

"You should have protected her, protected us."

He bends down, his face is so close to mine I can smell his breath.

"Do you think I didn't know Hugo had behavioural problems? We were working to help him, his mother and I. I said

294

to your stupid sister, don't break it off with him yet. I knew he might do something truly terrible if she did, and I was the Chief Constable of Whitbrook with my eye on being the Mayor. I couldn't have my son be publicly ousted as a psychopath. I said to her, just do whatever he wants. Fuck him. Suck him. I don't care. Do whatever it is that he wants from you, and eventually he'll tire of you. He always does."

"You're as crazy as he is, you sick piece of shit."

"Language, little Molly. You don't get to talk to the grown-ups like that. Don't get angry because your whore of a sister didn't listen back then. She didn't listen and look what happened. Hugo is better now. He has his issues under control. He has a family, a standing in the community. She should have listened and given him what he wanted."

He lifts the phone to his ear.

"Yes, this is Edward Hennessy, I need assistance—"

I quickly push myself off the wall and take three steps forward. I position myself and pray that my small plan is going to work.

"She wrote it all down, you know. Right here." I tap the book.

He snaps his phone shut and turns around to face me.

"Give me that," he says, extending his arm. He steps forward and swears in pain as his foot becomes wedged into the space where I've pulled the floorboard, just as I'd hoped.

I bolt.

"Get back here!" His hand reaches out to grab the back of my parka, but his foot is stuck just long enough to give me clear path and I'm out the door.

I run around the corner and see that Jacob is sitting in his car, with his eyes closed.

I bang on the roof so hard it makes him jump.

"Go!" I scream. "Now!"

FORTY-NINE

I turn to look at Jacob. He looks white. We left Edward Hennessy behind, his arms flaying.

"I swear to you Rachel, Molly, whoever the fuck you are, if you lied to me and I get arrested—"

I've reached into the pocket of the parka I'm wearing, Jacob's parka, and I'm holding out the small black mic. "I turned it on. Did it work?"

He snaps his head around. There's a small red light blinking on the box. "Yes, it's on," he says. "What just happened?"

I tell him. I show him the book. He listens to me, his hands gripping the steering wheel, his knuckles white. We've driven a couple of miles by now and he swerves off the road, stopping the car with a screech of tyres. He gets out, retrieves a small soft bag from the boot and pulls out the sound recorder. He puts headphones on and I watch the shock in his eyes as he hears the recording I just made.

"Jesus, Rachel, I mean Molly, I mean—shit, I'm so sorry I didn't believe you. That was insanely scary in there. I just couldn't believe that—" then it must dawn on him where we are, because he throws everything back in and in seconds he's behind the wheel again. "I'm taking you back to London," he says.

I lean back in my seat and for the next hour I read Grace's memory book, in silence. There's so much about our lives that I had forgotten. I miss her so much. The sadness slices at my heart, but there's relief too, that it's almost over. I feel her so close to me right now.

I realise with a start that we're halfway there already. "Can I have your phone?" I ask.

"You're not going to take the SIM card out, are you?"

"I want to call Matt."

I call my own mobile, the one I left behind at our flat. Matt answers.

"It's me."

"Rachel, where are you? Everyone's looking for you!"

"I know. I'll explain everything. I'm almost home."

"Oh, Rach," his voice breaks.

"It's okay, love. It's going to be okay, I promise."

"No, it's not."

"Yes, it—"

"It's Gracie," he says, and my heart stops. Then with a sob, he adds, "She's missing."

"Gracie's missing," I tell Jacob. "Go faster! Please!"

He just nods and puts his foot on the accelerator. I don't think he cares about the speed limit anymore.

I call Vivian.

"Give me his phone number," I say the moment she answers.

"Rach, I'm sorry, I'm so sorry. I didn't know." She wails.

"Where is he?"

"I don't know," she sobs.

"What happened?"

She tells me that after I disappeared from the hospital, Matt called her and asked her to look after Gracie. Vivian took Gracie back to her place, as she's done before on a handful of occasions. But Peter was there, waiting outside her flat. They all went inside and that's when he got the call, from his father.

"And then?" I am almost folded in half in the car seat. The phone is pressed hard against my ear.

"Oh Rach, he went completely crazy. I was so scared. He trashed my place. He was like a hurricane. He grabbed anything he could find and smashed it against the walls. Gracie was screaming. I begged him to go, to leave us. He punched me, in the face. He continued to smash things. I ran to the bedroom with Gracie and I put my hands on her ears. I called the cops. Oh, Rach—"

"Where is she now?"

"I braced myself against the door, trying to keep him from coming in, but it was no use. He kicked it and came into the bedroom and he looked at Gracie like he'd only just noticed she was there. He asked me if that was Grace. I screamed at him to leave, that I'd called the police, but he just ripped her out of my arms," she crumbles into sobs.

"Where did he go?"

"I don't know," she wails.

"Did he say anything at all?"

"No."

"What's his number?"

"I'm so sorry, Rach, I'm so, so sorry!" she sniffs, "The police are here. Where are you?"

"What's his number Vivian? Give it to me now!"

"Hang on," she sniffs again, there's a pause then she reels it off.

I hang up.

"Where to?" Jacob asks. We're just coming into London.

"I don't know yet," I say.

I punch in the number.

"Hello," he says, almost in sing-song voice.

"Hugo, where's my daughter."

"Well hello! Little Molly! I heard you escaped from the nuthouse."

"Where is she?"

"Where is who?"

"That's enough!" I yell. "Where is she?"

"You mean your brat? She's right here. Say hello to mummy, Grace."

There's a moment where the phone moves away from him. I can hear voices, traffic. They're outside somewhere, in a public place.

"Mummy?" I nearly faint in relief from the sound of her voice, but I clench my hands and focus.

"Oh my god, Gracie, my love, are you all right?"

"I—yes, are you coming, mummy?" Her voice is trembling, she's hiccupping from tears.

"I'm coming for you right now, sweetie. Can you tell me where you are?"

"I—"

He's snatched the phone away from her.

"Do you have the diary with you? Your stupid sister's fucking diary?"

"Yes."

"Bring it."

"Where are you?"

"The Millennium Bridge," he says, before hanging up.

. . .

I stand at the beginning of the bridge, on the St Paul side. Hugo is only a few metres away. He has Gracie sitting on the railing, facing out towards the river. His hands are on her waist. Passers-by are noticing. They don't think it's safe, and they're giving him stern looks, though no one is interfering, yet.

Matt is standing next to me. I've never seen him like this. Not even when he thought I was in a psychotic breakdown. His face is white and drawn. He's as terrified as I am.

He grabs my hand. He can't look at me. It's all come down on him, on all of us, so fast. That I was telling the truth all along, that Peter really is Hugo, and now he has our daughter and he won't hesitate to kill her if he thinks it will help him.

The police are here, but they're not moving yet. They're staying in the background. They wanted to clear the bridge and we had to make them understand that he will throw our little girl into the Thames if he is threatened. We, I, have to give him what he wants. So they're unseen. For now.

"I'll take it, Rach. Just give it to me," Matt says.

I squeeze his hand, hesitate. I want to do it, but I'm scared that I can't and we don't have room for mistakes. I give Matt the memory book.

He lets go of my hand and starts to walk towards Hugo. I hold my breath.

"Uh, uh, uh. I don't think so!" Hugo says, lifting one hand off Gracie's waist to shake his finger at me. Matt freezes in his tracks. "It's you I want, Little Molly. Not your boyfriend. Go back there, Matthew. Let Molly to come for a walk."

Matt is only a couple of steps away from me. He turns

around and looks at me. His eyes are filled with fear. He knows I can't cross a bridge. He turns back towards Hugo.

"Listen—" he says.

"Matt," I reach across and grab his arm, pull him back. "I'll do it."

I have been here before with Hugo, on a different bridge. And I know, without a doubt, that facing him again, right now, is like completing the journey across that other bridge, twelve years ago. Except this time it's my daughter he is going to hurt.

I take one step, one short step onto the bridge. *One.*

People are walking past us. Most of them are ignoring us, some of them are wondering what we're doing.

"Hugo," I say loudly. "Put Gracie on the ground."

"Don't be ridiculous. Give me the diary first."

I take another step. *Two.*

"Gracie, hold on to the railing please. With both hands," I say.

Her little fingers wrap themselves around the metal.

Three.

"I have it here." I lift my hand and show him the memory book.

Four.

"Good girl," he says. "Bring it over, why don't you."

Five. My legs are wobbly, but I won't give in. I look at my brave little girl. I can do this. I know I can.

Six.

"Can you hurry up, please? I don't want to stand here all day," he says.

I take another step, and another one. *Seven. Eight.* My heart is beating fast, but I can do this. I'm doing it. I focus on Gracie. *Nine.* I think of what this man has done to my sister.

Ten.

I'm close now. Close enough so we don't have to shout. I can see Gracie's teeth chattering. *Eleven.* She's holding on to the railing with both hands, knuckles white.

Twelve.

I hold up the memory book. "Let me have Gracie and I'll give it to you."

I watch him for any sharp movement, but he stays very still. He peers at the cover I'm holding up. He can see the photo of Grace and me. He can see it's the real thing.

"That's a trade, Molly."

I am there in an instant. Hugo snatches the memory book from me at the same time as I bring an arm around Gracie's waist and pull her back. Her feet land on the bridge. Hugo has opened the book at random pages and quickly scans the writing. He's frowning. He looks up at me, his face is awash with hatred. "This wasn't the deal, Molly."

Matt is there. His hands shoot out as he grabs Gracie from my arms and turns to run. The police are right behind him.

"You will pay for this, bitch," Hugo says, but he's not looking at me. He's looking at my daughter's retreating figure as Matt runs her to safety.

I don't understand what happens to me after that, all I know is that with a force I didn't know I possessed, I shove Hugo Hennessy over the railing of the Millennium Bridge.

Then I take a nice, deep breath.

FIFTY

I didn't give Hugo Grace's memory book. I asked Matt to bring mine and that's what I gave him instead. But before that, I had removed the plastic cover from hers and wrapped it around my own. My memory book is at the bottom of the Thames somewhere, and I don't care. I don't need it anymore.

They fished Hugo out of the river and he's in jail now, along with his father. Other women have come forward to tell their stories of being raped and terrorised by Hugo. Hugo's mother has spoken publicly about the many times Edward Hennessy hit her, although never somewhere that was visible. It would have ruined his career otherwise. They were both evil as it turned out, but I knew that already.

I was finally able to go back to Whitbrook and collect my family's things. Most of them were sold, but the truly personal things—the family albums, the home videos—those I got back. Mrs Patel, our neighbour, the woman who worked with my father and the wife of the man who first walked in on my murdered family, fought the city for the permission to hold onto these things all this time. Mrs Patel said that I might be back someday, and that they belonged to me. All this time, there was one person who still believed I might be alive.

The media have been all over us, of course. I was once again the subject of news all over the nation. But this time, I got the headline I always dreamed about. *Molly Forster has been found.*

Mr Holloway did arrive from Australia, and I had to tell him his daughter was dead. He nodded, but he didn't cry. He said he'll track her grave down, Jane Doe's grave, and make things right.

For the first few weeks after that moment on the bridge, we just strove to be a family again. Matt and I needed time to heal, but I wasn't really worried about that.

It's been four months and he's still getting used to calling me Molly, and I'm still getting used to hearing it. When the media finally got too crazy, we decided to leave our flat for some peace and quiet. So we rented out a house in the French countryside with Matt's mum and his sisters. Next week, Vivian is coming to stay for a few days. Matt's mum still asks when we're getting married. We told her we're thinking of next spring and she cried with joy.

Before I left, the *South Hackney Herald* asked me to record the final episode of the podcast. I chose passages from Grace's memory book. An entry from the last Christmas we spent together, that told of how happy we all were, and the very last entry, the one where she described what Hugo had been doing to her, and how she tried to get his father to intervene.

Then I ended the long search for myself with a simple truth.

"You've been listening to Missing Molly. My name is Molly Forster."

ACKNOWLEDGEMENTS

I've had a few wonderful people help me with this book (my problem child, as I've been known to call it....) and I would like to thank Katrina Diaz Arnold and Katharine D'Souza for their invaluable help in crafting this story.

A special thank you to Frank Ahern for his time and invaluable advice on the complexities of fake identities.

As ever, my heartfelt gratitude to my friends and family, and especially to my husband who keeps me fed and watered while I ponder how to murder people. I couldn't do it without you.

And last but not least, thank you, dear reader, for choosing this book, and getting this far. It means the world.

Made in the USA
Monee, IL
01 February 2022